JUST THE
NICEST
FAMILY

BOOKS BY ALISON JAMES

The School Friend

The Man She Married

Her Sister's Child

The Guilty Wife

The New Couple

The Woman in Carriage 3

The House Guest

DETECTIVE RACHEL PRINCE SERIES

1. Lola is Missing

2. Now She's Gone

3. Perfect Girls

JUST THE NICEST FAMILY

ALISON JAMES

bookouture

Published by Bookouture in 2024

An imprint of Storyfire Ltd.
Carmelite House
50 Victoria Embankment
London EC4Y 0DZ

www.bookouture.com

ISBN: 978-1-83525-760-9
eBook ISBN: 978-1-83525-758-6

This book is a work of fiction. Names, characters, businesses, organizations, places and events other than those clearly in the public domain, are either the product of the author's imagination or are used fictitiously. Any resemblance to actual persons, living or dead, events or locales is entirely coincidental.

PROLOGUE

The swimming pool was the very best thing about the villa.

The surface of the water glinted and shimmered in the sunlight, bouncing light back from liquid blue depths ringed with warm, honeyed stone. The light was so dazzling, in fact, that they had to shield their eyes from it if they were not wearing shades. This, they thought, was the glamour of the Côte d'Azur. The glamour that the two weeks in France had promised.

Flanked by cushioned loungers and umbrellas, and with a well-stocked bar and showers in the pool house behind it, this was the automatic focus of their daily activities. Here they would spend hours chatting, drinking, reading and splashing in the sun-warmed water. And they would do so with no inkling of the events that turned the pool terrace into a place capable of shattering their happy world for ever.

A place of death.

PART ONE

ONE

LOUISE

Now

'How would you feel...' Louise's husband asked her when he returned from work that Friday, 'about two weeks in the South of France?'

Tim had returned from the vet's practice at 6.50 p.m. just as he always did, and walked into the kitchen to kiss her on the lips just as he always did, but his opening line was a complete surprise.

'Oh wow!' she said in response, dropping the pasta into the boiling water. 'Are you serious?'

'Completely,' he said with a broad grin. 'Two whole weeks, everything included apart from flights. Starting the week of 17th July.'

Louise frowned slightly as she stirred the pasta in the pan. 'Hold on... the kids are still at school that week. They don't break up until the 21st. Nor do I, for that matter.' She was deputy head at a local girls' high school.

'Surely we can work something out?' Tim pleaded. 'This is far too good an opportunity to turn down.' He glanced around as he reached into his bag for his laptop. 'Speaking of the kids, where are they? They need to see this too.'

'Harry's upstairs and Elle's at a playdate with Samira. She's being dropped off later.'

'Well let me show you, at least.' Tim poured a glass of red wine for each of them and opened his laptop. 'Look at this.'

Louise squinted down at the screen, which showed an aerial shot of an imposing golden stone building surrounded by trees and vineyards, below a brilliant blue sky.

'Le Mas des Flores. Which could be our home for the last two weeks of July. How fantastic would that be?'

'It looks amazing,' Louise agreed. 'But how? What's this all about?'

'Remember I mentioned that Swiss company VCM that owns the Healthipet cat and dog food brand, amongst a whole lot of other things?'

'I do.' She gave an eye roll. 'They're one of the bunch who throw big promotional jollies to try to bribe you vets into pushing their products.'

'Exactly,' Tim smiled, not rising to the bait. 'Well, Renée Weber, their CEO, is making a big name for herself in the veterinary world. She's out there buying up independent practices at an incredible rate.'

'Practices like yours, I'm guessing.'

'Exactly. It would be an incredible opportunity for us. And Vet Care Mondiale own this place. They use it for entertaining clients, and Renée has invited us down there so that she and I can discuss the deal in a bit more detail.'

'Ah,' Louise nodded. 'So there are strings attached.'

'Well sure, sweetie, but who in their right mind would turn down the offer of a trip like that.'

'It does look heavenly,' Louise agreed. 'And you're really thinking of selling to them?'

'Well...' Tim swirled his wine round his glass. 'There could be some big advantages to joining forces with them. There'd be some fantastic benefits for me personally, and I would have a hell of a lot less admin to do, which would leave me more time to actually treat the animals. And spend more time with you and the kids, of course.'

'Sounds exciting.' Louise hesitated. 'But it wouldn't just be us there surely? Not in a place that size.'

'No, I expect there will be other guests too.'

'I don't know, darling. I'm not sure how I feel about going on holiday with people I don't know. What if we don't get on?'

'I'm sure we will.' Of the two of them, Tim was by far the more confident socially. 'But it looks like the place is big enough to avoid them if not.'

Louise was now serving up the pasta, and Tim went to the foot of the stairs to call down twelve-year-old Harry.

After they had listened to a blow-by-blow account of his latest gaming achievements over bowls of pasta, and Harry's younger sister, Elodie, had been dropped off from her playdate, both children were shooed upstairs to get ready for bed.

Tim poured the remains of the red wine into their glasses. Louise sat down opposite him, reaching for his hand.

'So what do you reckon?' he asked her, looking into her face expectantly. 'Do we go for it? For the South of France?'

'It's only three weeks way. Not a lot of time to organise things. And we'd have to pull out of the booking in Polzeath.' The Cutlers usually took their main summer holiday on the coast of Cornwall: a wholesome fortnight of surfing and sand-castles.

'We can do Polzeath any time. Think what an amazing opportunity this would be for us as a family. The kids will love it, and it will be great for Harry's French.'

Louise gave a little shiver of pleasure. 'I've got to admit, it is pretty exciting.' Jumping up from the table, she headed upstairs to the bedroom, Tim hard on her heels, and flung open the doors to her wardrobe. She started flicking along the end of the rack where she kept her summer dresses, looking for anything that would pass muster in the South of France. 'I'm going to have to go shopping, obviously,' she said to her husband with a grin. 'I'll need more swimwear and beach cover-ups. Probably some evening dresses too. I expect there'll be fancy dinners, and the other guests will probably be super chic.'

'Oh, and that was the other thing.' Tim gave her a playful pat on her backside as she held up a dress in front of herself and looked at her reflection. 'Apparently there's enough space for us to invite a couple of friends along too.'

'Goodness. We'll need to think about who we ask.'

'Yes, we will,' Tim concurred, finishing his own glass in one gulp. 'Who gets the golden ticket?'

TWO

LOUISE

Now

The following morning all the Cutlers piled into the car and headed off *en famille* to watch Harry play a Saturday match for the local under-13s soccer team.

Several of his classmates also played on the team, and there were familiar faces among the supporting parents standing on the touchline. Elodie scampered off to play with some of her own friends and Tim and Louise approached the group together, with Louise hooking her arm though Tim's and leaning into him.

'Look at you two lovebirds,' said Mandy Fielding, a tall bossy blonde with an overbite who considered herself the queen bee of the school gate mothers. 'Literally joined at the hip.'

'Ignore her,' whispered Shona Prentice, a strikingly voluptuous redhead whose daughter was in Elodie's class. She was wearing tight black leather jeans and a leopard-skin top in some clingy synthetic fabric, both of which struck Louise as highly unsuitable for a football pitch on a warm June day. 'She's only jealous.' Shona watched as Louise unwrapped herself from

Tim's arm, only to have him reach instinctively for her hand, 'She has a point, though, you two are just too cute.' She was smiling, but there was the slightest edge of bitchiness in her voice.

Louise was used to this reaction. As though she and her husband were just too good to be true; that they couldn't really be this close, this happy. But they were. It *was* true.

Twenty years after they'd first met as students, she was unable to pursue the thought of never having met Tim. It was too big, too mind-bending. There was no world in which she wasn't Mrs Tim Cutler: the idea was simply impossible for her to comprehend. Their togetherness and their complete certainty of each other stirred up envy in other people, she knew that. Hence Mandy Fielding's sour remark and Shona Prentice's faintly patronising smile.

'I'm just going to go over and grab myself a coffee.' Shona tilted her head in the direction of the sports centre that adjoined the playing field. 'Can I get you guys anything?'

Louise requested an iced latte, Tim shook his head. 'Is your other half here?' he asked. Louise barely knew Shona, but Tim played squash with her husband Kevin and the two men were quite friendly. 'Wouldn't mind arranging a game while we're here.'

Shona pointed out Kevin in a group of other fathers, and Tim planted a kiss on Louise's bare shoulder before strolling off to join them. A few minutes later, Shona returned with the coffees. 'Got your holiday plans all sorted?' she asked briskly, tossing a lock of auburn hair over her shoulder.

'Well, I thought we had,' Louise said, unable to suppress a smile as she took a sip of the iced coffee. 'But something's just come up. Something incredibly exciting.'

She told Shona about the invitation to the Swiss conglomerate's villa in the South of France.

'Wow!' Shona's eyes widened. 'You lucky sods! I'd be there

like a shot. A luxury villa, all paid for? You'd be mad not to accept. I wish my bloody husband did something that came with perks like that.'

Kevin Prentice, belittled constantly by his wife, did something in insurance.

'I'm sure you'll be going somewhere just as lovely,' Louise murmured in a placatory tone, aware even so that this sounded insincere.

'As of right now, we're doing precisely fuck all this summer,' said Shona bitterly, closing her artificially filled lips round her straw and inhaling her frappuccino. 'Kevin was supposed to have sorted an apartment in Menorca but he cocked up over the flights and now they're all full for our dates. So we've had to cancel.'

'That's a shame.' Louise thought of the invitation to the French villa having been extended to include friends of the Cutlers, but decided against mentioning this. She didn't know the Prentices all that well, and the way Shona treated her own husband made her uncomfortable.

With the football match over, Tim bought burgers and fries for the children in the sports centre's café, then he and Louise walked hand in hand back to the car, with the children running on ahead. It was a breezy but warm June day, and as the sun broke through the clouds, Louise released Tim's hand to rummage in her bag for her sunglasses.

'I was thinking,' she said, as she put them on and rearranged her wavy brown hair, 'Rosie and Justin would be perfect to ask along to the villa with us, if we go.'

Rosie was Louise's first cousin, and the two women were close. Both the Cutlers liked her husband Justin, a genial, easy-going man who managed the family farm.

'Ah,' said Tim, 'about that...'

Louise experienced a sinking feeling as she guessed – correctly – what was coming next.

'...I mentioned it to Kevin just now, and he was very keen for them to be included. He told me they had something planned in Menorca, but apparently it's fallen through. I felt kind of sorry for him, actually.'

This was Tim all over; always a sucker for a sob story.

'But, sweetheart, we barely know them. And I'm not really friends with Shona,' Louise remonstrated, turning to face him. The children had reached the car by now and Tim waved the key fob at it to unlock the doors and allow them to climb in. 'And she's... well, to be honest, she's not really my cup of tea. Rosie and Justin would be a much better fit.'

'Yes, but they've got four kids, and I'm not sure the space in the villa would extend to an extra six guests. That might look like taking the piss. The Prentices only have the one, which is one of the reasons I asked them.'

And Violet Prentice was very much a stereotypical only child, Louise thought, with a trace of spite. Overindulged and overprotected.

'Can't you tell them that the Swiss woman...'

'Renée Weber.'

'...Renée Weber has changed the plan and we can't bring anyone else.'

'We could,' said Tim reasonably, opening the car's passenger door for her. 'But that would be a lie.'

This was also Tim: honest to a fault.

'Look, I'm sure it'll work out. Kevin's a good guy, and Violet will be company for Elodie. And from the sound of it, the place is big enough for us all to do our own thing. You'll be able to ignore Shona, I'm sure.'

He climbed into the driver's seat and started the engine, smiling confidently at his wife.

'Don't worry, sweetheart, it will be just fine.'

THREE

TIM

Now

Fairlawn Veterinary Clinic was housed in a purpose-built business unit a twenty-minute walk south of Winchester Cathedral.

On Monday morning, Tim sat through a long and depressing meeting with Glen Beane, the practice accountant, which convinced him more than ever that he needed to sign the deal to sell the practice to VCM. After it finished, Amy, the practice receptionist, stuck her head round the door.

'I know it wasn't booked earlier, but looks like we've got an emergency euthanasia coming in. Mrs Sullivan just phoned in floods of tears; says Rollo has taken a turn for the worse and started fitting.'

Rollo was an ancient chocolate lab that the practice had cared for over many years.

Tim sighed heavily. 'Of course. God, dear old Rollo... Call her back and ask if she wants me to go over there and do it.'

Occasionally, if circumstances allowed, Tim would put

animals to sleep in their own homes, and at this moment he quite fancied an excuse to get out of the building.

His mobile rang. 'Darling Wife', the screen display said.

'Hi, sweetie,' he said flatly.

'Are you okay?' Louise instantly picked up his tone of voice.

'Yes, sorry, I'm fine. Just about to send a beloved lab to meet his maker, that's all.'

'Oh no: poor you. I know those ones are always tough. I really don't know how you do it. I'd be a wreck... Listen, darling, I've just been in and spoken to Paul. About the South of France.'

Paul Garland was the head at St Agnes's Girls High, where Louise worked: an officious and rule-bound man in his fifties.

'It's not good news, I'm afraid. There's some kind of audit or inspection being done by the independent schools trust we belong to, and it's happening in the last week of term. There's no way I can take that week off; I'm so sorry.'

Tim squeezed his eyes tight shut, but said nothing.

'Is there any way we can put off your contact at the Swiss company till a bit later in the summer? It would be a lot easier for us all to get down there in early August.'

'No,' said Tim, his voice heavy. 'I don't want to mess them around by being awkward about the dates, and then risk the whole deal being off. We have to go for the weeks they've offered.'

'But, Tim, I'm telling you from my end that's just not possible.' There was steel behind Louise's words, and he realised this was the closest they had been in a long time to having a row. Normally they simply did not argue.

'Okay, look...' Tim stood up and unlocked the drugs cabinet. Distracted by the conversation, he grabbed a multipack of phenobarbital vials and tossed it into his open messenger bag, followed by a couple of IV kits. He usually took a pre-packed medical bag, but he had decided that after dealing with Rollo's demise he would clear his head with a walk along the banks of the River Itchen. This would mean parking his car on the street, and he made a point of absolutely never doing that with drugs left inside it, even if they were out of sight. There was a 'VET ON CALL' sticker on the back of the car, and the local druggies would happily break into his Land Rover if they thought there might be ketamine inside. 'I'll see if we can delay the trip by a couple of days. I'm sure that won't make much difference. And then I can travel out there with the kids, and you can follow on a few days later when your term is finished.'

'What about the Prentices?'

'They can come whenever. Maybe you can arrange it so you travel with them?'

'I suppose so. But... I don't know.' There was a catch in Louise's voice. She didn't need to finish her sentence. Tim already knew exactly what she was thinking and feeling. That they'd never travelled abroad without each other. That they had never even spent any time apart at all, other than Louise's two overnight stays in the maternity unit when the children were born. He could sense her anxiety, and irrational though it was, it filled him with an overwhelming sense of dread.

FOUR

TIM

Now

Le Mas des Fleurs was a huge stone farmhouse with a terracotta tiled roof, a few kilometres outside the chic village of Cotignac.

After a twisty climb into the hills, the car turned onto a long gravelled drive, with tall cypresses standing guard at the entrance to the property. Visible in the distance were the hazy purplish hills of Provence. The flowers in the property's name grew in abundance everywhere you looked: sunflowers, lavender, hibiscus and pink dianthus in stone-edged beds, with jasmine and bougainvillea climbing the walls and arches.

Tim, Elodie and Harry had flown to Toulon on Wednesday 19th July, leaving Louise to finish her term at school and travel to join them on Saturday morning. The adult Cutlers still felt uncomfortable at this compromise, but the children were so excited they were barely aware of the highly unusual circumstance of travelling abroad with just one of their parents. Being met at the airport by a chauffeur driven limousine only added to their high spirits.

'Where's the pool, where's the pool?' Elodie squeaked,

hurling herself out of the car once they'd driven them the sixty kilometres to the villa. 'Daddy, you said there was a pool, didn't you?'

She looked up at her father hopefully.

'Yes, there's a pool,' Tim sighed. He went to help retrieve the cases from the boot, but was waved away by the driver. 'And a tennis court too, I believe.'

'Am I going to have to share a room with Elle?' Harry groaned. 'I really don't want to.'

'We'll have to see how many rooms there are, but I think the plan is for Elle to share with Violet. So you'll probably have a room to yourself.'

The force of the sun was intense, bouncing off the pale stone and creating blocks of deep shadow. The combination of the heat, the loud droning of the cicadas and the powerfully heady scent from all the flowers was suffocating, and Tim felt suddenly dizzy. He looked around, blinking, wishing fervently that he could FaceTime Louise so that she could see what he was seeing. But she would no doubt be in a meeting with one of the school auditors.

A woman in a black uniform appeared on the steps and helped the driver carry the cases through the front door. Tim hung back uncertainly, but Renée Weber appeared on the steps wearing just a one-piece swimsuit and a stylish striped kaftan.

She was a well-groomed woman in her late forties, with immaculately coiffured brown hair. She sported an impressive tan and, while not slim, had a shapely pair of legs. The two of them had spoken on video calls but never met in person until now.

'Tim! Welcome!' she trilled, holding out her arms and embracing him through a waft of Joy perfume, giving a continental double kiss. Tim was acutely aware of his sweaty, travel-stained T-shirt, so it was no surprise when Renée said, 'You'll want to go and freshen up and change; Pascale will show you to your rooms. Come and find us by the pool when you're ready.'

They followed the uniformed housekeeper – Pascale – to the first floor of the house, where she explained in broken English that in the main building there were four suites, and a further two ground-floor rooms with a shared bathroom allocated to the children. A fifth guest suite with its own terrace was in one of the outbuildings near the pool. Altogether there were five terraces, an outdoor covered loggia for dining, a fifteen-metre pool and a clay tennis court. Tim had expected décor in French chateau style: battered antiques, gilt and brocade, but all the rooms had been decked out by the same high-end interior decorator. There was chic modern furniture, plain but expensive-looking drapes, circular mirrors and tasteful pieces of *avant garde* sculpture. The en suite in his room had a free-standing oval bath and a floor-to-ceiling window overlooking acres of lush green vineyards. The housekeeper demonstrated how to program the air conditioning, and once she had left to take the children to their rooms, he switched it to the coldest setting and luxuriated in the blast of chilly air.

After he had showered and changed into swim shorts, a fresh T-shirt and flip-flops, he went downstairs in search of Harry and Elodie. Harry had a small single room to himself, which he declared himself pleased about, and Elodie was to share a room with twin beds with Violet Prentice. The three of them headed outside again and found the path leading to the pool terrace, where a group of people were gathered. It was shaded with ancient olive trees, and had wooden decking along one length and a lawned area on the other. Ten wooden loungers were arranged in a neat row on the decking, separated by small tables, and there were a couple of larger round tables under umbrellas. Renée Weber was sitting at one of these with a handsome younger man who was wearing a pair of neon pink shorts, his bronzed legs gleaming with suntan oil and arranged in a way that suggested supreme physical confidence.

'Everybody, this is Tim Cutler, and Harry and Eloise.'

'Elodie,' his daughter corrected their hostess stubbornly.

'This is my partner, Jared Frayn,' Renée indicated the oiled man.

'Hi.' He had a strong American accent.

'And these are my friends Richard and Merry Stafford.' She pointed to a couple on the sunloungers. 'Richard is a very old, and very dear, friend of mine.' She caught Richard's eye and a slightly conspiratorial smile passed between them.

So, as Tim had expected, there were other guests of Renée's at the villa; people they didn't know. He would have to get past the slightly uncomfortable feeling this engendered, he told himself, if they were all going to be able to relax and enjoy the villa.

Richard Stafford held out a hand and shook Tim's, but Merry, her face hidden behind huge Gucci sunglasses, merely nodded. From what Tim could tell, she was at least a decade younger than her husband. He had always been hopeless at women's ages, but guessed she was around thirty.

'And these two you already know, of course.'

Stretched out on another pair of loungers, their exposed flesh glaringly white, were Kevin and Shona Prentice. Tim did a double take. When they had discussed travel arrangements, Kevin had indicated that they would be picking up a hire car in Nice and would arrive at the villa some time that evening. And yet here they already were; Kevin with a bottle of beer in his hand and Shona clearly at least halfway through a bottle of sparkling wine.

'Surprise!' she said tipsily.

'We switched to an earlier flight last minute,' said Kevin, having the grace to at least sound apologetic. 'Thought, rather than waiting, we might as well tip up here and wait for you lot to arrive.'

'Shame you missed lunch,' Shona said. 'It was amaaaaazing.'

Tim smiled, but inwardly he felt wrong-footed and a touch resentful. They had invited the Prentices on this holiday – not the other way around – and yet here the pair of them were welcoming Tim as though he was their guest. Violet was happily splashing around in the pool on a rainbow unicorn inflatable that they surely must have brought with them. Elodie was already kicking off her sandals and walking down the shallow, shelving steps that took up the full width of the pool, letting out a whoop of delight. Probably put off by this sudden shattering of the peace, Merry Stafford gathered up her things and stalked off.

'Why don't you have a beer?' said Shona, adding, as if this were her role, 'There's a drinks fridge back there in the pool room.'

'Here, I'll show you,' Renée said smoothly, and Tim thought he saw her throw a look of irritation in Shona's direction. He flinched. Tensions already and they'd barely arrived. But the cold beer helped him relax, and Pascale appeared with a tray of snacks: bread, olives and charcuterie, which would tide them over until dinner. Once he'd had a swim and felt the warmth of the Mediterranean sun on his limbs, his bad mood dissipated somewhat. The children were emitting delighted shrieks as they jumped in the water, quite content to be left to their own devices.

It's going to be fine, Tim told himself firmly as he sprayed factor 30 onto his chest. *And once Louise arrives, it will be perfect.*

Drinks were served on the terrace outside the main 'salon' at 7.30, with dinner to follow sometime later. Concerned that this would be far too late for an already flagging Elodie, Tim had a brief discussion with Pascale and it was agreed that the two girls would be served supper separately in the kitchen during cocktail hour, after which they could go straight to bed. Harry insisted that he wanted to stay up with the adults, but Tim suspected he would get bored and told him he could leave the dinner table once he'd had enough.

Over drinks, Tim chatted to the handsome and charming Jared. He had met Renée at a global health seminar in Geneva two years ago, he said, and they had been together for a year and a half.

'What is it you do?' Tim asked.

'I specialise in integrative medicine,' Jared said, as though this explained everything.

'So... are you a trained physician?'

Jared shook his head. 'I operate more as a health coach. I help people achieve their wellness goals with nutrition and lifestyle changes.' He spoke as though he was reading out loud from a promotional brochure.

'Ah, I see.' Tim nodded, thinking that the muscular American with his perfect teeth, shining hair and unblemished skin was at least a good advertisement for his own profession.

Richard Stafford ran a global logistics company, and judging from the Breitling watch, the Balenciaga print shirt and suede Hermès loafers, he was clearly doing very well out of it. His wife, Merry, sported a shocking pink Dior slip dress and now her ponytail was let down revealed a luxuriant waist-length mane of gold and caramel. She had a tiny, perfect nose, visible filler in her lips and narrow, unreadable eyes fringed with false eyelashes. It turned out her name did not fit her at all. Hovering near to her husband's elbow, she spoke only when spoken to, and even then only gave brief, monosyllabic answers. There was nothing in the least merry about her.

'Bit of a space cadet that one,' Shona Prentice slurred

waspishly to Tim. She had angry red patches of sunburn on her shoulders and cleavage, and had already drunk too much. 'But thinks she's better than the rest of us.'

Eventually, at eight thirty they sat down to dinner. The long table on the loggia was set with sparkling glassware and candles, with a huge centrepiece of grapes, peaches and fresh figs. The paved area was flanked at each end by a pair of huge terracotta urns that stood around five feet high and a canopy of vines curved over their heads. Above it, stars studded the indigo night sky. They were served with melon and prosciutto, then a delicious garlicky coq au vin, followed by a magnificent cheeseboard.

'Amazing place, isn't it?' said Kevin, who was seated opposite Tim.

'Amazing,' agreed Tim.

'And lucky old you, you get to enjoy it for three days without the old ball and chain. Let off the leash, eh?'

Tim wanted to tell Kevin to speak for himself, but he didn't want to come off as a joyless stick-in-the-mud, so he merely smiled in what he hoped was an enigmatic fashion and took a mouthful of the excellent Rhone red. Even so, in his mind there *was* no leash: quite the opposite. He felt only half himself without Louise there. Yes, this place was wonderful and he was very lucky, but he was missing his wife terribly.

Everything would be perfect, he repeated to himself like a refrain, as soon as Louise arrived. Only then would the holiday really begin.

FIVE

LOUISE

Now

The first thing that Louise noticed was the smell of the flowers: sweet and musky, like an expensive perfume. She stood on the driveway as the taxi driver unloaded her cases and inhaled it, but rather than being pleasant, she found it cloying. She was already brewing a headache after the journey, and the hot, scented air was making it worse. Her flight had been delayed for two and a half hours at Gatwick, during which time the plane had sat on the tarmac with nothing for the passengers to drink. Subsequently, she was dehydrated and out of sorts. It also meant that instead of arriving at Le Mas des Flores just after lunch on Saturday, it was now early evening. In addition to the scent of the flowers she could smell dinner being prepared: roasting meat that was probably lamb, with base notes of rosemary and garlic. Rather than making her feel hungry, this only intensified her queasiness.

Elodie and Harry hurtled around the side of the house, dressed in their swimwear, their hair still damp. Both of them were starting to acquire a nice colour: like their father, they tanned easily. Louise herself had pale Celtic skin which took an age to turn brown.

'Mum!' They threw their arms round her and started talking over one another in their eagerness to tell her all about the place. As Louise hugged them back, she felt an overwhelming sense of relief to be reunited with her children. The house in Winchester had felt horribly empty without them.

'Mummy, the pool's amazing! I swam twenty lengths!'

'There's this really cool games room in the basement with a pool table and a cinema screen! Renée says we can watch the latest Star Wars movie on it tomorrow night.'

Tim now appeared, wearing shorts, a polo shirt and flip-flops, and enveloped her in a long embrace.

'You okay, sweetie?' He must have felt her wincing slightly, because he pulled back and scrutinised her face.

'I've got the mother of all headaches coming on,' she said apologetically. 'I'm sure I'll be fine after some water and paracetamol.'

'Let's go straight up to the room and I'll dig out some painkillers. It's nice and cool up there: I've left the air con on specially.'

Louise smiled at him gratefully and followed him as he carried her luggage up to the first floor. Their room had a sumptuous cream carpet, an Eames lounge chair upholstered in paprika red and heavy drapes in slate-coloured silk dupion. The huge bed had a complicated arrangement of pillows and cushions and had clearly been remade by a member of the domestic staff rather than Tim. There was a large bottle of mineral water and glasses on a tray on the dresser, and Tim poured her a glass and handed it to her with a couple of Panadol. She swallowed them gratefully and sank down onto the bed, covering her eyes with her fingers.

'I really need a shower, but I'm not sure I'm up to it.'

'Poor darling... wait there.' Tim went into the bathroom and came back with a small towel soaked in cold water, which he applied to Louise's forehead.

'I think it's a full-on migraine,' she whispered. 'Sorry.'

She had suffered from migraines before, although infrequently.

'Aw, you poor thing... what rotten luck.' Tim continued to hold the compress on her forehead. 'Have you got any migraine medication with you?'

She shook her head slowly, wincing again.

'I'll go and ask the others if they've got something suitable. Or maybe Pascale has a medical kit – she's the housekeeper.'

He left Louise on the bed and returned a few minutes later, holding up a blister pack of pink pills.

'You're in luck: Merry had some diphenhydramine. It's really a sleeping tablet rather than a migraine cure, but it might do the trick. It'll knock you out.'

'Merry?'

'Merry Stafford. She and her husband Richard are Renée's guests.

'So there are other people here,' Louise said flatly.

'Well we knew there probably would be, given the size of the place.' Tim smiled reassuringly. 'It'll be fine; they seem perfectly nice. You'll meet them later. All in good time.' He went over to the window and drew the curtains to screen out the setting sun. 'But first, let's get these down you and get you feeling better.'

Louise woke the following morning to an empty bed.

The curtains were drawn back and the window opened, admitting a shaft of sunlight and the heavily scented air. Stretching, and pulling herself to a sitting position, she was relieved to find that the worst of her migraine had dissipated.

Her mouth was dry and she felt a little washed out, but largely better.

Tim had left a hastily scribbled note on the desk notepad.

Didn't want to wake you. Come down to breakfast (main terrace beyond living room) if you feel up to it, otherwise text me and I'll bring you something up. T xxx

She felt a vague, irrational sense of disappointment at being abandoned in this way.

The previous evening, when she had heard a light tap at the bedroom door, she'd hoped it would be Tim coming to check on her, but it had been Pascale bringing some soup and a fresh bottle of water. The woman seemed kind, but it felt odd having a stranger wait on her.

After showering, Louise dressed in a sage green linen dress, tamed her unruly chestnut waves as best she could, and headed downstairs. She followed the sound of voices and found the other guests, including her own children, gathered around a spread of baguettes, croissants, coffee and freshly squeezed orange juice. Instantly she felt conscious of her own white limbs compared to everyone else's golden ones. Even the guests who had arrived on Wednesday seemed to already be tanned.

Elodie rushed over to hug her and she was grateful to have her daughter at her side as the others all turned to look at her.

'How are you feeling?' Shona asked, without getting up to greet her.

'A lot better thanks,' Louise said, forcing a wide smile. The truth was she felt a little better, but still wobbly.

She was introduced to Renée and her partner Jared, and the Staffords, who were sitting at the far end of the table a little distance away from the others.

'It's you I have to thank for the migraine tablets,' Louise said warmly to Merry Stafford. 'That was so sweet of you; I'm very grateful.'

Merry, whose face was concealed behind massive shades, merely gave a brief smile.

'We usually loll around by the pool between breakfast and lunch,' Kevin turned to Louise after she had sat down and helped herself to coffee and a single slice of bread. 'But Sunday is Pascale's day off, so we have to organise our own lunch and dinner today. Which means someone needs to head to the supermarket.'

Louise felt a flash of irritation at Kevin presuming to tell her how the land lay. She wished they had been able to bring Rosie and Justin instead.

'Why don't you and I go?' Shona said to Louise. 'It'll give us a chance to catch up, have a bit of a girlie goss.'

Louise did not feel the need for a 'goss' with Shona, or any other form of catch-up. In fact, she was rather longing to have a swim and make a start on her own non-existent tan. So she hesitated for a few seconds, hoping that one of the others would jump in and insist that Louise, as the new arrival, should remain at the villa. No one did. She tried to catch Tim's eye, but he had just stood up and was heading to the kitchen to fetch more juice.

'Fine,' she smiled weakly. 'Great: let's do that.'

As far as Louise knew, Shona Prentice had no culinary skills to speak of. Which meant that having bought the food, she would probably be lumbered with cooking it.

'Wonderful!' Renée gushed. 'Tim told me he was married to an absolute angel, and now we know he wasn't exaggerating.'

Forty minutes later, Louise and Shona were heading to the hypermarket on the outskirts of Cotignac. Louise was grateful that at least Shona had volunteered to drive the large BMW SUV, which was one of the cars that came with the villa. She was wearing a white muslin dress with a lot of complicated flounces and a huge stack of gold bracelets that jangled constantly against the steering wheel. Her dark red hair was pushed back with an emerald green bandeau and her mouth was slicked with a thick layer of fuchsia lipstick.

'Any thoughts on what we should buy?' Louise ventured. She wasn't sure who was supposed to pay for it, but hadn't known how to broach the subject. Was Renée footing the bill with Mondiale's generous resources, or were they expected to pay their way?

Shona shrugged. 'You're the domestic goddess, not me.'

Louise bit back her response. She had been about to remind Shona that she had a career; worked full time. 'Let's just do charcuterie and cheeses for lunch,' she suggested. 'And maybe fish for dinner? Although maybe Sunday isn't the best day to buy fresh fish?'

Shona made a 'search me' face.

Having parked the car, they found a large trolley, which it seemed Louise was expected to push. She threw fresh tomatoes, salad greens, potatoes and haricots verts into it, then added grapes and melons, while Shona flitted aimlessly from one display of produce to another. At the fish counter, Louise selected two whole sides of salmon, then picked up a packet of ready-made puff pastry and a jar of pesto.

'I reckon I can do a very basic salmon en croute,' she told Shona. 'Maybe you can find us something for dessert while I get some cheeses and cold meats.'

Shona looked blank.

'Needs to serve eleven. And something the kids will like,' Louise prompted.

Shona eventually returned with a dark chocolate mousse and some ice cream, and once they headed to the checkout, produced a credit card that Renée had apparently insisted they use.

'I'm glad I got you on my own for a bit,' Shona said as they loaded the carrier bags into the boot of the car. 'I wanted to ask you about Jared.'

Louise looked at her blankly. 'Ask me about him?'

'Yes. What do you think of him?' Shona's tone was impatient.

'I don't know... I mean, I've barely spoken five words to him.'

'Gorgeous, though, isn't he?'

Louise frowned, trying to remember what he had looked like. 'Well, yes, I suppose he is very good-looking. If you like the buff, gym-going type.'

'I think he's soooo sexy,' Shona said with a little giggle.

'But, Shona, he's married to Renée.'

And you're married to Kevin, she could have added.

'They're not married actually,' Shona said, with an absurdly defensive tone. 'They're only dating. And I'm not sure what he sees in her – apart from her money, I suppose. She's old enough to be his mother.'

'Oh, come on,' Louise protested, as they took their seats in the car. 'She's not *that* old. I reckon the age gap's not much more than ten years.'

Shona pulled a face, her bracelets jangling wildly as she manoeuvred the car out of the car park.

'And also,' Louise said pointedly, 'she's our hostess. If it weren't for her, we wouldn't even be in the South of France.'

Shona pouted.

'How's Violet enjoying herself?' Louise asked, desperate to change the subject. 'And Kevin?'

'Violet's loving it. As for Kevin... well, frankly I don't really give a shit either way.'

· · ·

When they reached Le Mas des Flores, Shona helped carry the shopping into the kitchen but then disappeared, claiming she wanted to work on her tan.

Louise unpacked the food as best she could in the large, unfamiliar kitchen, then went upstairs and changed into a swimsuit and sarong, plonking a wide-brimmed sun hat on her head, grabbing a book and heading to the pool.

All the other adults were assembled on the row of loungers, some drinking beer or wine, while the three children splashed in the pool. It was clear that they had all become relaxed with one another because there was teasing and in-jokes. Jared was mocked for pronouncing Edinburgh 'Edin-boro', Harry was nicknamed Benny because of his obsession with the sugared beignets that Pascale baked to go with morning coffee. Once again, Louise felt like the incomer, as though she was starting at a new school where everyone else already knew one another.

She buried her nose in her book for a while, and once she could feel the sun's rays turning her pink, offered to go in and make a start on some salad for lunch.

Renée sat up on her lounger, scrunching her face up to indicate that she disagreed with this suggestion. 'You're very sweet, Louise,' she said in her excellent English, that only had the faintest hint of an accent. 'But we always have lunch a little later. Around two seems to suit people best.'

So there was already an established routine, one that Louise wasn't party to.

'Fine,' she smiled. 'Of course. I'll leave it a while longer then.'

She stood up and moved her lounger into the shade and returned to her novel, though she found herself reading and re-reading the same paragraph.

Tim stood up and stretched, but instead of checking on Louise, he walked over to Renée. 'Can I fetch you anything to drink, R?'

The 'R' irritated Louise. She told herself she was being irrational. Her husband was here to try to secure the sale of his practice to the woman's company; of course he was going to dance attendance on her.

'Tim, you read my mind!' She pronounced it 'Teem', and her tone was playful. 'I would love a gin tonic.'

'Coming right up.' Tim headed in the direction of the bar in the pool house. 'Want anything?' he called to Louise, as an afterthought.

She shook her head. 'I'm going to head inside in a minute.'

Kevin, who had been doing laps with Jared, hauled himself up onto the edge of the pool, streaming water as he did so. He grabbed one of the pale grey pool towels and gave himself a cursory rub down, before tossing the towel onto his lounger. It missed, and landed on the end of Shona's, covering her legs.

'Fuck's sake, Kevin!' she screeched at top volume. She had already downed at least two glasses of rosé.

'Relax, woman, it's only a bloody towel!'

'It's soaking! And it's got my phone wet! Look!' Enraged, Shona brandished her mobile, which had a few drops of water on the screen. 'You're so fucking careless with other people's stuff! You just don't give a fuck!'

The Cutler children were staring open-mouthed at this outburst, but Violet continued playing with her pool float, indicating that she had seen this many times before.

'Seriously, you're such a fucking moron!' Shona screeched, spittle landing on her husband's face. 'I don't know why the hell I married you, I really don't.' She screwed up the damp towel and flung it at him, before plonking herself down on her lounger again and turning her back on Kevin.

Renée looked furious, shaking her head in overt disapproval. Tim returned with the drinks, and Louise made eye contact with him, trying to signal that the Prentices were his guests, and that he should try to exert some sort of control over them. They certainly couldn't endure this for the remainder of the fortnight. But he merely gave her a helpless shrug and continued towards Renée, placing her drink on the table beside her with what looked to Louise like an obsequious little bow.

Feeling strangely unsettled, she picked up her book and her hat and headed back into the villa to prepare lunch, wrong time or not.

SIX

TIM

Then

It was dark when Tim set off to the networking event.

The last thing he felt like doing was driving to Basingstoke on a gloomy, damp October evening for work. Especially since Louise was in such a fragile state. At the moment he didn't like leaving her alone at night. But he was still a junior partner at Fairlawn, and his boss, Desmond Amblin, had told him he wanted the practice represented at the Curadex Animal Health function. It was one of the major veterinary pharmaceutical companies in the region, and Desmond felt that someone should be there to keep an ear to the ground, pick up tips, find out what competitors were doing. And, of course, come away with free samples of the latest drugs.

Tim phoned Louise on his car's Bluetooth as he filtered onto the M3.

'How are you, my darling?' he asked tenderly.

'Not too bad.' He could tell his wife was trying to inject a little brightness into her voice so as not to worry him, and his heart ached with love for her. Two months earlier, she had suffered a late miscarriage. It had been their first pregnancy, and they had been so excited, so full of hope for the start of their own family. Louise had endured a bout of depression afterwards, and had been signed off sick for several weeks from her teaching job. She was now back at work, but he knew that she was still struggling a little.

'I wish I didn't have to go to this bloody thing,' he told her, watching the windscreen wipers work slowly to and fro as he drove. 'But Desmond's got an emergency equine colic to deal with, and he wanted someone to go in his place.'

'It's okay, darling. I'm going to open that bar of Dairy Milk and watch *The Apprentice*, without having to listen to you moaning on about how all the candidates are morons.'

He laughed. 'Fair enough. Save me some chocolate though.'

'You might get a couple of squares if you're lucky.'

'I'll try not to be back too late, but don't wait up, okay?' He cut the call.

The event was a meet and greet with drinks and canapés, held at a chain hotel between the M3 and the ring road. There were the inevitable promotional stands set up at the edges of the conference room, manned by Curadex drug reps handing out free products in branded tote bags.

Most of the floor space was taken up with little gaggles of people talking. The majority were vets, and the remainder company executives who were easy to spot because of their suits and ties. Vets never wore suits. Tim had put on a jacket for the occasion, but certainly no tie.

Glasses of warm wine and soft drinks were being handed round by girls dressed in white shirts and black miniskirts who were probably students at the local catering college. At the end of the room where Tim wound up – talking to a fellow Exeter graduate that he knew slightly – there were two waitresses, working as a team. The one that stood out immediately had very pale silver-blonde hair, a colour so light it rarely occurred naturally. Yet when she was up close handing him a glass of apple juice, he could see that it definitely hadn't been dyed. The other girl was shorter and had dirty blonde hair with brassy highlights and a diamond stuck onto one of her incisors. She tried to offer him red wine, and when he shook his head, saying he had to drive, she stared for a second, narrowing her eyes at him in a way he found unsettling. The two girls retreated to the side of the room with their drinks trays, and Tim caught sight of them glancing over in his direction, whispering behind their hands. He was used to his looks garnering a certain amount of female attention, but this felt unsettling.

After the drink and food was cleared away, the CEO of Curadex stood up on the stage at the far end of the conference room and called for quiet. He then embarked on the inevitable presentation, bragging about the company's excellent relationship with the veterinary profession and urging the assembled professionals to prescribe his company's products. Unable to consume any more alcohol and keen to get home to Louise, Tim edged his way to the back of the room and headed back towards reception, his Curadex tote in his hand.

As he got out to the car park, the threatened autumn storm arrived with full force, turning the drizzle into a biblical downpour. The rain clattered off hard surfaces and bounced out of puddles and a frenzied wind whipped through the branches of the trees. Covering his head with the tote, Tim ran to his car and climbed in, sending up a spray of water as he turned out of the car park and onto the road.

Then he saw her. There was a bus stop a hundred yards or so from the hotel and he spotted one of the waitresses who had served them drinks. Not the one with the silver hair, but the other one. She had a thin black cardigan over her waitressing outfit and her legs were bare. Despite huddling under the bus stop shelter, she was already drenched.

Tim indicated left and pulled up at the kerb, winding down the passenger side window. 'Can I give you a lift anywhere?' he asked. The poor girl was shivering violently. 'Where do you live?'

'Kempshott,' she said, naming a suburb on the south side of the town.

'That's fine, I'm driving that way anyway,' Tim said with a smile. 'Jump in.'

And that was the moment that changed everything.

SEVEN

CHRISTINA

Then

'D'you know what you and I should do while we're at work?'
Hannah Messenger said to her co-worker Tina Locke.

'What?'

'We should try coming on to some of these men.'

'Why?' Tina demanded. 'Why would we want to do that?'

She and Hannah were filling trays of glasses with wine at a
Chamber of Commerce function.

'You've seen how they look at us: they're all up for it,'
Hannah said, with a sly sideways grin. 'Gagging for it, to be
honest. And I figure we could use it to our advantage.'

'Like, how?'

Their supervisor, Kath Hughes, was coming towards them
now in the corporate navy suit she wore to events, signalling
that she was in charge. 'You girls need to get those trays circulating,' she said sternly. 'There are people out there who don't have
a drink yet. Come on: chop-chop!'

Tina rolled her eyes behind Kath's back.

'Let's talk during our break,' Hannah whispered, draping a

white napkin over her forearm before balancing the circular tray on it. She executed a smooth swivel and set off into the crowded room.

Tina watched her for a few seconds before loading up her own tray. It was easy to track Hannah's progress because of the extraordinary colour of her hair. What was even more extraordinary was that the creamy silver shade was natural. She was tall too, which made her even easier to spot. Tina, at four inches shorter, felt swallowed up by the throng of guests.

An hour and a half later, the waitresses had earned their only twenty-minute break. Hannah and Tina met in the bin store outside the kitchen, braving the March chill so that they could enjoy a cigarette. The two of them lived on opposite sides of the town and had never attended the same school, instead meeting on the Greenleaf Catering induction course. Hannah was aiming to boost her college fund and Tina had a dream of training as a beauty therapist: both needed extra cash.

'So, what have you got in mind?' Tina pulled her black cardigan around her, shivering as she puffed smoke out of the corner of her mouth.

'Well...' Hannah tipped her head back and inhaled deeply on her own cigarette. 'The way I see it is this. At least half of the people at these do's are male, right? And most of those must be married.'

'Yeah, because they're all ancient,' Tina observed grimly, flicking her ash.

'True, but what have all older men got plenty of?'

'Viagra?'

Hannah let out a giggle, coughing on the smoke as she did so. 'Money, you plank!'

'What are you saying?'

Tina looked at her more closely now. Hannah was privately educated and, to Tina, seemed worldly and sophisticated.

Where her superior confidence led, Tina was only too happy to follow.

'So we should try flirting with them.'

'And then what?'

Dean, one of the more experienced waitstaff, stuck his head out of the kitchen door. 'Oi, girls! You're due back on shift. Now.'

They both dropped their cigarettes and ground the butts under the identical black pumps that Kath Hughes insisted they wear.

Hannah shoved her mobile into Tina's hand as they headed back inside. 'Why don't you come over to mine after this thing's over, and we can talk about it some more. Put your number in my phone and I'll text you the address.'

Hannah lived in Chineham, a leafy suburb on the northern edge of Basingstoke.

After an argument with her mother, Tina secured a lift from her as far as the town centre and caught a bus the remainder of the way.

'I don't see why you want to go out again at this time of night, not when you've been working all evening,' her mother grumbled as she eventually reversed her battered hatchback off the drive of 7, Rowan Drive.

'Mum, it's only ten o'clock,' Tina said with an exaggerated sigh. 'It's not that late. And we've just wasted about an hour arguing about it.'

'Don't exaggerate, Christina, it's only been about ten minutes.'

Donna Locke drove fast and aggressively, crunching the gears and barely stopping as she pulled up at the bus station. As soon as her daughter was out of the passenger seat, she left with a screech of tyre rubber and no backward glance.

As soon as Tina had got off the bus and turned onto Maynards Lane, it was immediately obvious – if Tina didn't already know it – that Hannah's parents had better careers and made more money than her own. She stood for a few seconds looking enviously at the handsome three-storey detached house with a gravelled driveway and mock-Tudor gables before ringing the doorbell.

Hannah put her finger to her lips as soon as she had pulled the front door open, and pointed upstairs to indicate that her parents were already in bed, and they should keep the noise to a minimum. They went into an expansive, well-lit kitchen, where, with casual largesse, Hannah offered her guest a choice from a dedicated drinks fridge. Or there was espresso from a huge chrome coffee machine, or tea made with boiling water from a special tap. Tina felt shabby and self-conscious in her cheap market-stall leggings and chain-store hoodie. Even more so when she was led up to Hannah's bedroom, professionally deco-rated in shades of raspberry and cream, with a double bed. Tina still had to sleep in a bunk bed, with her younger stepsister Jodie sharing it half the time.

They sat on the window seat, Tina drinking the Diet Coke she had chosen and puffing smoke out of the open window.

'We need to flirt with the men every opportunity we get,' Hannah said, her lips curling in a smile around the filter of her cigarette.

'But only when Kath's not looking.'

'Yeah, obviously. We need to be a bit subtle about it. Just enough to get them to cross the line. Then they'll be feeling guilty in case their wives find out. So they'll do what we want.'

'You mean ask them for money?'

'We could do. Or even just take it when they're not looking.'

'What if one of us gets money and the other doesn't?' Tina looked doubtfully at Hannah's long legs and mesmerising hair.

'We have to report everything we make, and we split it fifty-fifty.'

'So, like a business?'

'Like a business, or a gang.' Hannah turned her head towards the window to expel a gust of smoke. 'Have you ever heard of the Forty Elephants gang?'

Tina shook her head.

'It was this all-female gang of thieves in the 1920s. They saw it as a way of having some sort of power in a man's world. There's a book about them in our school library.' Hannah flicked a column of ash into the garden below. 'I think we should be like the forty-first and forty-second elephants.'

'You're saying what we do will be... illegal?' Tina felt a little frisson of excitement, the thrill of the forbidden.

Hannah grinned. 'Borderline illegal.'

On their first night of operation, they made £25.

They were serving lunch at an away day for employees of the local council, being held in a country house hotel. Tina had no luck at all with the men, but managed to get £5 from one of the female guests when she encountered her in the ladies' cloak-room, after giving her a sob story about needing to buy tampons. Hannah allowed a male guest to put his hand on her backside in the lift, and when she lied that she was obliged to report any advances to Kath Hughes, he slipped her a twenty-pound note to buy her fictitious silence.

'Do you think we should actually have sex with them?' Tina asked when they divided their spoils that evening. True to Hannah's word, the £25 was split into equal halves, so she had done better out of their enterprise so far. 'They'd surely pay loads for that.'

'God, no!' Hannah was shocked. 'We don't need to go that far. That would make us hookers.'

It turned out she had a boyfriend, Levi, and Hannah claimed he would dump her if he found out. Even so, the stakes were generally lower for Hannah. She lived in that big house in Chineham, just her and her parents since her older sister had left for university, and they gave her a generous allowance. Tina, on the other hand, lived in a small house, crowded in with her younger siblings, her mother and stepfather and step-siblings who came and went according to their shared-custody arrangement. Space was tight, and so was money. Tina couldn't wait to get away.

She and Hannah now made a point of being available for every waitressing job that came up, and asked Kath Hughes to roster them on the same jobs, which she seemed happy to do. As they became bolder and more daring, their side hustle started to make more money, but Hannah continued to do much better than Tina. They split their earnings equally, but still Tina was frustrated by her role as second string. For her, it started to feel like a competition.

She spent some of her money on new make-up and perfume, and went to a salon to have bleached highlights put in her mousey hair. Her mother told her they looked cheap, and Hannah's silver-pale locks were still more eye-catching, but it gave Tina an extra boost of confidence. At the next event, she racked up a total of £30 by getting into the back of a taxi with a drunk guest and allowing him to feel her breasts, then using Hannah's line about reporting him to Kath Hughes.

Her stepfather offered to lend her his bike to get to and from catering jobs, but she turned him down. The encounter in the taxi had planted the seed of an idea.

'We should pretend to the guests we need lifts home,' she told Hannah during one of their cigarette breaks. 'If you get a man alone in a car, then he'll do anything. Easy pickings.'

And, sure enough, when she stood helplessly by the side of

the road after the next event, an older man in a Jaguar pulled up.

'Need a lift, dear?'

Dear. Who the hell ever used that term of endearment anymore?

Inside, the car smelled of leather and cigar smoke and expensive aftershave. The man had a moustache and wore a camel coat with a velvet collar, in contrast to Tina, who only had her thin cardigan over her tight work blouse.

'Sexy little thing, aren't you, dear?' he said, sounding like an actor in an old black and white film.

When he leaned in to kiss her, the taste of cigars on his breath made her want to gag but she held her nerve. His fingers between her legs were rough and insistent, however, and she couldn't prevent herself letting out a little whimper.

'How old are you, dear?'

'Fifteen,' she whispered, and watched him rear back in shock.

'I'm sorry,' he muttered. 'You won't say anything, will you?'

'That depends,' she said coyly.

Thirty seconds later, she was standing on the side of the road with five twenty-pound notes in her purse; more than either of them had made on one night so far.

She had done it. She had cracked the code, and beaten Hannah into the bargain.

Tina shared the £100 with Hannah, but didn't tell her how she had managed to make such a large sum. It wouldn't work for Hannah anyway, she reasoned. Since she was a lot taller than Tina, function guests were unlikely to believe that she was underage. And also there was the Levi issue. But Tina wanted to maintain her secret advantage. She didn't want to go back to being the underdog, the lower earner.

Their gang of two continued making money until the summer, grossing them an average of £600 per month on top of the wages paid by the catering company. Hannah went away travelling with Levi over the summer and Tina found a temporary job in the local branch of Boots, but by September, their two-woman incarnation of the Forty Elephants gang reconvened.

Then, in October, at a veterinary supply company function, Tina saw someone who interested her.

'Look at that one,' she whispered to Hannah, nudging her and pointing.

'Which one?'

'The one with the very dark hair.'

'You mean the young, good-looking one?' Hannah giggled.

'Yeah...' Tina breathed. 'He is, isn't he? And he's also on the soft drinks, which means he's probably got his car with him.'

'Toss you for him,' Hannah said with a laugh.

'I saw him first,' Tina said, shooting her a look.

'Okay, okay.' Hannah held up her hands in a gesture of defeat. 'Knock yourself out.'

Their shift was two hours long, and as it ended, Tina was delighted to discover that an autumn storm had blown in. Rain lashed the windows and wind shrieked round the corners of the hotel buildings. This was perfect timing, because only the most hard-hearted could fail to offer a lift in these conditions.

She positioned herself at the nearest bus stop to the hotel and popped a piece of gum into her mouth so that her breath would smell fresh. Her cardigan already drenched, her bare legs ice cold.

And then she spotted him, at the wheel of a silver family-sized car. Edging nearer to the kerb, she positioned herself so that he couldn't fail to spot her. Sure enough, he pulled over and wound down the passenger side window.

She held her breath, waiting. Would he fall for it?

And then he spoke. 'Jump in.'

EIGHT

LOUISE

Now

Having committed to cooking fish for dinner, Louise had to shower, change and head back to the kitchen just before six to make a start on the preparation.

To her surprise, Renée appeared a few minutes later, wearing an elegant black maxi-dress and a lot of chunky silver jewellery. Her hair was a stiffly quaffed helmet: a style that Louise thought of as female politician's hair.

She smiled warmly, and pointed a ringed finger in the direction of assembled ingredients. 'How can I help?'

'No, really,' Louise protested, blushing slightly. 'That's very kind, but there's no need. Everything's pretty much sorted.'

'Nonsense,' said Renée firmly, taking what must have been Pascale's apron from the back of the door and tying it around her waist. 'I'll do the potatoes.' She produced a potato peeler from a drawer and started peeling one with long, confident strokes.

'I was just going to bake them in the oven, to make—'

'Pommes purée will be much nicer, I think. We have butter, yes?' Renée marched to the fridge, her Louboutin sandals making a loud clatter on the stone flags. 'Pascale has plenty of butter, of course. She knows what I like.'

Retrieving a block of it, Renée returned to her potato peeling, while Louise set about rolling out the pastry and smearing pesto generously over the salmon sides before sealing them neatly in their crust and washing them with beaten egg.

'You are an accomplished cook, I can see that,' observed Renée. 'Tim is a very lucky man. A good-looking man, also. So – you are a lucky woman,' she added with what Louise thought of as European bluntness. 'I'm excited that Tim and I will be in business together.'

'Do you get to cook very much?' Louise asked, wanting to change the subject from this admiration of her husband.

'Not so often, regrettably.' Renée put the cut potatoes into a large pan. 'But I enjoy it. It relaxes me.'

She went on to explain how her mother, who had been an excellent cook, had passed on her culinary skills when Renée was young, believing they were necessary to prepare her for a successful marriage.

'She was disappointed, I'm afraid,' she said with a rueful smile. 'Because here I am, forty-seven years old, and never married.'

Having set the potatoes to boil, she went to the fridge and retrieved a bottle of Puligny-Montrachet and poured out two glasses, handing one to Louise without asking if she wanted it.

'Have you never wanted to marry?' Louise asked, as she set about topping and tailing the green beans.

'Not really,' Renée shrugged. 'I have had relationships, of course, and once... well, let's just say I thought that once it might happen. But my career has always come first. But now...' There was a softness about her now, and she looked suddenly girlish. 'I think maybe it's not too late.'

'How long have you and Jared been together?'

Renée did a double take, as though her mind had been elsewhere. 'About a year and a half,' she said, gathering herself, 'which is not so long. Sure, there is an age gap. He is only thirty-four, and I can't give him children. So, maybe in the future...' She shrugged.

'You two seem great together,' Louise lied. The truth was she had barely seen them interact.

'We are. And you know what?' Renée took a triumphant slug of her wine. 'Who knows what might happen? You never know, right?'

Louise nodded, grateful that Renée did not seem the type to indulge in relationship drama, and that beyond their business dealings she seemed to have no interest in Tim. Yes, there had been a little surface flirting, but that was all part of the dance of their contract negotiations. Louise was relieved about this, not least because she was starting to feel that Renée was someone she could trust.

'And you, Louise... did you always want children?' Renée asked a little later, as the two women loaded the food onto platters ready to carry to the table.

Louise hesitated. 'Was I always sure? To be honest, no. My own childhood was not easy. Full of disruption. So I wasn't very confident about having a family of my own. I had no example to model it on.'

'Really?' Renée set about whisking some salad dressing in a ceramic bowl. 'You do surprise me. You're such a natural with your children. And you and Tim seem so happy.'

'We are,' agreed Louise. 'We're very lucky.' She shrugged, as she picked up the platter with the fish and headed for the kitchen door. 'But, you know, no family is perfect, right?'

After the group had assembled for lunch and exclaimed about how delicious it was, Renée caught Louise's eye and raised her wine glass in a little salute. But it was not herself and

Tim that she focused her attention on, Louise noticed. It was Richard and Merry Stafford.

NINE

TIM

Then

The waitress climbed into the passenger seat with a grateful smile that rendered her rather hard face much prettier. Her eyes were a little too small, her nose a little too large, her chin a little too square, but there was something about the combination of her features that was rather attractive. Her wet shirt clung to her torso, revealing a slim but curvaceous body, and she was wearing a strong, sweet perfume that smelled of vanilla, mingling with a faint top note of cigarette smoke. Tim supposed that objectively she would be considered sexy.

'What's your name?' he asked her, desperate to normalise the situation.

'You don't need to know that.' She gave him a smug little smirk.

He shrugged. 'Okay, suit yourself. And the other girl – the tall one with the pale hair – she's a friend of yours?'

'Yeah, she is.' She looked into the back of the car, where his clinical kit was on the back seat next to the sodden Curadex tote. 'So you're a vet?'

'That's right, yes.' He nodded in the direction of his kitbag. 'Always have to travel with supplies, just in case I'm called to an emergency.'

'Cool,' she grinned at him, and carried on chewing.

When they reached Kempshott, she directed him to a development of boxy newly built homes just off Winchester Road. He pulled over outside the house she pointed to and waited for her to get out of the car. But although she had unclipped her seat belt, she didn't open the door. She turned towards him instead.

His heart racing, Tim stared at her. He somehow knew what was about to happen. In fact, it was as though he had made it happen by having the unbidden thought that she was sexy. She removed the gum, and with the slimy nugget still between her fingers, started to kiss him. Her mouth tasted of gum and cherry lip gloss.

He wanted her to stop, of course he did. He hadn't asked for this, or expressly invited it. And yet he was frozen, passive. And although her advances were unwelcome, it was also wildly exciting because of its sheer unexpectedness. His head was saying firmly that no, this was absurd, he didn't want this. But his body, shut out from any physical intimacy with Louise for months, was saying something else entirely.

With a surprisingly practised move, her hand slid down to his crotch. Somehow pulling his mouth away from hers, Tim managed to croak 'No! What the hell are you doing?'

'What the hell do you think I'm doing?' she asked in a teasing tone, a triumphant smile playing across her face. She unclipped his seat belt and climbed onto his lap, pressing her damp breasts against his chest. Her body was compact and surprisingly strong. And he was aroused, of course, he was. His most basic instincts had kicked in, despite himself.

He still continued to protest, but somehow she had unzipped his fly and slid his erection inside her. What had happened to her underwear? he wondered. Was she even wearing any? She was straddling him and rocking to and fro in time to the rain pounding on the roof of the car. In a blind panic he tried to pull away, but there was nowhere for him to go, he was trapped in the seat. And he was having sex with her, even though he didn't want to. Gasping, he pressed the flat of his hand against her chest and tried to somehow dislodge her, but it was pointless.

A few seconds later, it was all over. The girl climbed off him, gave him a suggestive little smile and disappeared into the teeming rain. Tim turned the car towards Junction 7 of the M3 and drove the twenty-five miles back to Winchester, shivering violently despite having the heating turned up high.

What have I done? What have I done?

The words repeated themselves on a loop in his brain. He hadn't wanted sex; he hadn't asked for it. And yet he'd just had it with a complete stranger. He was a lot bigger and stronger than her, so why hadn't he stopped it? He could have opened the driver's door, pulled himself out from under her. And yet he'd been so frozen with shock, he hadn't done so.

He arrived home fifteen minutes later. The Cutlers' five-year plan was to buy a large family house with off-street parking, but for now he was stuck with trying to find a free space in the road of Victorian terraces where they'd bought their first marital home. Once he'd manoeuvred into a tiny space, he sat in the car for a long time, afraid to go inside in case Louise sensed the waves of despair radiating off him. The two of them had always been unequivocally honest with one another. They'd made a pact at the start of their relationship that what-ever happened, however badly wrong they got things, they would tell one another everything. But his wife was grieving the baby they had just lost, and recovering from a debilitating bout of depression. How could he possibly honour that pact now?

As he climbed out of the front seat, he noticed a piece of paper in the footwell. Something that must have fallen out of the girl's cardigan pocket as she extricated herself. He unfolded it and saw that it was a payslip; the sort that was inserted into a brown envelope with cash wages. It was for £27.40, paid by Greenleaf Catering to a Christina Yorke. She hadn't wanted him to know her name, but now he had it. He shoved the slip into the inside pocket of his jacket, some instinct telling him that he needed to hang on to this piece of information.

When he let himself in, the lights in the living room were still on and Louise was asleep on the sofa. He stood looking down at her for a few minutes; at her full mouth with its dimples either side, the long eyelashes resting on her cheek, the soft brown curls of her hair. His sweet-natured, trusting, precious Louise.

He couldn't tell her about this. He simply couldn't do it.

TEN

CHRISTINA

Then

Tina did two things in the days that followed.

She carried on with Hannah's moneymaking scheme as though nothing had happened. Hannah had texted her afterwards: *How did it go? Get any money from him? x*

No, she had typed back eventually. *Nothing doing x*

It was the truth, after all. She had received precisely nothing – not yet.

The second thing Tina did was to set about finding out more about Timothy Cutler, FRCVS. Online stalking, some people would call it. Tina preferred to think of it as valid research. He'd been wearing a name badge at the event after all.

As it turned out, there wasn't a great deal to find. She quickly found the practice in Winchester where he was a junior partner, and through the bio on their site learned that he had qualified at the University of Exeter. There was a headshot of him looking smiley and trusting, which she screenshotted to her phone. Other than that, he had no social media presence other than an old Facebook account. It hadn't been updated in a while, although it did reveal that in 2006 he'd married someone called Louise Gilbert. The wife had a Facebook account too, but its privacy settings were like Fort Knox. A little more 'research' showed that she was a teacher at a girls' school in Winchester. Her photo revealed an unremarkable-looking woman with a pleasant face and wavy brown hair. She looked like... well, one of Tina's own teachers.

Unsure what to do next, Tina did nothing for a couple of weeks. She could show up at his work, she supposed. Or even, after a bit more digging, find his home address and show up there. But both of those options were too public. The police might be called. Or, God forbid, her mother. No, it would have to be something more private. But first she needed a phone number for him. She went back onto the website for the veterinary clinic, and under his contact details there was a mobile number listed as 'Emergency and out of hours'. She composed a text and hit send.

Hi, I'm the one you gave a lift to Kempshott last month, I need to talk to you.

To her slight surprise, a reply came back straightaway.

Who is this?

Whoever it was had not denied the lift. So it must be him, surely?

You don't need to know, she typed.

Have it your way. Where shall we meet?

Her heartbeat sped up. It *was* him, otherwise why would whoever was on that number want to meet up? A little thrown by how easy this had proved to be, her mind went completely blank when it came to a venue.

Don't mind.

He eventually texted her again, after what seemed like hours but was probably only twenty minutes or so.

There's a Starbucks in Kempshott on the main Winchester Road. Meet me there tomorrow at 2.45?

There was no reason that Tina could not make this time, but she didn't want to make things too easy for him.
Earliest I can do is 4, she typed, picking the time at random.

Fine, see you then.

There was no doubt in Tina's mind what she needed to wear for this assignation. She went into the wardrobe used by her stepsister when she was in Rowan Drive and borrowed her school blazer, tie and lace-up shoes, digging out a pair of white knee socks from her own overflowing chest of drawers. No make-up, obviously, and hair tied up in a ponytail.

It worked like a charm. He was already there when she arrived, which was a relief. It had occurred to her that she would arrive and find some other random man waiting for her. But no, Tim Cutler was sitting in the corner with a black coffee, and when he saw her, he looked as though he'd seen a ghost. Whatever he'd been expecting, it wasn't this.

He doesn't even know your name, she reminded herself. *If this all goes tits up it won't rebound on you.*

She strolled over to his table with her can of Coke and sat

down, waiting for him to speak. He had such a nice face, she thought. She really liked the contrast between his round, almost childlike chestnut-brown eyes and the very masculine black stubble that covered his chin like iron filings. He cleared his throat.

'I'm glad you got in touch, because I think we need to talk about... the other night.'

Tina flicked her hair over her shoulders, feeling suddenly out of her depth. She covered her nerves by smiling at him in what she hoped was an enigmatic fashion.

'It really shouldn't have happened,' he was saying. 'It wasn't what I intended when I offered you the lift. And it wasn't something I wanted.'

'Are you serious?' she demanded hotly. God, this was insulting. 'If a man doesn't want it, then he can't do it, can he?'

'Unfortunately, that's not the case. A man can be mentally unwilling but certain physiological responses kick in anyway.' He looked self-conscious, as though aware he sounded pompous. 'And obviously we didn't use protection.' He was looking around them now, clearly terrified someone would hear what he was saying. 'So the responsible thing now we're here is for me to make sure that there were no unintended consequences.'

She assured him that she wasn't pregnant. Then she played her trump card, and watched with satisfaction as his face turned ashen.

When she informed him that what happened next was going to cost him, she wasn't actually thinking about the money, but a burning sense of rejection that had welled up from nowhere. This man wasn't interested in her, not in the slightest, beyond the fact that she wasn't going to mess up his nice little life by getting accidentally pregnant. Her father hadn't been interested in her: he'd left when she was three. Her mother was too busy with her job and her new husband to be interested in her. Her stepfather merely tolerated her to keep the peace. And now Tim Cutler, with his sweet, handsome choirboy's face, was only too happy to cast her aside as soon as he'd had sex with her. It was this final rejection that sealed the ruthlessness in her.

'Look, I'm very sorry that we're both in this situation, but if you're sure you're not pregnant...' He screwed the cap back on his water and stood up to go. This was her cue.

She reached in her blazer pocket for the pre-prepared note and pushed it into his hand. 'Set up a new email account no one else knows about and use it to message me. Then I'll tell you what you need to do next.'

'No.' He seemed to have found his nerve at last, and was shaking his head at her. 'No, if you think I'm going to let you extort me, then you can forget it. It's not happening.'

She mustn't lose her own nerve now. She had to make him think she was serious. That this *was* happening.

'Fine.' She stood up and pushed rudely past him. 'I guess you'd rather go to prison.'

ELEVEN

LOUISE

Now

On Monday morning, Pascale returned and the domestic routine of the household returned to normal. Louise was privately a little disappointed. She had quite enjoyed being a catering team with Renée, and Pascale unnerved her slightly. Every time she looked up, the woman was there; hovering, watchful.

But since she was freed from the demands of being temporary chef, Louise decided it would be good to get away from the villa for a while, without Shona Prentice this time. She suggested to Tim that they take the children into Cotignac to browse the shops and galleries, spend some of their holiday money.

'Just us Cutlers, though,' she said firmly. The Staffords had already headed into the village in a taxi, for Richard to order a consignment of wine from one of the local wine merchants.

Tim frowned. 'Don't you think we ought to ask Renée and Jared at least? To be polite.'

'No, I don't. They won't miss us for a couple of hours, and

besides, Renée told me last night that she's got a beautician from a local spa coming over to give her a facial. It'll be fine.'

So they drove the five kilometres in the villa's BMW, parking just south of the river. The heat was stifling, making the children complain as they walked the five hundred metres over the bridge and into the town. It was an arrestingly pretty place, with its honey-coloured stone squares, ornate ironwork, fountains and shady plane trees. Tim and Louise sat at a pavement table in the main street and drank coffee while the children headed off on their own to buy ice cream and investigate the shops.

'This is nice,' Louise sighed, as the waiter set down two iced lattes. 'The villa's amazing, but it's also lovely being just us two.'

She covered Tim's hand with her own, and he squeezed her fingers. Other tables at the café were filling now, and shoppers were convening around the boulangerie and greengrocer's stall across the street. The warm air smelled of ripe fruit: melons and peaches.

'Where are you with the takeover deal?' she asked. 'When I was talking to Renée yesterday in the kitchen, she gave the impression she was still pretty keen for it to go ahead.'

'I hope so,' he said fervently. 'She's said we're going to have a sit-down sometime to go over the figures and the small print in the contract. Not sure when, though. Before the weekend, at any rate.' The Cutlers were due to fly back to the UK on Wednesday of the following week, 2nd August.

'I like Renée,' Louise said thoughtfully, stirring sugar into her glass with a long-handled spoon. 'It was sweet of her to come and help me make dinner when no one else offered.' She knew Tim would understand she was referring to Shona. 'We had a nice chat while we were preparing the veg.'

'I'm glad, sweetie.' Tim reached for her hand again. 'It can only help oil the wheels if you two are getting on.'

'What do you make of the Staffords?'

'They seem perfectly all right,' Tim said carefully. 'He's an old friend of Renée's, but she seems to barely know Merry. I talked to him a bit about his business on the first night, and I found him quite engaging. I haven't got a whole lot from her. She's pretty reserved.'

'No,' Louise agreed. 'I've barely spoken to her, apart from asking her to pass the bread or the cheese. She's very attractive, though, isn't she?'

'Is she?' Tim grinned. 'You know me, darling, I never really notice other women. I don't really look at them.'

'Those hair extensions of hers must be very uncomfortable in this weather,' Louise mused. 'I'm sure they're heavy. And make your head sweat.'

'Is that what they are?' Tim laughed. 'I thought she was just blessed with an inordinate amount of hair.'

Then, very suddenly, he tensed, his whole body stiffening. He pulled his hand away from Louise's abruptly and gripped the edge of the table. Underneath his new tan, and his omnipresent dark stubble, he looked very pale.

'Are you all right?' Louise stared at him, concerned. She motioned to the waiter to bring some water.

'Yes, yes,' he said, gathering himself. 'Probably just a touch of heatstroke.'

Tim, who had Maltese blood on his mother's side, was supremely unaffected by heat, in fact positively relished it. In all the time she had known him, Louise had never known him suffer heatstroke. She poured him a glass of water from the jug the waiter had brought and watched him anxiously as he drank it.

'How do you feel now?'

'Fine. It was just a passing thing.'

And, sure enough, the colour had started returning to his face.

He drained his coffee and got to his feet. 'Come on,' he said brusquely. 'I fancy a swim. Let's go and round up the kids and head back to the villa.'

They got back to Le Mas des Flores just as Pascale was setting the table on the loggia for lunch.

Delicious, garlicky aromas were wafting from the kitchen, and from the pool area there were sounds of laughter.

'If you run and get changed, there's just time for a quick dip before we eat,' Louise told the children.

She and Tim went up to their room together, and straightaway she stripped off her T-shirt and shorts and headed into the bathroom to fetch her bikini, which was drying on the towel rail. When she came back into the bedroom, Tim was sitting on the edge of the bed, still fully dressed.

'Aren't you coming?' Louise asked, reaching for her book and suntan cream.

He shook his head. 'I don't fancy it.'

'But you were the one who wanted to come back for a swim.' A tinge of exasperation crept into her voice.

'Sorry, sweetie; I still feel a little weird. Maybe midday sun isn't the cleverest idea. I think I'll go dig out the practice paperwork and go over some figures, ready to talk to Renée.' He indicated his messenger bag, which was propped against the wall next to the red lounge chair.

'Okay, fine. See you at lunch?'

He nodded without looking up and, feeling slightly unsettled, Louise dropped a swift kiss on his cheek and headed down to the pool.

The first thing she saw was the back of Shona's head, her dark red hair tied up in an elaborate arrangement with a twist of bright coloured fabric. She was sitting on the edge of the pool with her legs in the water, and her back was suffused with bright pink from too much exposure to the hot sun.

'I think you need to put on some SPF,' she called as she approached the decked area. It was only when Shona twisted her body around to see who was talking that Louise spotted Jared Frayn. He was in the water, his elbows leaning on the edge of the pool, his large white American teeth bared in a grin. There was no sign of Renée. Or Kevin.

'Hi there, Lou,' he drawled, and she felt a flash of resentment. Only Tim and her closest friends were allowed to call her Lou.

'Your back's burning,' she said to Shona, ignoring Jared. 'You might want some of this.' She waggled the bottle of factor 30.

'No, it's okay, we're going in in a minute.'

Louise noted the easy use of 'we' to refer to herself and Jared, and experienced a queasy sensation in the pit of her stomach.

The two of them continued their conversation in low voices, so she picked up a towel from the wicker basket on the deck and walked over to the loungers. The only other person sunbathing was Merry Stafford, her body toned and slim in a delphinium blue bikini.

'Hi.' Louise raised a hand in greeting.

'Oh. Hi,' Merry returned without enthusiasm.

'Richard not about?'

'He's on the tennis court. Renée arranged for a pro to come and play with him.' This was the longest sentence she had ever heard Merry utter.

'How did you two meet?' Louise launched into small talk to fill the awkward silence.

'He was a client.'

'Oh really? What kind of client?'

'I worked in a spa, at a hotel near Zurich. He was living out there at the time, doing logistics for Mondiale.'

So that must be how he knew Renée.

'Ah. How long ago?'

'About three years.' Merry picked up her glass of sparkling water and took a sip.

'So when you say he was a client...?'

'I was a trained massage therapist and beautician.'

'Oh, fantastic!' Louise enthused, because she couldn't think of anything else to say. Merry showed no reciprocal interest in her own backstory, so she ploughed on. 'And do you still do that?'

She shook her head, the long tendrils of amber hair waving around her shoulders. 'I don't need to work anymore.' Her tone was matter-of-fact, unapologetic.

'But you don't have children yet?'

'God no.' Merry gave a brittle little laugh. 'I don't want them.'

At that moment, Louise's own children came charging down the path to the pool, arguing loudly, and Merry took this as her cue to leave.

Over lunch, it was once again as though the two women had never spoken. Louise attempted to get more information about the spa in Switzerland, but Merry was so monosyllabic she gave up. When Shona wasn't bickering with Kevin, she was giving long, sultry looks at Jared. Tim, usually extremely enthusiastic about all French food, was pushing the langoustines and aioli around his plate.

'Are you still feeling off colour?' Louise whispered, resting her hand on his bare arm.

'I'm fine. Please don't fuss.' His tone was curt, and he edged his arm from under her fingers.

She felt stung. Tim never spoke to her like this. Not ever. They were no rows or arguments; rarely even disagreements.

After lunch when everyone retired for a siesta, they went

up to their room, but Tim sat on the bright red lounge chair rather than lying on the bed next to her. She barely felt capable of broaching the strange sense of disconnection between them.

'Are we okay?' was all she could say.

He rested his chin on his hands. 'I'm sorry, darling. I guess I'm just anxious about getting this VCM deal tied down.'

He managed a smile, but Louise still felt a creeping unease. They were alone in their room, but it no longer felt as though they were together.

TWELVE

TIM

Then

It took several days for the shock of that night to wear off.

Days when Tim had to force himself to act naturally, to behave as if nothing was wrong. And then, when the disbelief subsided, it hit him. He had not only had sex with a girl he didn't know, it was unprotected sex. What if she was pregnant?

The thought tormented him, the pain of it all the sharper because of the Cutlers' own recent baby loss. Surely it would be too harsh a punishment if he and Louise were unable to have children of their own, but this girl did? This idea was so horrific that at first he tried to push it away. But eventually he accepted that he could not just leave the question unanswered. To do so would mean he never knew a minute's peace. He could only justify not telling Louise about what he thought of as 'the incident' if it was definitively over.

No, Tim had to be sure that there were no unintended consequences. And to do that, he had to find her.

He retrieved the payslip he had found in his car and then did a search on Greenleaf Catering. The office was in

Basingstoke and the manager was listed as Kath Hughes. Tim waited until he was alone in the surgery and phoned her, using the practice's landline, to make his query seem more official.

'Hi, my name's Tim Cutler, one of the guests at the Curadex event last week. I'm trying to get contact details for one of your waitstaff. I don't know if you remember, but that was the night of the storm and it was tipping down, so I offered a lift to one of your waitresses...' The best lies, he reasoned, had a large element of truth in them. '...Only she left her purse in my car. It must have fallen out of her coat pocket.'

'Do you know which one?' Kath Hughes asked.

'Which one?'

'Which girl?'

'Um...' He couldn't exactly describe her as the sexy one. 'She was the one working with her taller friend with the unusual light blonde hair. I think she said her name was Christina.' He knew full well that was her name, but he didn't want it to look as though there'd been reason for him to remember it.

'Ah yes, that'd be Tina Locke. Give me a minute.'

There were background sounds of filing drawers being opened and papers flicked through. Then Kath came back on the line.

'Got a pen and paper?'

She gave him Tina's mobile number. He put it into his phone as 'Curadex'.

Much as he wanted the business over with as quickly as possible, Tim realised that there would be a minimum window of a couple of weeks for a possible pregnancy to be confirmed. So he waited. In November, sixteen days after the event in Basingstoke, he was about to compose a text to Tina when, unprompted, he received a message from 'Curadex'.

Hi, I'm the one you gave a lift to Kempshott last month, I need to talk to you

He was taken aback that she had got hold of his number. She must have found it on the practice website, which meant she knew his name. This was not good. He was already having nightmares about her turning up on the doorstep of their house or, worse still, at the school where Louise taught.

The text was unsigned, and just to test the water, he typed back *Who is this?*

He expected someone her age to be on her phone constantly, and so it was no surprise when a five-word response came through five minutes later.

You don't need to know.

Have it your way. Where shall we meet?

Her next text unnerved him, because it revealed how young she was. *Don't mind.*

To be on the safe side, he decided they had to meet in a public place. Not an actual pub; that would seem far too cosy. Instead, he chose a Starbucks on the far side of Kempshott and suggested they meet there the next day, at 2.45. Before it was dark outside, and with no suggestion of a meal or alcohol.

Earliest I can do is 4, she replied.

Tim checked his appointments for the next day. He had a minor surgical list in the morning and had planned to leave for Basingstoke immediately afterwards, then go straight home after he had seen Tina. He could still do that, but would just be back a little later. He texted her that 4 p.m. was fine. Of course it didn't feel fine. None of this was fine.

. . .

Desmond came into the operating theatre the next morning as Tim was suturing the abdomen of a freshly spayed cat.

'Been meaning to ask you, how did the Curadex shindig go? Any interesting gossip?'

Tim shook his head. 'Nothing of note. Except a bulk order discount on offer; usual sort of deal.'

'Maybe Amy can set it up for us.'

'Probably easier if I do it. Not sure accounting software is her strong suit.'

'Fair enough. Better get back to seeing outpatients.'

Desmond strode out of the theatre and Tim watched as Claire, his veterinary nurse, lifted the unconscious cat off the table and carried it through to the recovery area. His mobile buzzed in the pocket of his scrubs. *Message from Darling Wife.*

What time will you be back? Thought I'd cook us something special xxx

Tim sighed heavily. If only he could drive straight home now and never see Tina Locke again.

Not late, he typed. *Love you xxx*

Once he'd pressed 'Send', he changed out of his scrubs, told Amy he was going to meet up with a veterinary supplies rep and drove to Kempshott. He arrived a few minutes early. He ordered an Americano and a bottle of water and sat at the back of the seating area, in the darkest corner he could find.

At five past four, the door opened and Tina walked in. She bought a can of cola at the till and his throat tightened as she turned in his direction to walk over to the table.

She was wearing school uniform.

'I'm glad you got in touch, because I think we need to talk about... the other night.'

Tim cleared his throat. He hoped he had outwardly recovered his composure, even though his pulse was still thundering in his ears. So she was a teenager. Oh God, this was even worse than he had thought.

Tina looked at him, flicking her badly highlighted hair over her shoulders but saying nothing. He found her expression impossible to read. Was she nervous, or amused, or... what? For a second, he'd have sworn she almost looked pleased with herself. When they'd met she had had a full face of make-up on. Now her face was scrubbed clean, and she looked a lot younger.

'It really shouldn't have happened,' he blundered on. 'It wasn't what I intended when I offered you the lift. And it wasn't something I wanted.' He looked down at the rapidly cooling coffee that he didn't want either.

'Are you serious?' she sneered, and he could see a ball of chewing gum on her tongue. 'If a man doesn't want it, then he can't do it, can he?'

'Unfortunately, that's not the case. A man can be mentally unwilling but certain physiological responses kick in anyway.' He was aware that he sounded old and stuffy, but ploughed on. 'And obviously we didn't use protection. So the responsible thing now we're here is for me to make sure that there were no unintended consequences.'

'You mean, am I pregnant?' That smug smile again.

'Yes.'

'No, I'm not pregnant. I'm on the pill. But I am fifteen.'

Tim felt the blood drain from his face. Under the table, his left knee began to shake uncontrollably. He had no sisters and had been educated at an all boys' grammar school. The true age of teenage girls was something he had no feel for at all.

'Fifteen?' he repeated, in a whisper.

'Yes. Fifteen,' Tina said calmly. 'I'm not legal yet. And that's going to cost you.'

Tim still hadn't touched his coffee, and he wasn't going to

now. He felt as though he would vomit if he did. Instead he uncapped the water bottle and took a sip.

'If I'd known...' But he let the sentence trail off. It was no use saying, 'If I'd known, I'd never have done it,' because that would imply he would have been happy to have sex with her if she were older. And that wasn't the case. She could have been twenty-nine – the same age as him – and still he would never have wanted to have sex with her on the front seat of his car.

'But you're employed by the catering company,' he said instead.

'You can legally work in this country if you're fifteen,' she said scathingly. 'As long as it's part-time hours. Loads of my friends have part-time jobs in the evening, or on Saturday.'

He shook his head slowly. 'Look, I'm very sorry that we're both in this situation, but if you're sure you're not pregnant...'

He started to push back his chair. Despite the November chill, the coffee shop was hot and airless, and Tim was starting to sweat profusely. He just wanted to get out of there and never see this girl again.

Tina did not stand up, but instead handed him a small piece of paper. On it was an email address – Fortytwoelephants@hotmail.com. What had made her choose that? he wondered. It was clear she still didn't want to give away her real name. He felt a frisson of petty one-upmanship that she was unaware he already knew it.

'Set up a new email account no one else knows about and use it to message me. Then I'll tell you what you need to do next.'

Tim stared down at her, trying to glean clues from the girl's appearance. This was one of Basingstoke's less wealthy suburbs, but she was clean and well presented. Her shirt and socks were spotlessly white, and the puffa jacket she wore over her uniform was a designer brand. Nothing suggested deprivation or a desperate need for money. What exactly was her endgame?

'No.' He shook his head. 'No, if you think I'm going to let you extort me, then you can forget it. It's not happening.'

'Fine.' Tina stood up, and he got another whiff of her sickly vanilla perfume as she brushed past him. 'I guess you'd rather go to prison.'

Once she'd left the coffee shop and disappeared from sight, Tim sat down at the table again.

He googled the law on sex with a minor. It was complicated, that was the first thing he discovered. Very complicated, with a huge number of variables around consent, coercion and grooming. As far as he could tell, given that there was no element of premeditation and the act had been consensual, the maximum sentence was probably five years. But bearing in mind that he had a spotless record, that he had also been ignorant of Tina's age, and had not initiated or asked for physical contact (that would be difficult to prove in court, he knew), it seemed the likelihood was a suspended sentence. He would rather just come clean and take the consequences than sit in fear indefinitely while handing over God knew how much money. Louise's suffering was the sticking point. How would his wife react?

She would be able to deal with it, he decided, as he drove back down the M3. Because the one thing that was certain in this life was that he and Louise knew each other, as well as two human beings ever could know one another. She knew who Tim was, to the very core of his being. And because she did, she would believe him. She would believe that he hadn't either sought or desired what had happened. That the worst he was guilty of was weakness in not physically fighting the girl off.

His mobile rang. It was his mother. He ignored the call, and again a second time, but when she tried a third time, he realised there must be something wrong and he answered on Bluetooth.

'Mum, I'm on the motorway, can I call you back?'

'I just needed to tell you about Uncle Arthur.'

Arthur was his great-uncle; his late grandfather's brother. He had no children of his own and had always been very involved in the lives of Tim and his brother Phil.

'You know his health hasn't been good these past months, and I'm afraid he passed away last night. I'm sorry. I know you were fond of him.'

'Oh no.' There was a catch in Tim's voice. He felt suddenly overwhelmed with tearfulness, as much at the sound of his mother's voice as the news about poor Arthur.

'I'm sorry, love,' his mother repeated. 'But it was very peaceful at the end.'

'Let me know about the funeral, okay? Sorry, Mum, I'm going to have to go.'

He was on the outskirts of Winchester now, and as soon as he had hung up his thoughts slammed back to his own terrible dilemma. To 'the incident'. He was going to have to tell Louise. There was no other way.

When he let himself into the house, he was greeted by music, warmth and delicious cooking smells.

'I thought I'd roast a chicken,' Louise said, kissing him. 'And I've lit a fire.'

She was smiling and there was more colour in her cheeks than of late.

'Great,' Tim kissed her back. 'This calls for wine.' He was suddenly desperate for a drink, for the comforting numbness of alcohol. He pulled a bottle of Chilean Malbec from the wine rack in the tiny kitchen and uncorked it, before reaching for two wine glasses.

'No,' said Louise. 'Not for me.' She was smiling as she said it, and her arms wrapped around his waist. 'I'm not drinking.'

He stared at her, and his stomach lurched.

'Yes,' she nodded, and her eyes were sparkling. 'I'm pretty sure I'm pregnant. But I wanted to wait till you were home before I did the test, so we could find out together. It's what we wanted, isn't it?'

'Yes,' said Tim, trying to hide the anxiety he was feeling. 'It is.'

'Let's just pray that this time nothing goes wrong for us.'

THIRTEEN

LOUISE

Now

'Morning, darling.'

Louise woke to Tim standing over her with a glass of the delicious freshly squeezed juice that was served at breakfast.

'I brought you this.' He handed the glass to his wife and pulled back the heavy drapes, opening the full-length window to admit the persistent floral scent. 'Call it a peace offering if you like.' He sat down on the edge of the bed and stroked her bare arm as she drank. 'Look, I'm sorry I was off with you yesterday, sweetie. It's not us, is it, behaving like that?'

Louise shook her head.

'To be honest, I wish we hadn't done this. Come here, I mean. It's not easy being on holiday in these circumstances. Trying to combine business and pleasure. If I'd known it would actually be this stressful maybe I'd have said no to Renée. But...' He held up his hands. 'We are where we are. Just got to make the best of it.'

Louise considered this. 'How's your heatstroke?'

For a few seconds, Tim looked as though he didn't know

what she was referring to. 'Oh, that's all fine now. I feel better for a good night's sleep and some of Pascale's rocket fuel.'

Another of the private jokes Louise had arrived to was the strength of the housekeeper's coffee.

'Have you eaten?'

He shook his head. 'I was waiting for you. Throw some clothes on, and let's go down together.'

When they arrived in the shaded loggia, everyone was assembled, apart from Merry Stafford, who rarely ate breakfast, often not emerging from the couple's suite in the outbuilding until noon.

The three children were squabbling over who got the pain au chocolat as opposed to the plain croissants. Kevin and Richard were talking about Formula One racing, watched resentfully by a sulky-looking Shona. Louise noted that the burnt skin on her back was starting to peel.

'Can I get you more coffee, babe?' Jared asked Renée solicitously, touching her fingertips.

Renée nodded stiffly, barely managing a smile even when he handed her a cup with a gallant little flourish.

'Morning,' murmured Louise, resting her hands on Harry's shoulders and kissing Elodie on the top of her head. Her dark hair, the same colour as Tim's, smelt of coconut shampoo and chlorine.

Tim took the empty seat on the other side of Renée, who gave him the briefest of smiles before downing her cup of coffee and standing up, tossing her linen napkin onto her plate.

'If you'll excuse me, I need to get ready.'

'Renée, I was hoping you and I could get some time for a sit-down today.' Tim caught Louise's eye as he spoke and she gave him what she hoped was an encouraging look.

'I'm sorry, Tim, it will have to wait. I have business at the

VCM offices in Marseille, and I'm going to stay overnight. Perhaps tomorrow when I'm back.'

She left the table, but Jared didn't follow her, instead heading to the pool as the table was cleared. Louise noticed Shona give a little smile of satisfaction as she stood up and followed suit.

With Renée gone for the day, Shona clearly felt free to flirt openly with Jared.

Louise saw the Staffords raise eyebrows at one another as Shona pawed the American's muscular naked shoulders. So it wasn't just her who had noticed it. She looked over in Kevin's direction, willing him to assert his connection with his own wife, but he seemed hell-bent on ignoring it, instead focusing on teaching the backstroke to his daughter. Violet was a skinny, timid child with thin mousey hair and an overbite. Alternately smothered or ignored by her mother, Louise felt it unsurprising that she lacked confidence compared to the buoyant and outgoing Cutler children. Her own two, who were both strong swimmers, were currently holding a diving competition at the far end of the pool.

However, at the lunch table, Elodie started complaining of a stomach ache.

'I don't feel very well,' she moaned, clutching her sides.

'Probably all that pool water you've swallowed,' Tim observed.

It was decided that the children would take an afternoon off from swimming. Elodie and Violet settled down in the cinema room to watch *Frozen II*, while Kevin challenged Harry to a game of table tennis.

'I really don't feel like lounging by the pool this afternoon either,' Louise confessed to Tim as they lay down for their customary hour's siesta. 'It gets kind of repetitive.'

'Why don't we explore the vineyards,' Tim suggested. 'We're slap bang in the middle of a six-hundred-hectare wine estate after all.'

Armed with sun hats and bottles of water, ten minutes later they left the villa, holding hands just as they always did. The pool area was on the south-eastern side of the property, and the Cutlers headed to the south-west, leaving behind the manicured path and flower borders and striking out along a rough stony track. It dipped down a steep slope and then up again, flattening out in a broad expanse of vineyards fringed with ancient, gnarled oak trees. The vines were heavy with fruit that was turning from green to pinkish-purple.

Tim bent to pick a grape, wincing at its sourness and swigging from his bottle of water to wash away the taste.

'I think we can agree they're not ready for harvesting just yet.'

Louise lifted the hem of her T-shirt and dabbed at her sweating face. Although the sun was getting lower in the sky, there was no breeze and the heat was still oppressive. 'What do you think the temperature is?' she asked, reaching for the water bottle.

'Must be close to 90. Let's head over to where those trees are, and we'll get a bit more shade.'

They walked on in silence. Louise knew her husband so well that she could tell just from the way that he was holding her hand that he was still finding it difficult to relax.

'It's a shame Renée went off on her own today,' she said as they reached the shadier stretch of track. 'But hopefully you'll get a proper chance to talk to her tomorrow.'

'Fingers crossed,' Tim sighed. 'I don't think it's helping her mood seeing Shona's bloody antics. Fawning all over her meathead of a boyfriend.'

'You've noticed that then?'

'It's pretty hard not to. And more to the point...' Tim

uncapped the water bottle and took a long draught. '...It's obvious Renée has noticed it too.'

Louise shook her head slowly.

'And because we invited the Prentices here, it feels like we're responsible.'

'Well, we're not.' Louise decided against pointing out that it was Tim who had invited them, and that she had been against it.

'I know, but you couldn't blame Renée if she resented us for our choice of holiday companions. At the very least, she's going to be unimpressed. And my worry is: will that make her think twice about going into business with me?'

'Surely not,' soothed Louise. But the very same thought had already occurred to her.

When they returned to the villa, Elodie was hunched miserably under a blanket in the screening room, claiming that her stomach pain was worse.

Louise sent her to bed with a glass of ginger ale, and Pascale fed Violet and Harry pizza in the kitchen, since neither of them wanted to try the octopus a la niçoise she was preparing. The Staffords had gone out to dinner in Aix-en-Provence, leaving numbers at the dinner table reduced to five. Shona, dressed in a plunging black jumpsuit that revealed her breasts, was giggling vapidly at everything Jared said, and Kevin's reaction to his wife's behaviour was to drink glass upon glass of wine. By the time the cheese course had been cleared, he was so steaming drunk that Tim had to half drag him, half carry him up to the Prentices' room.

'He's passed out,' he said to Shona, returning to the table as tarte au citron and coffee were being served. 'I've taken his shoes off and put a bucket and a bottle of water next to him.'

'Fucking idiot,' she scoffed, before turning back to asking

Jared about his stint as a lifeguard in California before he trained for his current job. As far as Louise could tell, his work just involved charging wealthy people a lot of money to recommend various supplements and alternative therapies.

After eating his dessert, Tim excused himself to go and check on the children, but Louise lingered for a while, aware that when she got up from the table, she would be leaving Shona and Jared alone.

Eventually, unable to stand the palpable sexual tension any longer, she excused herself and headed upstairs to bed.

Just after midnight, she was woken by her phone bleeping with a text.

Glancing down at the screen, she saw that it was from Harry. He had recently been given his first mobile phone, while Elodie was still considered too young.

Mum I think I can hear Elle throwing up you'd better come

Sighing, Louise glanced over at Tim. He was snoring faintly, so deeply asleep that he didn't even stir when she switched on the light. While nowhere near Kevin's levels of consumption, she had noticed her husband drinking heavily at dinner since she had arrived.

Pulling on her robe, she took a bottle of water from the fridge and a towel from the bathroom and headed downstairs to the room the girls shared. The light was on and Elodie was leaning back on the pillows, her face pale and sweaty. Violet lay on her side on her own bed, blinking sleepily.

'I've been sick, Mum,' Elodie wailed.

Louise soaked the towel in cold water and wiped her face, just as Tim had done to her when she had her migraine. 'How many times?'

'Only once.'

'Is your tummy feeling better or worse now?'

'Tiny bit better.'

'Well, that's a good thing. Drink some of this water, but just sips, okay?'

She fetched a plastic bowl from the kitchen and placed it next to the bed, sitting beside her daughter until eventually she drifted off to sleep. Violet was asleep too.

Leaving the bedside light on, Louise left the room and headed out into the hallway.

And then she heard it.

From outside, there was a faint but distinct shriek of laughter. Knowing what she was going to find, but feeling the need to confirm her suspicion, she slipped through the kitchen door and down the path to the pool, the stones on the path digging into the soles of her feet. The night air was heavy with the cloying scent of jasmine and nicotiana. As the decked terrace came into view, the underwater floodlights illuminated Shona and Jared's bodies. Their naked bodies. They were skinny-dipping, that much was clear. And who knew what else, given that Shona's arms were wound around Jared's neck kissing him, her legs wrapped round his tanned, gleaming torso.

Shivering, despite the warm air, Louise turned on her heel and hurried back into the villa.

FOURTEEN

TIM

Then

Louise was indeed pregnant.

And how, Tim asked himself, could he now possibly tell her that he was at risk of being prosecuted for a sexual offence with a minor? He couldn't. Of course he couldn't. What if the stress made her lose this baby too? He was well and truly trapped.

His first move was to set up a burner email account and reluctantly do as Tina had demanded. He sent a blank email to fortytwoelephants@hotmail.com. Sure enough, he received bank details by return and an instruction to pay fifteen hundred pounds a month into the account, or risk her reporting him to the police. He wondered how she had come up with that amount. Either way, he didn't have it, not to spare. He earned decent money compared to a lot of people, but his net salary after tax went into a joint account. There was no way he could siphon off fifteen hundred pounds each month without Louise knowing.

Then he remembered the standing order to Curadex that he had just set up on the Fairlawn account. Desmond left such administrative chores to him and wasn't much interested in the balance sheet. What if he somehow manipulated the practice accounting system to make regular outgoing payments to Tina's account, subbing it with his own salary. He wasn't exactly sure how that would work, but there must be some way of balancing the accounts. Perhaps he could do some extra locum work to make up the difference in his earnings, so that Louise didn't notice that they had less money in their joint account each month. Just until the baby was born and all was well, and then he'd stop. He'd stop and face the music.

But no, he then told himself. Apart from being immoral, that would be risky. If the accountant spotted the payments, then questions would be asked, and he could end up being struck off for financial mismanagement. So what was he supposed to do? He felt suffocated by the bind he found himself in.

He spent a miserable weekend, during which his mind was stuck in an endless agonising loop, but he was having to pretend to be nothing but thrilled about the new pregnancy when his pleasure was tainted by the Tina situation. And then on Monday evening his mother came to the rescue. She phoned him and told him that his great-uncle Arthur had left him and his brother thirty thousand pounds each.

'What did your mum want?' Louise asked when he hung up and came back into the kitchen. She was standing at the stove stirring pumpkin soup, which she claimed was currently the only thing she could face eating.

'Just stuff about the funeral.' This wasn't a lie: the funeral date had been mentioned.

'You didn't tell her about the baby?' Louise asked anxiously. 'Only this time I don't want to tell anyone until I'm further along.'

'No, my darling.' He leaned in and kissed her cheek. *Thirty grand*, he was thinking with relief. *That will help keep Tina*

Locke at bay. 'I kept schtum. Maybe we can think about telling her and Dad and your folks at Christmas?'

Louise did the arithmetic on her fingers. 'I think that will just about be okay. As long as nothing goes wrong.'

After they'd eaten, Tim texted his mother.

Can you ask A's solicitor to make cheque out just to me and send to Fairlawn? We're reorganising finances (complicated work/tax stuff) and don't want it to wind up in household account x

When the cheque for thirty thousand pounds duly arrived, Tim opened up an account in his sole name at a different high street bank to the one he and Louise used.

How about I set up a transfer for a grand a month? he emailed Tina. *Surely that's more than fair?*

But this elicited a reply of only three words. *No. Fifteen hundred.*

After setting up the standing order, he agonised each month as the total dropped by fifteen hundred pounds. The arrival of the accounts made him burn with anger each time. That money should have been used as a deposit on a bigger house. Or to allow Louise to take longer than the statutory amount of maternity leave. The statements arrived at the practice address, but since he didn't want Amy finding them and asking awkward questions, he brought them home with him and stashed them at the back of the desk drawer where he kept expired passports and old chequebook stubs.

But this state of affairs would last just until the baby was born. Once all was well at home, he would come clean about the situation and place himself in the hands of the criminal justice system. But although Harry was born at term, he had a congenital abnormality of his gastrointestinal tract requiring an operation soon after birth and a second surgery at three months. Louise crumpled under the stress and developed a bad case of postnatal depression. She ended up needing to take longer than the statutory leave anyway – an irony not lost on Tim.

And so he didn't dare end the payments, at first until they knew Harry was going to be okay, and later until Louise was fully recovered and back on her feet. But by then over a year and a half had passed since the incident.

All of Uncle Arthur's legacy was used up. He had no money left to pay Tina Locke.

FIFTEEN

LOUISE

Now

Louise lay awake for most of the night, wondering whether she should tell Tim about what she had seen at the pool.

By the time pale golden sunlight was penetrating the gap in the curtains and pooling on the carpet, she had decided that she would not. It would only add to his already high stress levels, and Louise had no wish to do that. Nor would it stop Shona from doing what she was doing. Not unless she was openly confronted, which in turn would make Renée angrier and more inclined to abandon the plan to buy out Fairlawn Veterinary Clinic. Keep things calm and copacetic, she told herself. No rocking of the boat: not yet. A boat that could nonetheless be heading for complete disaster.

As they went downstairs for breakfast, they found Merry Stafford standing alone in the front hall dressed in a crochet maxi-dress and wedge-heeled sandals, her customary huge shades on top of her head. She did not greet the Cutlers, but merely dropped her shades rendering her expression unreadable. Through the open door, Louise saw Laurent, the gardener cum handyman who also doubled as part-time taxi service, bringing the BMW round to the front door.

'Are you off somewhere?' Louise asked Merry brightly.

The sunglasses were raised briefly. 'I just need to do a bit of shopping.'

'Oh, lovely.'

'Yes.' Merry's features arranged themselves into a smile, but her deep-set eyes did not join in.

Laurent jumped out of the car and held the rear door open, and Merry walked out and climbed into the back seat without a word or a backward glance.

Richard Stafford was at the breakfast table along with all three Prentices, Harry and Elodie, who was well enough to devour one of the prized *pains au chocolat*. To Louise's relief, there was no sign of Jared. Shona and Kevin were ignoring one another, and Kevin was pale and unshaven.

'How are you feeling?' Tim enquired. 'Only you were in a bit of a state when I left you.'

'Yeah, sorry, mate... thanks for doing that.' Kevin drained his cup of coffee and poured a second one from the jug. 'Nothing a bit of grease and caffeine can't fix.'

On cue, Pascale appeared from the kitchen with a plate of fried eggs and sausage, which she placed in front of Kevin.

There was a sound of wheels on gravel and through the pillars of the loggia there was a glimpse of a long black limousine. A minute later, Renée appeared on the terrace dressed in a black linen suit and heels, her helmet hair sprayed into place.

'Welcome back,' Tim greeted her warmly.

'Thank you, it's nice to be back. I can't wait to change and have a swim.' She looked around the table. 'No sign of Jared?'

Glancing at Shona, Louise shook her head. 'He hasn't come for breakfast, no.'

'I'll go and find him. Tim; let's talk this afternoon, yes?' She turned to go.

'One second, Renée.' Kevin held up his fork, and egg yolk dripped onto the front of his T-shirt. 'Just wanted to ask you something... we've got some friends – the Farrows – staying in Saint-Maximin, just up the road, and I wondered if it would be okay if they came over for lunch and a swim.'

If Renée objected to this suggestion, she didn't show it, merely replying smoothly, 'Of course. Just make sure you tell Pascale about the extra numbers for lunch.'

Louise, on the other hand, glared at Kevin furiously. The Prentices were already guests of guests. They had no business inviting yet more people to the villa.

The Farrows were due to arrive at one, but only appeared a few minutes before two.

A dusty white Mercedes jeep disgorged two adults and two boys who looked a little older than the Cutler children.

'I'm Jerry,' boomed the male half of the couple. 'Jerry Farrow.' He was a large square man with heavy jowls and longish hair slicked back with styling gel. He wore over-tight white jeans, a top with 'Balenciaga' emblazoned across it, a gold necklace and bracelet and blue suede loafers on his bare feet. His wife, Debra, had sharply bobbed platinum hair and wore head-to-toe Gucci and enormous platform soles. Their two sons, Bodhi and Xavier, were like miniatures of their father, and maintained a sullen silence.

Pascale had prepared aperitifs and canapés to greet them on arrival, which meant that lunch itself was very late being served. The villa's resident children were bored and hungry by this point, and in Harry's words 'over it'. Louise steered them away from the bite-sized morsels of seafood and caviar and into the kitchen, where she persuaded Pascale to serve them some of the fried potatoes that were to accompany lunch.

As she was returning to the assembled group in the salon, the front door opened and Merry Stafford came in, her face as ever obscured by her eyewear. She lifted the sunglasses briefly to squint at the newcomers, curling her lip in disdain before hurrying past and heading through the hallway.

When they finally sat down to lunch, Jerry Farrow was next to Renée. He drank a lot of the excellent white wine, and was soon slurring slightly.

'So what is it you do then, Renie?' He leaned in far too close.

'Renée,' she corrected him. 'I work for Vet Care Mondiale. It's part of the Mondiale food group.'

At the far end of the table, the younger Farrow boy was kicking his feet repeatedly against his chair. His mother told him feebly to stop, but he continued.

'Very nice,' Jerry said, slurping more wine. 'I know them: massive company. And exactly what do you do for them?'

'I'm the CEO,' she said stiffly.

'Amazing. That's amazing, isn't it, Debs?' He stuffed in a mouthful of salad. 'Tell you what,' he went on, leaning even closer. 'You might want to invest some of that lovely Swiss cash with us.'

'Really. And who is that exactly?'

'FitStyle International. We're based out of Luxembourg. Revenue nearly three billion last year.'

'Is that so?' Renée countered coldly. She knew, as did most of the people round the table, that FitStyle was a multi-level marketing company.

Tim was screwing up his face in second-hand embarrassment, trying to catch Kevin's eye in the hope he might stop his friend attempting to involve their hostess in a pyramid scheme. In vain, Louise willed Jerry not to say anything further.

'I reckon with your credentials I could get you in as an investor at quite a high level,' he went on.

Kick, kick, kick went the Farrow boy's designer trainers.

In the end it was Jared who came to the rescue. 'Hey, let's not waste this wonderful lunch talking about business. How about we try religion or politics instead?'

There was strained laughter and Shona beamed at Jared.

'If you'll excuse me, I'm afraid I have a headache.' Renée stood up abruptly, her expression stony, and walked away from the table, Tim staring helplessly after her.

After lunch was over, he and Louise went back to their room for an hour, then joined the Prentices and Farrows at the pool. Debra Farrow was stretched out on a lounger wearing a swimsuit with a series of complicated cut-outs and Louise – self-conscious about her own pale limbs – was secretly pleased to see ugly orange-brown tidemarks from Debra's badly applied fake tan. The Farrow boys amused themselves scooping insects out of the pool and throwing them at one another. Renée did not reappear, nor was there any message for Tim about the two of them meeting.

'This is a disaster,' he said later as he emerged from the shower and changed into a fresh shirt. The Farrows had dropped hints about staying for dinner, which fortunately had been ignored. 'Just as I'm finally about to sign the deal, Kevin's bloody shyster of a pal tries to wring money out of her and she's offended. And who can blame her? Bad enough Shona flirting with her boyfriend, but this is the icing on the bloody cake.'

Louise thought about what she had seen at the swimming pool the night before and decided to change the subject. 'No sign of the Staffords all day: I wonder if they'll be at dinner.'

Tim shrugged. 'Didn't she go off to burn through Richard's credit cards?'

'Yes, but she came back this afternoon.'

And it was only then that Louise realised what had been

niggling in her brain since then. When Merry had returned after five hours away from the villa, she had had no shopping with her. Nothing at all.

It seemed everyone at the villa had some sort of secret.

SIXTEEN

TIM

Then

In the summer of 2012, Tim was forced to take stock.

Harry – now a toddler – was thriving, so much so that he and Louise were thinking tentatively of having another child. She was back at work on part-time hours and it was going well. Tim himself had been promoted to partner, but even so he wasn't earning so much that fifteen hundred a month wouldn't be missed. And he had spent all the money he'd inherited. No, 'spent' implied he had got something out of the transaction. He had received nothing, not even peace of mind. The money had simply leaked away into someone else's bank account.

This was absurd, he told himself. Okay, so what he had done was not great, but between himself and Tina Locke, who was the greater sinner? Admittedly paying her off did not help his case much. But when they'd had sex – a few brief seconds that had left his life in such a horrible mess – she had known she was underage and he had not. And she was not underage now. She was almost certainly seventeen, above the age of criminal responsibility. He did some googling and found the sentences for blackmail were on a par with those for sexual offences. This girl was calling his bluff, surely. She didn't want to risk a decade of her life in prison any more than he did.

After the last payment was transferred from the account he had opened with Uncle Arthur's money, he simply closed it. No account, no payment, no comeback, he told himself. But even so, he continued to check the burner email, and sure enough, a week later there was a message. It contained no text or subject line, simply a link to a news article.

Married teacher, 39, pleads guilty to sex with teenager

A primary school teacher, James Bartlett, was today sentenced to ten years in prison after pleading guilty to rape and sexual activity with a child. He will also be placed permanently on the sex offenders register. Reading a statement in court, his victim told how she had been completely destroyed by his actions.

'Are you all right, sweetheart,' Louise asked him that evening after they had bathed Harry together and put him to bed. 'You're awfully quiet?'

'Fine,' he smiled at her. 'Just tired. How about you? How was your day?'

'I think you could say it was pretty interesting...' She smiled, showing the dimples he had fallen in love with all those years ago, before rummaging in her bag and pulling out a white plastic stick. It took Tim a few seconds to realise that it was a pregnancy test.

'Was it...?'

'Positive? Yes.' Louise beamed. 'Harry's going to be a big brother.'

'Wow, that's amazing! You clever thing!' Tim pulled his wife into a hug, hoping she couldn't sense the aching tension in his body.

'I know. We're going to have everything we ever wanted.'

The next morning, Tim told Amy that he needed an emergency dental appointment, and took the morning off work. He was not going to play Tina Locke's game for the duration of a second pregnancy. That simply wasn't going to happen. He would tell her in person that he wasn't paying her any more money, and if she objected, then he would go to the police himself and tell them everything. How Louise would react was something he pushed to the back of his mind. It wouldn't come to that, he reassured himself. Once he had made Tina see sense, it never need get that far. The matter would be closed.

He still remembered the exact location that he had dropped her that night. He had stared at the street sign, Harebell Close, for several minutes after she had got out of the car, and the name was etched into his memory. However, she had just disappeared into the darkness and he had no idea which house she had gone into, if any of them. Checking on Google Maps, he found that the nearest secondary school was Coppice Hill Comprehensive. He put the coordinates into his satnav and headed back onto the M3 in the direction of Basingstoke.

Only as he pulled up outside the school gates did it occur to him that the school year was now over. It was early August, with the London Olympics underway and everyone in the United Kingdom was fully in holiday mode. But he hazarded a guess that the school office would be open in readiness for a new year's registration, and sure enough found one harassed-looking middle-aged school secretary toiling away at a computer terminal.

'We're not supposed to give out pupils' personal information,' she said doubtfully when Tim told her he was looking for Tina Locke. 'The head's very strict about that.'

He pleaded for her to at least tell him if she was currently registered at the school, and swayed perhaps by his boyish good looks and unthreatening demeanour, she agreed to consult their records.

'No,' she said eventually. 'We don't have a Christina Locke on our roll. That's all I can tell you, I'm afraid.'

Tim tried phoning the other secondary schools within a radius of a few miles and got the same answer from all of them: they did not have a pupil called Christina or Tina Locke. It occurred to him that if she had decided to leave school after her GCSEs then she wouldn't feature on any school roll anyway.

He stopped to get coffee, avoiding the Starbucks where he had met Tina, then drove to the South Ham Community Library and asked to see the electoral register. He found a couple of Lockes in the local area: a Barry Locke and a Winifred Locke, but they were not in Kempshott and there was no means of knowing if they had any connection with Tina.

Emerging into the glaring midday heat, he felt drained and frustrated. Then he remembered how he had found Tina in the first place. The catering company. He googled the number for Greenleaf Catering and phoned it once again. A different woman answered this time; apparently Kath Hughes had moved on.

And so had Tina Locke. 'Sorry, she's not active on our books any more. I can see from our records that we haven't used her for a year and a half.'

No wonder, she doesn't need the money anymore, thought Tim bitterly.

'Do you still have her contact details though?'

'We've still got her original address on the database, yes.'

Just as he was scrabbling for some plausible reason why he would need it, the woman on the line read it out loud, seemingly without thinking.

'We've got 7 Rowan Drive for her... does that sound right to you? Only it doesn't look as though it was ever updated.'

'Yes, yes, that's probably it,' Tim said, hastily opening his maps app. Sure enough, Rowan Drive ran perpendicular to Harebell Close. 'Thanks for your help.'

Number 7, Rowan Drive was a modest semi-detached new-build identical to the others in the street. A gaggle of children circled the driveway on their bikes, and from a garden somewhere, Tim could hear the sounds of children playing in a paddling pool.

'Yes?' A harassed-looking Asian woman opened the door.

'Sorry to disturb.' Tim managed a self-effacing smile, hyper aware of the sweat patches on his shirt. 'I'm looking for the Lockes.'

'Sorry.' She shook her head, backing away and pushing the door closed. 'They don't live here.'

'Did you buy the house from them?'

'We're renting.' She shook her head again. 'Only been here six months. Sorry.'

Tim tried the neighbours on either side, but no one answered. The occupants were probably away on their summer holidays. Seething with frustration, he headed for the nearest pub, where he cooled off with a beer under an umbrella in the garden.

It hadn't really occurred to him that he wouldn't be able to find Tina, but the implications of this slowly started to sink in. How far would he get now if he went to the police with a complaint of blackmail against her? They might make some cursory enquiries, and then conclude that it wasn't worth more of their time. And what hope did he have of resolving the problem if the girl had disappeared?

SEVENTEEN

CHRISTINA

Then

Tina was rather pleased with the email username she came up with. *Fortytwoelephants*.

There was nothing in the reference to the infamous Forty Elephants gang that gave any clue to her real identity. Only she chose not to disclose this particular enterprise to her partner in crime. As far as Hannah was concerned, they were still making the occasional ten or twenty pounds by threatening to expose the advances of guests at the functions where they waitressed. They had come to view it as a sort of generous tipping system.

And after Christmas, Hannah resigned from the catering company's books anyway. She and Levi were going travelling in Australia for six months, prior to her starting a marketing course the following autumn. Tina resigned too. Because, to her slight surprise, she now had fifteen hundred pounds landing in her account each month. She hadn't thought Tim would go through with it. She thought he'd call her bluff, making her scheme fall apart as quickly as it had started. But no: the money was there. This was real.

She had arrived at the sum by chance, because what did she know about how much blackmailers made? The house in Rowan Drive was now up for sale because her stepfather had a new job in Southampton, and she'd heard the sum of fifteen hundred pounds a month being mentioned in the context of rent for a temporary home when they moved. So that was the price she named. It was a huge sum to her, and yet it seemed that Tim Cutler could easily afford to pay it. So be it.

She desperately wanted to avoid moving to Southampton with the rest of the family, and this money allowed her to achieve that. It gave her independence. She moved to a studio flat in Sutton, on the southern outskirts of London, and initially secured a job as an apprentice in a beauty salon in Purley; waxing the legs and painting the nails of women with too much time on their hands. She learned from these women; removing the diamond stud from her tooth and wearing braces to improve her smile, upgrading from the cheap, brassy highlights to something more subtle and expensive-looking.

But she was also ambitious, and saved up enough from her wages and her payments from Tim Cutler to undertake a prestigious training course at the British Aesthetic Academy in central London. The market in cosmetic injectables was mushrooming, and she knew that once she could correctly administer Botox and fillers, she would never be out of work. One day she would open her own salon, she decided. It was possible if she continued to save most of the money Cutler sent her.

But then, in July 2012, the payments stopped without warning. She waited for a few days, but there was no email to the fortytwoelephants inbox, no explanation. Tim had clearly decided that he no longer needed to continue. It was up to her to convince him otherwise.

Tina's online research revealed an absolute goldmine of news headlines. There were so many men being prosecuted for sex with minors that it proved hard to pick one. In the end, she settled on 'Married teacher, 39, pleads guilty to sex with teenager'. The man in question was sentenced to ten years. That should do it.

And yet, two weeks later, she still hadn't heard anything. Clearly, she would have to try harder. She phoned St Agnes Girls' High and asked to speak to Louise Cutler.

'I'm sorry, I'm afraid Louise isn't in yet,' the receptionist told her, and since she was clearly indiscreet, went on in a confidential tone, 'She's usually in a bit later than the other teachers because she drops her little boy at nursery on her way here.'

Little boy. So they'd had a kid.

Tina had vaguely thought about asking to meet with Tim's wife and relying on her reporting this back to him. But now she probably didn't need to. She googled daycare centres within a quarter of a mile of St Agnes, and, sure enough, there was one about five hundred yards away: First Steps. She still had to take half a day's leave and take a train down to Winchester, but when she got there all she needed to do was take a photo of the entrance to the nursery with the sign clearly visible and email it to Tim.

It was a guess that this was the nursery the Cutler child attended, but as it turned out, a correct one. Because three days after she had sent the photo, the fifteen hundred pound payments to her account resumed.

EIGHTEEN

LOUISE

Now

After another restless night, Louise rose early and went out for a walk, leaving Tim asleep.

She liked the place best at this time of day. The sky was still faintly hazy, the air cool and the scent from the flowers less oppressive. Instead of droning cicadas, the only sound was birds engaged in a joyful dawn chorus.

At the end of the path, she decided against taking the track to the vineyard, turning in the other direction to walk through the olive groves. Once she'd reached the top of the slope, she stopped to look back and admire the hulking purplish outline of the Ardèche mountains.

Joining the path to the villa again, she heard a faint rhythmic slapping sound. She turned right along the path to the pool, then stopped and stared. Merry Stafford was in the pool. Merry, who never swam. Her luxuriant tresses were knotted on the top of her head, and she was wearing a sporty navy one-piece. Louise watched, fascinated, as she powered up and down the length of the pool in a strong, confident crawl. The rippling turquoise water looked inviting, but Louise sensed that joining Merry would be unwelcome. In fact it didn't even seem right to interrupt her by speaking, so she turned on her heel and went inside to shower.

As the lunch dishes were cleared, Renée waved across the table at Tim.

'Tim, shall we take our coffee into the blue salon and have a chat?'

The room she referred to was a small informal sitting area just off the kitchen. It had a state-of-the-art log burner built into the wall, a flat-screen TV and a sofa and matching ottoman upholstered in stylish blue-grey fabric.

'Sure,' said Tim. 'Give me a minute and I'll go and fetch my paperwork.'

After he and Renée disappeared, Louise followed the children down to the pool. There was no point trying to take a siesta because she wouldn't be able to rest with so much at stake for Tim's business, so instead she engaged in an energetic game of Marco Polo with all three children and Jared, who had introduced them to this transatlantic form of tag.

An hour and a half later Tim appeared, wearing his swim shorts. He smiled at Louise and gave her a discreet thumbs up, but it was only after they were back in their room that he told her his news.

'It's all happening,' he said gleefully, spinning his wife round in his arms. 'Renée got their legal team to draft the contract of sale, and we went through it all together: pre-conditions, liabilities, et cetera. She's emailed a copy to the practice solicitor for him to check, but that should just be a formality. Hopefully we'll be signing tomorrow.'

'That's fantastic, darling!' Louise kissed him squarely on the lips. 'Clever you.'

The mood over dinner was jovial and relaxed. One reason for this was Shona's absence, excusing herself on the grounds that she'd had too much sun and was feeling dizzy. Jared was sitting next to Renée, and when Louise looked discreetly in their direction, they seemed perfectly at ease with one another. Renée even lifted Jared's hand to her lips and kissed his fingertips in a rare public display of affection. Louise remembered what she had said about not ruling out marriage. Was she planning to propose to Jared?

After dinner, the two girls were sent straight to bed and Harry, who was allowed to stay up until ten o'clock, challenged his father to play table tennis.

Since Kevin had followed Richard Stafford out to one of the terraces to drink Armagnac and smoke cigars, Louise decided that she should go and check on his wife. She did so with some reluctance, since not only were she and Shona not close friends, but she had been unable to shake the mental image of a completely naked Shona wrapping her legs round Jared Frayn.

The Prentices' room was next to their own, with Renée and Jared's suite at the far end of the same landing. Louise tapped gently on the door.

'Shona?'

'Come in.'

Louise opened the door a crack but stayed on the landing. 'Just wanted to make sure you're okay. Can I fetch you anything? Some water?'

'I've already got wine.' Shona was sitting up on the bed dressed only in black lace underwear, with a glass in her hand and a half-empty bottle on the floor beside her. 'Come in a second.' She patted the empty half of the bed.

This was exactly what Louise had not wanted. She did not want a cosy exchange of confidences with this woman whose presence and behaviour she now resented furiously.

'I need to go and check that the girls have got their light out. As long as you're okay...' She started to back away from the door.

'Just for a minute. There's something I need to tell you.'

With a sinking feeling, Louise perched on the edge of the bed. The room was similar to theirs, but the window, which was smaller, had dark orange drapes and the Eames lounge chair was mustard yellow. She would have preferred to sit on that, but it was heaped with discarded clothes, and the floor space was strewn with shoes, bags, bras and a pair of Kevin's boxer shorts. Shona's auburn hair hung in unbrushed clumps, and her mascara was smudged into semicircles beneath her eyes.

'Jared and I are having an affair.'

Louise closed her eyes and held her hand over her face. 'I was afraid you were going to say that.'

'You can see the chemistry, right?' Shona poured more rosé. 'I mean, surely everyone can, by now.'

'Define affair,' said Louise carefully. She didn't want to get dragged into a discussion about sexual chemistry.

'We're sleeping together.'

'Sleeping? How have you managed that?'

'Well, banging then.' Shona could not resist a smirk.

Louise sighed heavily. 'Shona, why are you telling me this? I really don't want to get involved.'

'Because I'm going to leave Kevin. Our marriage is over. It's been dead in the water for years really.'

'And Jared? What does he think about that?'

'He's going to leave Renée.'

'Are you sure about that? Only at dinner tonight they looked pretty happy together.'

'Obviously he's having to pretend, isn't he?' Shona scoffed, taking a mouthful of wine. 'For now. Until we can figure out what we're going to do.'

Or how he's going to replace the lifestyle subsidy Renée Weber is providing, thought Louise. Out loud, she said. 'Please, Shona. Don't do anything for now.' She stood up and walked over to the door. 'Take some time and think this through properly.'

Tim's response, when she relayed this conversation, was much more extreme than she had anticipated. He was incandescent with rage, swearing loudly and stamping around the room. Louise couldn't remember ever seeing her normally placid husband like this.

'This is exactly what we didn't need!' he stormed. 'Just as Renée is about to sign on the dotted line, our moronic friend throws over her marriage for Renée's own partner. It's like something from a bad soap opera. In fact, it would be laughable if it wasn't putting the whole sale to VCM at risk.'

Then he collapsed onto the end of the bed like a balloon that had lost all its air. He hunched forward, and Louise realised with horror that he was crying.

'Sweetheart!' She hurried over to him and cradled his head against her as if he was one of their children.

'Lou, I haven't told you this before because I never want you upset...'

'Told me what?' There was a cold thud of dread in her chest.

'We're completely reliant on this deal going through. It's not just desirable, it's essential. Fairlawn is going under financially. It can't keep going if we don't sell to VCM.'

Horrified, Louise let go of him and took a step backwards. 'Oh my God. Surely not?'

'I'm afraid so.' He was shaking his head sadly. 'It's the same for most small practices. Since the pandemic, our clients have been sourcing products and services online, and to an extent they've stayed there. The practice margins have always been really tight, but now they're unsustainable. So we have to stop this nonsense between Shona and Jared. I don't care what it takes, we have to put an end to it.'

NINETEEN

TIM

Then

By the time he made the hot drive back to Winchester that afternoon in August, Tim had convinced himself that Tina Locke's disappearance was a good thing. If she had moved out of the area, surely that implied she had now moved on with her life. Found a boyfriend. Started studying at college. She'd had all the money he inherited; that was enough.

For a blissful couple of weeks, he almost managed to forget about her. Then the notifications on his burner account showed that he had new mail. Once again there was nothing in the subject line. He opened it and stared at the screen in his surgery, unable to make out at first what he was looking at. And then he realised and his stomach lurched.

It was the entrance door to First Steps, the nursery where Harry was looked after while Louise was teaching.

It did not take Tim long to process the implications of this message. It told him that not only did Tina Locke know exactly who *he* was, but she also knew that he was married and had a child. It told him she had stalked him.

It was impossible not to view this photo as a threat. It suggested some sort of harm might come to Harry. That he might even be abducted from the nursery. Different scenarios played out in his brain: Tina Locke pretending to be a friend or relative and persuading the staff that she was collecting Harry. Or even getting a job at the nursery herself. Okay, so the scenario sounded far-fetched, like something from a TV drama. But the harm it would cause to Louise if it was even threatened was unthinkable. She might even miscarry again. It was too great a risk: he would have to go on paying.

He was about to ask his brother Phil if he could borrow some money, when he got a stroke of luck. A literal stroke, in this case. Desmond Amblin suffered a minor stroke and decided it was time to retire, leaving Tim to step into his shoes as senior partner. And as senior partner – and sole partner – he had complete control over the practice's finances.

The books were still audited annually by Glen Beane, so Tim still needed to be a little careful. He emailed Curadex to tell them that he would no longer be paying them by standing order but would revert to being invoiced for drugs he ordered. Keeping the name 'Curadex' on the roster of outgoing payments, he changed the payee account details to Tina Locke's account, and set a monthly amount of £1500. So she was now effectively being paid out of the practice's profits.

To compensate for short-changing the business, Tim signed up to do locum night-time cover twice a month. The fees he received for each session – approximately £750 a time – went straight into the practice account, more or less covering the liability of Tina Locke's extortion payments. And as far as Louise was aware, when this happened he was simply doing on-call stints for Fairlawn. She accepted this without question, even though, with Elodie's arrival the following spring, she was caring for their newborn alone on those nights. He occasionally questioned how long he could keep this up for, but for the most

part his life was too full with the twin demands of young children and a demanding career. All he could do was muddle
through.

When it came time for Glen, the practice accountant, to see
the books, Tim simply produced a dummy set which obscured
the incoming credits for his private locum work. There was the
monthly outgoing payment to 'Curadex', but Glen never questioned this, and any real purchases from the company were
simply filed under 'sundry drugs'. Tim hated doing this to Glen,
who he liked and respected, and on a couple of occasions came
close to confessing the whole thing. But it wasn't hurting Glen
Beane, he reasoned, who had always had his professional fees
paid on time. The only person this hideous house of cards was
harming was himself.

And then in early 2020, with no warning, the outgoing
payment to Tina Locke's account bounced back.

There were many, many occasions during the previous
decade that Tim had come close to confessing to Louise. He
despised himself for breaking his promise to always be honest
with her. For lying to her for so long: even if they were lies of
omission. What kept him from doing so was his deep sense of
shame. Because the sum that he had handed over amounted to
over one hundred and fifty thousand pounds. Enough to put
both children through university. Or to give them each a size-
able deposit on their own home. The thought of what that rainy
night had cost sickened him to the core of his being.

Wanting to be sure of what this meant, he phoned the desti-
nation bank and quoted the error code that had appeared in the
credit column next to the returned payment. The call centre
representative informed him that it meant that Tina Locke's
account had closed. It no longer existed.

Relief hit Tim like a body blow. It was over.

TWENTY

LOUISE

Now

'I thought I might head into town alone this morning,' Tim said to Louise as they lingered over their coffee. Everyone else had left the breakfast table and either gone to change or headed straight to the pool.

'Really?' Louise was a little taken aback, but at least her husband seemed to have regained his composure after last night's meltdown.

He smiled at her, reaching out to give one of her brown curls a playful flick. 'It hasn't escaped my notice that we have a wedding anniversary in a few weeks. I thought I might try and buy something special in one of those fancy little Provencal boutiques. After all, if everything goes to plan, I'm not going to have much time for shopping after we get back to the UK.'

Louise leaned against his shoulder. 'Have I ever told you you're the perfect husband?'

'And about the other thing...' Tim picked up a slice of baguette and started picking at the crust.

'You mean the Shona and Jared fiasco?'

'Exactly. Look, with any luck, we'll be signing the contracts later today, when we get final approval.' He lowered his voice slightly. 'But, Lou, it's desperately important it all goes through. I wasn't exaggerating last night: if this doesn't happen, the practice could go under. So can you at least try to stall Shona. Try to stop her rocking the boat for just a little while longer.' He looked at her pleadingly.

Louise sighed. 'I'll do my best, but I think she's demonstrated that she doesn't want to listen to anything I have to say.'

After being in France almost a week, Louise had lost her desire to lie by the pool working on her non-existent tan and cringing at the Prentices' antics. Instead, armed with a book, she positioned herself in a hammock on one of the lawned areas outside the house.

'Hi! Louise!'

A shadow fell over her, and she looked up to see Richard Stafford. He was dressed in a Lacoste polo shirt and was brandishing a tennis racket.

'I wondered if you fancied a game.'

Louise squinted at him. 'I don't really play...'

'It's all right, I'm pretty crap myself, to be honest.' He smiled encouragingly. 'Come on. Just a little knock up. We can be crap together. There are spare rackets in the lobby area behind the kitchen.'

'All right then,' Louise agreed, hauling herself out of the hammock. 'Let me just go and put my trainers on.'

It would be good to get some exercise, she decided. She wasn't used to sitting around doing nothing all day, and didn't really enjoy it. Being constantly busy was more her speed. And, in truth, she wasn't a total rookie when it came to tennis. She occasionally played with her friend Yasmin, who had a court at the bottom of her garden, and at work she had sometimes had to stand in for the PE teacher and put the Year Sevens through their paces.

A few minutes later, armed with a racket and some water, she joined Richard on the clay court behind the house. The sun was beating down relentlessly and she was very quickly sweaty and breathless, but found she was quite enjoying herself. Far from being the corporate dullard she'd taken him for, Richard was genial company: quick-witted and self-deprecating, and refreshingly down to earth.

'It's a shame you and I haven't talked very much before now,' he said when they sat down in the shade for a break. 'But you and Tim always seem so loved up and happy in your own company.'

This wasn't the first time Louise had been told this. 'I'm sorry,' she said with a rueful smile.

'Don't apologise: I think it's charming. How did you two meet?'

'In a student bar.'

And, instantly, Louise was transported back to that moment. She had been in the student union bar in Exeter when she first saw Tim, at the start of her second year of undergraduate study. Someone had knocked a glass of red wine off the edge of a table and, seeing it happen, she'd sidestepped it deftly, just avoiding the arc of crimson liquid that spattered the floor. Looking up with a smile of triumph, she'd caught the eye of the man nearest the bar, seemingly the only other person who had clocked the athletic speed of her reflexes. He'd smiled back at her, and she'd liked the humour in his expression as he did so. Something had uncoiled in her gut and expanded, a sensation that was both sharp and warm. It was a feeling she'd never had before. Later she would describe this as the sensation of falling in love at first sight.

The man was slightly above average height, with hair so dark it was almost black, and round brown eyes. His lower face had a thick layer of black stubble, and she'd guessed he was one of those men who despite shaving in the morning was well on the way to a beard by nightfall. It was early autumn and he had the remains of a summer tan. His arms, exposed by his T-shirt sleeves, were well-muscled, suggesting he'd been doing manual labour over the long vacation.

He had looked at Louise and she had looked back at him. Just as it seemed as though he was about to say something, or offer a drink, he had been intercepted by a group of acquaintances. There was loud back-slapping and hugs of greeting, and then to Louise's disappointment he had followed his group of friends out of the bar. Not without turning back to look in her direction when he left.

Louise had visited the union bar nearly every evening from then on in the hope of seeing him again. Eventually, after two weeks, she did. Their eyes had met with a flicker of recognition, and this time he came straight over to her with the words, 'I was hoping I might see you here.'

He'd told her his name was Tim Cutler and he was studying veterinary medicine.

'Louise Gilbert.' She'd shaken his hand formally. 'I'm doing a PGCE. Teacher training,' she'd added, in case he didn't understand the acronym.

He'd kept hold of her hand just a fraction longer than politeness required, and their eyes met. And there it was again; that churning, intense feeling in her gut.

'Can I just say, I haven't been able to forget the way you swerved that wine,' he'd said with mock seriousness. 'Those are some impressive footwork skills. Are you an acrobat, as well as a trainee teacher?'

She had laughed, shaking her head. 'No, but maybe I should look into it. I always wanted to join the circus when I was little. It was my dream.'

'Mine too.'

They had looked at each other again, and later were to agree that it was in that instant that they knew. They both knew.

Tim had bought her a drink, and they were still talking ten hours later, long after they'd moved on from the bar to her room. And they'd been together ever since.

'Renée and I weren't much older when we first met,' Richard said, with a smile.

'Oh,' Louise was temporarily taken aback. 'I didn't realise you two went quite so far back. Was it... were the two of you an item?'

He shook his head. 'No. It never quite got that far. I suppose we could have been, but her work took her all over the place and I ended up meeting my first wife. And now I'm with Merry, of course.'

'Of course.'

Richard must have caught something in Louise's expression, because he went on, 'Merry doesn't always make it easy, I know that. She's not exactly chatty. She's actually a bit shy.'

Louise made a neutral sound, not wanting to be rude and disagree.

'Look, I'm fully aware people think she's a trophy wife. Given she's a fair bit younger than me. And a hell of a lot better looking,' Richard said ruefully, lifting his water bottle to his mouth. 'I mean, I know she's not as into me as I am her. I'm not an idiot.'

Louise was surprised by this revelation. 'You two get on all right though?' she asked eventually, avoiding Richard's eye as she drank some of her own water.

'Oh yes, we get on great. We may not be like you and Tim, but we're really very happy. We have an extremely nice life-style, and Merry's very organised, runs everything for me, takes care of all the domestic stuff.'

Knows which side her bread is buttered.

'She's not what you imagine, you know,' Richard said with a

faint smile, as though he was reading Louise's thoughts. 'She may be glamorous and well-groomed, but she's no airhead. There's a steadiness about her, a focus. She really looks after me, which is more than I had in my first two marriages.' He stood up then and headed back to the service line, turning to Louise as he did so and saying, 'There's a lot more to my wife than meets the eye.'

'Where's Dad?' Elodie demanded as they all sat down to eat lunch.

All of them apart from Tim, that was. Louise had expected him to return after a couple of hours. Shopping really wasn't his thing. But he had messaged her and said that he was going to grab a bit of lunch while he was in Cotignac and head back later.

Love Pascale's cooking, but really craving something different, he texted. *Going to source a burger and fries! X*

'He'll be back in a bit,' she reassured her daughter, though she didn't know if this was true.

Elodie pouted. 'Me and Violet have worked out this cool new handstand trick underwater. I wanted to show Dad.'

'Tell you what, I'll just change into my swimmers, then I'll come down to the pool and you can show me.'

Louise watched the two girls scurry off down the path, then hurried back into the villa. She had just seen Shona heading into the kitchen alone, and decided to seize the chance to confront her. She heard the jangle of Shona's bracelets before she saw her: predictably helping herself to a bottle from the huge stainless-steel wine fridge. The other woman frowned when she saw Louise and went to push past her. Louise blocked her path.

'I need to ask you something. It's important.'

Shona, who was wearing a gauzy zebra-striped kaftan over

one of her neon bikinis, folded her arms across her chest. 'I know what you're going to say.'

'The thing is, the reason we're here – why all of us are here – is for Tim to go into business with Renée. That creates pressure for us, and if you and Jared are—'

'I'm sorry, Louise, I really am, but we want to be together. I can't go back and change it now just to suit you.'

Louise was taken aback by her sheer self-centredness. She also doubted that this was what Jared wanted. As far as she could tell he was perfectly happy with the life of luxury Renée provided. 'Can't you at least leave things a little longer?' she pleaded. 'Until you're more sure. And until Tim knows where he is with this deal. Please, Shona. It's very important.'

'I've told you: I have to end things with Kevin.' Shona pushed past her. 'And I'm going to tell him today.'

Louise stood in the kitchen doorway, watching her helplessly, before trudging up the stairs to change into her swimsuit.

As she left the room and headed downstairs, her phone buzzed with a message from Tim.

Just on my way back. See you in 10 X

'Louise.'

Merry was standing at the foot of the staircase, her impressively toned physique displayed to full advantage in a strapless cream playsuit. Her long tawny hair coiled over her shoulders in artfully created waves, and without the ever-present shades her face was visible for once. She had small, neat features that verged on blandness. If her mouth had been a little wider, her eyes a little bigger, she might have been beautiful. As it was, her looks stopped just short of beauty.

She placed a cool hand on Louise's arm for a few seconds, making her flinch in surprise.

'Look, tell me if I'm speaking out of turn, but I wanted to say something about your friend. About Shona...'

Louise knew what was coming next.

'...A couple of days ago I went back to the pool to fetch my sunglasses case, and I saw her and Jared on one of the loungers. You know.' Merry raised a perfectly groomed eyebrow. 'In a clinch.'

'Yes.' Louise sighed heavily. 'I'm aware of the situation.' Mindful of Tim's paranoia about this spreading to Renée, Louise didn't want to say much more.

The hand was there on her arm again. 'Poor you. This must be terribly difficult for you. Awkward, I mean. You're kind of stuck in the middle, aren't you?'

'I am rather.' Louise smiled gratefully. Her position had made her feel permanently on edge when in the group, and it was nice to have that acknowledged. Merry Stafford, an ally: who would have thought it? Today was turning out to be full of surprises.

'Actually, Louise, I'm glad I found you. I was going to ask if I could have my tablets back. I've got a migraine of my own coming on.'

'Yes, sure. I'll just pop up and get them.'

'No need. You've only just come downstairs, and I know the girls are waiting.' Another sympathetic smile. 'Just tell me where they are, and I'll go and fetch them.'

Louise hesitated, but then dismissed her concern as ridiculous. They were all sharing the same house, and she would be perfectly happy to fetch something of her own from the Staffords' room to save them the trouble.

'Sure. Our room's the one at the far end when you turn left,' she said, returning the smile. 'I think they're on the bathroom vanity unit, to the right of the sink. Excuse the mess.'

Merry glided up the stairs, not looking in the least like someone who was coming down with a migraine. As Louise watched her tanned calf muscles contract with each step, she thought about seeing her swimming the previous morning. About her impressive physical power. And Richard Stafford's words came back to her.

There's a lot more to my wife than meets the eye.

It would be nice to think of Merry as being on her side, but Louise was still unsure. With the intrigue that was going on behind the villa's closed doors, she wasn't sure of anyone. Anyone at all.

TWENTY-ONE

TIM

Now

By the time the Cutler family arrived at Le Mas des Flores in July 2023, Tim had not thought about the night of the Curadex party for many months.

Or perhaps it had lurked in the back of his mind when the realisation sank in that he would probably have to sell the Fairlawn Veterinary Clinic. He might have thought momentarily about how the practice would have been in better financial shape without the drain the blackmail had made. The extra hours' work he had had to do to make up the practice books. But for the most part the issue was done and dusted.

Until the morning when he and Louise took the children to explore Cotignac. The morning that he saw *her*.

He and Louise were enjoying cappuccinos under the shade of plane trees on the broad central promenade. Despite the heat, the village was bustling with tourists and shoppers. Louise asked him about the progress of the takeover deal, revealing that she and Renée had talked while they prepared Sunday's evening meal together. He was relieved that the two women had struck up a rapport. It could only help oil the wheels of their business relationship.

They then compared notes on the Staffords, with Louise wanting to know if he found Merry Stafford attractive. If he didn't know how to answer, it was because he genuinely hadn't given the woman a thought.

'Those hair extensions of hers must be very uncomfortable in this weather. I'm sure they're heavy. And make your head sweat,' Louise observed with a trace of cattiness that made Tim laugh.

'Is that what they are? I thought she was just blessed with an inordinate amount of hair.'

It was at that precise moment that he caught sight of her. She was several metres away, but it was unmistakeably her. It's possible to not set eyes on someone for years and yet there is something about them – their gait, the way they hold their body, the angle of their head – that allows them to be identified in an instant.

He felt as though all the air was being sucked out of his lungs. His body immediately became rigid, the muscles in his jaw going into spasm. Louise had covered his hand with hers and he automatically retracted it, clinging to the table like a drowning man to a lifebelt.

Get a grip, Tim, he told himself.

But he was instantly taken back to that night in October 2010. Trying not to seem too obvious, he watched her cross to the far corner of the square and disappear into a bar with a striped red and black awning and a handful of small wooden tables outside.

'Are you all right?' Louise beckoned to the waiter to bring him a glass of water.

'Yes, yes. Probably just a touch of heatstroke.'

Of course it was nothing of the sort: he had never been affected by the heat in his life. It was shock, plain and simple.

He made a point of drinking the water that had just been placed in front of him, aware he was gripping the glass far too hard. After a few minutes, his heart rate slowed and he managed to reassure Louise that he felt all right.

'Come on,' he said, getting to his feet. Suddenly all he could think about was getting out of Cotignac. 'I fancy a swim. Let's go and round up the kids and head back to the villa.'

Tim tried telling himself that he had been mistaken. That it wasn't her. It was just a young woman around the right age who looked like her. After all, what were the chances? The odds of a coincidence like that must be a million to one.

But inwardly he knew. He knew it had been her. It was as though he'd always known that this would happen. That despite all his hard work to cover his tracks, it had only been a matter of time. And this question gnawed away at him: if coincidence was too far-fetched, then did her presence imply he was once again to be targeted in some way?

After several days of turning this around and around, he decided that he had to talk to her in person. It might not make much sense, given that he now seemed to be off the hook. It surely made more sense to let sleeping dogs lie. But still he felt the need to have just one conversation, to try to find out why the hell it had happened.

On Friday morning he came up with an excuse. Their wedding anniversary was in September, and he told Louise he was going to go into Cotignac and buy her a gift. He sensed a wariness in her, which was quite understandable. On Monday night, he had snapped at her when she asked how he was feeling. Quite apart from the unexpected sighting, there was so much riding on the outcome of their holiday at the villa. He had been struggling to relax anyway. And now this. Now *she* was here.

The first thing he did was to go and buy the gift, at an antique shop that had caught his eye. He chose a vintage signet ring in eighteen carat gold, featuring a carnelian engraved with an image of Venus. The goddess of love was highly appropriate for a wedding anniversary, the shop's owner assured him, and rings like this intaglio were very rare and very sought after. It cost a lot more than Tim had intended to spend, but the combination of feeling guilty and being short on time swayed him. With the ring box expertly wrapped in paper and ribbon, he headed to the bar with the black and red striped awning.

It was called Le Bar des Vignobles, and it didn't open for another hour. Tim messaged Louise and told her he was going to have some lunch, then went back to the café where they'd had coffee on Monday. He ordered a citron pressé and a hamburger with frites and settled down to wait.

Just before the hour was up, he saw her. She was wearing a white T-shirt, black jeans and espadrilles, and carrying a straw bag on her shoulder. She stopped at the door and pulled a heavy set of keys from the bag, sorting through them until she found the key she was looking for and used it to unlock the door of the bar. A few seconds later, the metal shutters were raised and she came outside again and arranged the chairs around the tables, placing ashtrays and beer mats on them. So she was not in Cotignac on holiday, she was working at the bar. She lived here. This unexpected revelation threw him temporarily.

He watched as a few of the older villagers arrived at the bar and took up their positions at the tables, smoking, drinking red wine and gossiping. Then he paid his bill, and with his fingers touching the wrapped box in his pocket like a talisman, walked slowly over to Le Bar des Vignobles.

He was going to confront her.

TWENTY-TWO

LOUISE

Now

'I'm going to have to speak to Kevin, aren't I?' Tim sighed, when Louise relayed her conversation with Shona. 'Far be it from me to interfere in someone else's marriage, but I don't really see that we have a choice.'

They were in their room in the dead time between the mid-afternoon swim and pre-dinner drinks. Tim had returned from Cotignac a few minutes after her conversation with Merry and joined her and the children at the pool. When she asked about the success of his trip, he merely tapped the side of his nose and warned her not to go rooting around in any drawers.

'Shona has made it abundantly clear she's not going to listen to me.' Louise rubbed her freshly showered hair with a towel before standing in front of the circular mirror and pulling a comb through it in a vain attempt to tame the waves. 'In fact, I get the impression that the more I push her, the more likely she is to blow the whole thing up by telling Renée.'

Tim glanced at his watch. 'It's five now: I'm due to sit down again with Renée in an hour and hopefully sign the papers.' He made a fervent fingers-crossed gesture. 'So there isn't any time to waste. I'll go and find Kevin right away.'

He returned twenty-five minutes later, as Louise was applying her make-up in front of the bathroom vanity mirror. The smartest outfit she had packed – a pale blue polka dot silk wrap dress – was on a hanger on the back of the bathroom door in order to get out some of the creases.

'How did it go?' She addressed Tim's reflection.

'Kevin's agreed to leave tomorrow,' he said heavily. 'Tonight would have been better, frankly, but that wasn't an option.'

'Really? Are you sure he means it?'

'I stayed with him while he rearranged their flights. Leaving from Nice at midday. So it's definitely happening. They'll miss the last four days of the holiday, but they've had over a week, so...'

'But what did you tell him? About Shona, I mean.' Louise set down her lipstick and turned to face him.

'Well, I didn't go so far as to tell him his wife is having an affair, if that's what you mean. I reckon that's Shona's job, don't you? I alluded to her constant drinking, and inappropriate behaviour making people uncomfortable. Stressed the importance of not offending Renée. But he knows exactly what's going on, he must do. He's got a pair of eyes in his head, after all.'

'Well done, darling.' Louise blotted her lips with a tissue, then kissed her husband on the cheek. 'I'm sure it wasn't easy, but it's for the best.'

'He's not going to say anything to Shona about the changed flights just yet though, so you mustn't either, okay? He's going to leave it until first thing tomorrow, so she can't kick off over dinner and ruin everything. We've just got to try to keep a lid on her for one more night.'

Louise thought back to Shona's words to her when they'd

been in the kitchen and wondered whether this was even possible.

'Just one more night,' she repeated.

With the sale of the Fairlawn Veterinary Centre duly signed and sealed, Renée announced that there would be an extra-special celebration that night.

It started with the opening of a jeroboam of vintage Dom Perignon, which was drunk on a rooftop reception area that overlooked the vineyards. All the women had made an effort with their appearance, Merry's elegant column of steel-coloured satin contrasting with Shona's plunging leopard skin. Renée, resplendent in emerald green chiffon and sparkling diamond earrings, made a brief speech about how happy she was to be going into business with Tim and the exciting plans for the future of the new Vet Care Mondiale, Winchester. It was practised and slickly delivered, and despite the beaming smiles and the arm placed around Tim's back, Louise had to remind herself that Renée had done this many times before. It meant everything to Louise and Tim but was nothing special to her, even though she seemed to have a genuine soft spot for the charming Tim Cutler.

When they eventually went down to the loggia for dinner (lobster thermidor and more champagne), Louise pulled Harry to one side.

'There's an extra ten euros spending money for you if you sit next to Jared,' she whispered.

Harry frowned at her. 'Why?' he asked loudly.

She touched a finger to her lips, and shook her head slightly to indicate that she couldn't explain.

'When do I get the money?' he demanded.

'Tomorrow. Just do it. Go.'

Renée was already seated on Jared's left, and Harry obediently took the chair on the other side. He raised his eyebrows dramatically at his mother, who just beat Shona to the chair opposite Jared. Louise pulled Elodie into the seat to her left and Tim was opposite Renée, so with what resembled a chess move they had effectively blocked Shona from flirting with Jared. She sat at the end of the table between her husband and Richard, and shot daggers in Renée's direction. Her expression was sulky, but Kevin must have stuck to the plan and not mentioned that they were to leave the villa the next day, since there was no overt quarrelling. Instead, Shona downed glass after glass of champagne.

'Well, that went pretty well,' Louise said with satisfaction as they eventually headed up to bed. She felt a little tipsy herself and had to sit down on the edge of the bed to tug off her heels. 'We managed to see off potential disaster.'

'There's still another twelve hours for things to go tits up,' said Tim gloomily.

'Let Shona do her worst,' Louise said, tossing her strappy sandals across the room and rubbing her sore feet. 'She's got to be on that plane tomorrow, and the contract is signed. What's the worst that can happen?'

On Saturday morning Louise was roused by the sound of car tyres rolling over the gravel. The clock on the nightstand said it was 9.03 a.m.

Her head was pounding from all the champagne she had drunk the night before and it was a struggle to orientate herself. Then she remembered that the Prentices were heading to the airport that morning. This must be their taxi. So they were actually leaving: thank God.

Her relief was short-lived. Footsteps pounded along the landing.

'Mum! Mum!' The bedroom door was flung open and Harry ran in.

Her first thought was that he must have come to collect the extra cash she had promised him the night before. But then she saw the distress on his face, and his pallor under the healthy tan. This was not like her usually laidback son. Her own heart started to pound wildly. 'What is it, sweetheart? What's wrong?'

'Mum, something awful's happened. It's... I don't... I don't know.'

Instinctively, Louise jumped up from the bed and started pulling on a pair of shorts.

Tim was awake now. 'What's going on?' he asked, rubbing his fingers over his stubble and blinking.

'I've just seen something terrible. I'm scared, Dad. Please, you need to come.'

Downstairs, the smell of fresh bread and coffee emanated from the kitchen, along with the clattering of plates and the electronic whirr of the juicer. Harry led his parents outside and down the path to the edge of the pool terrace, where he stopped and pointed.

And there, on one of the loungers, was the lifeless naked body of a young woman, her long golden hair fanned out around her head.

PART TWO

TWENTY-THREE

LOUISE

Now

Oh my God, it's Merry Stafford.

That was Louise's first, shocking thought when she saw the body. The body of a slim young woman with long hair streaming over her naked shoulders.

Her second thought was to protect her children, so she looked away after only the most fleeting of glances.

'Harry,' she said, her voice sharp with shock. 'Go back into the house.'

'But Mum—'

'Do as I say!' she barked in her best deputy headteacher's voice. 'Go and make sure your sister's all right and stay with her. Inside.'

Harry stared at her for a few seconds, still pale and wide-eyed, then turned on his heel and ran up the path.

Tim pushed past his wife and approached the body. He stood staring down at it, his arms rigid at his sides, hands clenching and unclenching.

'Tim...' Louise's voice now came out in a croak. 'Is she...?'

Tim had the equivalent of a medical degree, she reassured herself. He'd be able to tell.

He held his fingers against his temples for a second or two before stepping forward and squatting on his haunches. Lifting the woman's left wrist, which hung over the edge of the lounger, he pressed his fingers to the pulse point. After a few seconds, he stood up again, shaking his head slowly.

'Yes,' he said, with a heavy exhalation. 'She's dead.' He turned to Louise, and she saw sweat breaking out on his forehead despite the relative cool of the morning. 'Lou, I need you to go and find Renée. Tell her to call an ambulance. And the police, I suppose.'

It was difficult not to just stand and stare, but Louise roused herself from her stupor and with legs that felt like jelly stumbled along the path and headed upstairs to Renée's suite. Jared answered the door, and as calmly as she could Louise relayed Tim's instructions, then returned to the swimming pool, followed closely by first Jared and then Renée, talking urgently into her mobile.

The warm air had started to dry the woman's hair and Louise saw with relief that instead of being dark golden blonde the loose strands were a pale platinum colour.

'It's not Merry,' Renée said at the exact moment the same realisation hit Louise. 'Thank God for that, at least.'

Sure enough, a dazed-looking Richard Stafford appeared to find out the source of the commotion, and confirmed that his wife was safe and sound in her room.

'So who the hell is this?' Jared demanded aggressively.

But nobody knew.

Renée was asked if it was perhaps one of the local girls who sometimes came to help Pascale clean the rooms, but she thought this unlikely. Pascale, summoned from the kitchen and crossing herself fervently at the sight of the body, confirmed that this woman had never worked at Le Mas des Flores.

The dead woman was a complete stranger.

The next few hours were a confusing blur.

Louise remembered helping search everywhere for the woman's belongings – clothes, shoes, a bag – but they found absolutely nothing. Nor was she wearing any jewellery that might identify her, apart from plain gold hoops in her ears.

'This is bizarre,' Richard Stafford said as he and Louise combed the bushes around the pool terrace. 'But I guess it's one for the authorities.'

'I've called my lawyer,' Renée said, walking back down the path with her phone in her hand. 'As well as the police, naturally.'

'Your lawyer?' Tim queried. He had fetched a large towel from the pool house and now draped it as discreetly as possible over the corpse's upper body and face, leaving just a few locks of silvery pale hair visible.

'Yeah, sure – think about it,' Jared drawled. He positioned himself next to Renée and put a protective arm round her. 'I mean, she didn't drown, did she? Otherwise how the hell did she get out of the pool and onto the lounger? Unless it was, like, that secondary drowning thing.'

'Someone must have dragged her out and put her there,' Richard stated firmly. Merry had appeared at his side and stood shivering in a flowered silk kimono, her arms wrapped tightly across her chest.

'Exactly. Foul play.'

'That makes no sense,' Louise protested. 'There's only us here, and none of us could have done this. Someone else must have come onto the property during the night. Apart from this woman.'

'Where are the Prentices?' Merry asked.

'They were picked up in a cab about an hour ago,' Tim said, then suddenly looked doubtful. 'At least I think they were.'

'Has anyone checked?' Renée demanded. Her voice was drowned out by the rhythmic wailing of sirens and, seconds later, four uniformed gendarmes surged down the path in pale blue uniform shirts and combat trousers, their pistols visible at their waists.

With a lot of gesticulating and commands in guttural French, they ushered the villa's guests away from the pool and back into the house, cordoning off the area with tape. More officers arrived, a couple with sniffer dogs, and they started combing the grounds.

'Looks like there's a forensic team arriving too,' said Tim, watching through the window of the main salon. Sure enough, several people in white paper Tyvek suits went past carrying kitbags.

Renée, who had gone outside to speak to the senior officer, came into the room looking strained. 'Apparently they will need to drain the pool,' she said in a low voice. 'I keep telling them that we have no idea who the woman is and no idea what happened, but given... how she ended up... well, I suppose that must seem somewhat unlikely to them. They're checking the CCTV from the front gate now, and have asked us to all stay in here for the time being. Pascale's giving a statement, and once she's finished I've asked her to bring in coffee and pastries.'

'Can you explain to them that the children are on their own in their rooms, and I need to go and check on them at least?' Louise asked, and was told to go and bring the children to join the six adults in the salon.

A makeshift incident room was set up in the formal dining room and one by one they were taken in there to be questioned. It was a frustrating process. The senior officer, Capitaine Palomer, spoke English with such a thick Provencal accent that it was difficult to understand him. The other officer – Lieutenant Cabrit – barely spoke any English at all. The children, who were intrigued and excited at first, quickly became bored and started to complain about not being able to swim.

Outside the Provencal heat shimmered, the cicadas droned, and the guests were all effectively imprisoned in the house as the forensic investigators did their work. Eventually, a body bag was stretchered past and loaded into a windowless van, and they were given permission to go outside onto the loggia, but no further. Pascale served a buffet-style lunch which they ate in silence. Jared asked for a beer, but everyone else avoided the customary afternoon wine consumption.

Louise took the children through to the blue salon and, after a certain amount of arguing, got them to agree on a movie they both wanted to watch.

'Mummy, will we be able to swim in the pool tomorrow?' Elodie asked.

'I really don't know, angel,' Louise said heavily, giving her daughter a hug. 'Let's try and help the police do their job by not asking too many questions just now, okay?'

Easier said than done, she thought as she went to join the others for coffee in the loggia. Richard looked suddenly grey and exhausted, and a solicitous Merry had her arm linked through his, murmuring quietly to him. Louise remembered his words on the tennis court the previous afternoon, which seemed like a lifetime ago now: '*She really looks after me.*'

Renée, who had gone back to speak to Capitaine Palomer, returned to the table and held up her hands for quiet.

'Okay, listen... I have an update from the gendarmes. They have requested backup from a bilingual interpreter to ensure that statements are taken accurately. That person will be arriving tomorrow morning, and, until then, no one is to leave the premises. They are currently doing a search of the house, and ask that you wait here on the loggia until it's completed.'

'What about the Prentices?' asked Louise. 'For all we know,

one of them could have seen or heard something.' It had now been confirmed that they had left in a taxi at 9 a.m. as planned.

'By the time the officers started taking our statements, they were boarding their flight back to the UK,' Renée said, her expression suggesting she was not sorry about this. 'But, naturally, they need to be questioned also. I have told the gendarmes that you or Tim will give them their contact details, and they will request that the police in Winchester take statements as soon as possible. If it looks as though they need to return, then it will be arranged,' she said smoothly, adding: 'But let us all hope that is not necessary.'

After an equally silent supper, they were all instructed to go upstairs to their rooms while the downstairs rooms were searched. Louise looked out of the bedroom window into the inky black sky. Below her, on either side of the front door, two armed police officers stood to attention. Were they being guarded, or imprisoned? she wondered.

Tim joined her and she leaned back against him, trying to release some of the tension of the awful day. 'This is surreal,' he murmured. 'It's like something out of an Agatha Christie.'

She turned to face him, her expression grim. 'If it was an Agatha Christie, you know what we'd all be asking... who's next?'

TWENTY-FOUR

LOUISE

Now

Louise liked Guillaume Hall instantly.

He was the bilingual interpreter who arrived the next morning to help the local gendarmerie take full statements. A well-built man who could have been anywhere between thirty-five and fifty, he had light brown hair tinged with grey that had started to recede at the temples. When he smiled – which he did frequently – he exposed a distinct gap between his front teeth, and his pale grey eyes crinkled attractively at the corners.

Renée had already given a full statement in French, so didn't need to be interviewed again. Jared was the first of the guests to be dealt with, and then Louise was called into the dining room. Lieutenant Cabrit had a large black digital recorder in front of him, while Guillaume had a pad for taking notes. He introduced himself and explained that as someone who lived locally and had one French parent and one English, he was often subcontracted by the local police force, primarily helping in incidents that involved British tourists.

'Oh dear, are there a lot of them?' Louise asked nervously.

'You'd be surprised,' Guillaume smiled at her.

The recording machine was switched on, and Guillaume started.

'So, you're Mrs Louise Cutler... correct?'

She nodded.

'And you've been here at Le Mas des Flores for how long?'

'I arrived last Saturday. The rest of my family got here a few days earlier.'

'Oh? How come?'

'I was working. I teach at a high school, and term didn't finish until July 21st.'

'Okay... let's start with Friday night. The day before yesterday. Can you tell me what you did? Starting with when you last were at the pool.'

Louise thought back. 'Let's see... we were all at that pool in the afternoon. Myself and my husband and the children. And the Prentices too, I think. They're not here anymore; they left to fly home just before... before the body was found.'

'What time was it; do you remember?'

'I think it was about two when I headed down there. After lunch. Tim didn't join us until later.'

'And why was that?'

'He'd been doing some shopping in Cotignac.'

'On his own?'

'Yes. On his own.'

Guillaume looked up at her, eyebrows raised slightly, then made a note.

'We must have stayed down there till around four thirty. There or thereabouts. I know we were back in our room by five, because I'd just showered when Tim told me he had a meeting with Renée in an hour's time, at six.'

'This was to discuss Ms Weber's purchase of your husband's business, is that right?'

'Yes. And after their meeting we all had a drink to celebrate, on the roof terrace. Then we went down for dinner, on the loggia, as usual.'

'You didn't at any point go back to the pool?'

Louise shook her head, and Cabrit tutted and pointed impatiently at the recording device. 'No,' she said firmly.

'And as far as you're aware, no one else did?'

Louise thought back. There'd been a lot of champagne and wine consumed, and her memory wasn't as clear as it could have been. She remembered manipulating the table seating to avoid Shona being near to Jared, and bribing Harry to help.

'No,' she repeated. 'We didn't start eating until quite late, so by the time the meal had finished, everyone was tired and headed straight upstairs to bed. Apart from the Staffords, of course. Their suite's in one of the outbuildings in the grounds. Just past the swimming pool.'

'So the next time you yourself went to the pool, it was the next morning?'

'Yes. Just after nine o'clock.'

'And the reason for that was?'

'Harry – my son – came into our room and told us he'd seen something terrible at the pool.'

'Did he say what it was?'

Louise started to shake her head, then remembered the recording. 'No. He was too distressed, so we just followed him down there. And straightaway, that... that was when we saw her.' She hung her head and pressed her palms over her eyes as if trying to erase the visceral, haunting memory of the lifeless body.

'Why don't we take a break for a moment?' He gestured at the empty water jug, slipping easily into flawless French. 'Bastian, *peut-être aller chercher plus d'eau.*'

Cabrit stopped the recording and went to the kitchen to get more water.

'Do you live in Cotignac?' Louise asked Guillaume.

'No, Aix-en-Provence. It's just under an hour away. Here...'
He reached into the pocket of his linen jacket and pulled out a
business card, which he gave to Louise. '*Guillaume J. Hall,
Detective Privé*' it said, with a business address, email and
phone numbers.

'You're a private investigator?' she asked, surprised.

'I was in the *police judiciale* in Paris for several years...
that's a bit like Special Branch in the UK. But now I'm a free-
lance investigator. And a police interpreter, obviously.' He indicated the recording machine.

'Wow... good for you,' Louise said, not sure how else to
respond. She tried to hand the card back, but he waved it away.

'Hang on to it; it might prove useful.'

When Cabrit returned and they resumed the recording,
Guillaume asked her what happened after she'd seen the body.

'When I first saw her, I assumed it was Merry... Mrs
Stafford.'

Guillaume raised an eyebrow and scribbled on his pad.
'And what made you think that?'

'She looked to be the same age, similar build, long blonde
hair like Merry. But quite quickly I realised it wasn't her. The
hair was the wrong shade.'

'Did you touch her?'

'No, I didn't get that close. My husband felt for a pulse, and
said she was dead. But to be honest you could tell that by
looking at her. Not that I've seen dead bodies before,' she added
quickly. 'But, you know, you can just see that... they're gone.'

'And then?' he prompted.

'Then I sent my son away to check on my daughter, and
went back to the house and woke Renée. She and Jared came
down to the pool with me and she phoned the police.'

'And you're quite sure you'd never seen this woman before?
You didn't recognise her?'

'One hundred per cent sure,' Louise said firmly.

Guillaume consulted his notes, looking thoughtful. 'So if I can just take you back to the days preceding these events... did you notice any of your fellow guests behaving in a way that struck you as strange, or out of character? Did you see anyone unknown to you in the grounds of the villa, or even visiting the house for some reason?'

'Kevin and Shona... the ones who've gone home... they did invite some people over for lunch one day: a family they knew. What were they called...? The Farrows. Kevin Prentice will have contact details for them, I'm sure. But they were only here a few hours. They just had lunch and a swim. And that definitely wasn't her. Debra Farrow, I mean.'

'You're sure?'

Louise thought back, momentarily uncertain. But no, Debra definitely had short hair. 'I'm sure.'

'And what do you know about these people, the Farrows?'

'Not much,' she admitted. Oh God, she thought suddenly, what *did* they know? She thought back to Jerry Farrow's gelled hair and heavy gold jewellery. He had certainly looked like someone with criminal connections. Acted that way, given his attempt to rope Renée into some sort of pyramid scheme. Could he be involved?

'We'll make some enquiries... Anything else?'

Louise reached for the water jug and poured herself a glass, sipping it slowly to play for time. She didn't really want to go into the Shona and Jared affair, but if she never mentioned it and it later came to light, wouldn't she seem dishonest? It struck her as absurd that she was automatically feeling guilty, even though she had done absolutely nothing wrong. That was the effect being questioned by the police had, she supposed.

'Actually, there had been a bit of tension, on and off,' she ventured.

Guillaume fixed his grey eyes on her. 'Go on.'

'Shona Prentice... well, she developed a bit of a thing for Jared. Renée's boyfriend.'

He nodded.

'They were flirting a lot and it made the rest of us uncomfortable. I spoke to her about it, and eventually... well, Tim confronted Kevin and asked them to leave. That's why they flew home yesterday morning instead of on Wednesday with the rest of us. They changed their flights.'

Louise decided to stop short of telling him that Jared and Shona were having sex. That was up to Shona to reveal when she was eventually questioned.

'And now, can we just go back to the night before the body was discovered... Did you leave your room at all?'

'No. No I didn't.'

'And your husband. He was there with you the entire night?'

'My husband?' Louise blinked at him in surprise. 'Yes, of course he was.'

'You can be sure of that?'

A hot, panicky sensation unfurled in Louise's chest. 'As sure as anyone can be. I woke a couple of times, to get some water and to use the bathroom, and he was there next to me. I'm a very light sleeper; I'm sure I would have known if he'd left the room in the middle of the night.'

Oh God, should I have said that? Putting the idea of Tim creeping out into their heads.

Guillaume was scribbling furiously at this point, and she was relieved when he looked up and, prompted by a nod from Cabrit, said: 'Interview terminated at 11.44.' He gestured to Cabrit to switch off the recording. 'Thank you, Mrs Cutler, I think that's all for now.'

'So what happens next? When will the police be finished? Only it's hard not knowing, with the children...' Her voice tailed off.

'I understand that this process isn't exactly pleasant. But I hope you understand why certain questions have to be asked.' He stood up and walked to the door with her. 'The pathologist completed the autopsy yesterday, and the cause of death will determine what happens next...'

Louise nodded, her fingers turning his card over and over in her pocket. For some reason, it made her feel safer.

'Of course, it's very challenging progressing an investigation when you have no idea who has died. But...' he went on, 'Cotignac is a very small place. I'm confident someone will know who this woman is.'

'What if she came from somewhere else?'

Guillaume smiled. 'Like I said, someone will know who she is.'

Louise was relieved that her interview with Guillaume Hall had been straightforward.

'That wasn't too bad,' she told Tim as he was about to go into the dining room. 'You'll be fine.'

'Will I though?' His voice was flat, his tone grim. 'You can't be sure of that.'

She scanned his face anxiously. 'Why, what do you mean?'

'That in the circumstances we can't be sure of anything. Or anyone.'

After he had been through the same procedure, he was tense and restless, unable to settle. 'I just want to get out of here,' he kept saying.

'It'll all be over soon.' Louise attempted to calm him. 'The police will be gone and things will get back to normal. Well, as normal as possible, given what's happened.'

'It might be a while before the pool can be refilled though,' he fretted, pacing up and down on the loggia.

The forensic team had just arrived to conduct what Cabrit

referred to as *'une recherche secondaire'*. They had headed up to the suites on the first floor, and the guests had been asked to remain downstairs while they worked. Renée was on her laptop in the blue salon, Richard and Jared had been given permission to play tennis and Merry was sunbathing on one of the other terraces,

Tim pulled out his phone and started an online search. 'Maybe we should try to find a local hotel that can accommodate us, so that the kids can still swim.'

'But, darling, we've only got Monday and Tuesday, and then we fly home anyway. 'It's hardly worth it.'

'Everywhere's booked bloody solid.' He flung his phone onto the table in exasperation.

'Well of course it is,' Louise said reasonably. 'It's peak season now.'

Through the window, she could see through the salon and into the hall. Two white-suited men were just reaching the foot of the stairs, one of them carrying something carefully in gloved hands. And then Louise realised with an icy stab of shock that it was her husband's leather messenger bag.

Palomer said something and pointed, and the bag was carried out of the front door to where the forensic van was still parked. Palomer and Cabrit had their heads together in a hushed conversation, occasionally glancing in the direction of the loggia.

'Tim...' Louise grabbed his arm. 'Tim, I just saw—'

But before she could finish her sentence, the two police officers came through the French windows of the salon, with Guillaume close behind them.

'Tim Cutler, *vous êtes en etat d'arrestation,*' Cabrit said.

Louise's hand flew to her mouth.

'Vous avez le droit de garder le silence...'

Guillaume translated as the rights were read.

'This is absurd,' Tim said to him, pleading. 'Please tell them there's no way I could do anything like that. I was in bed with her...' He turned and gestured wildly at Louise. 'Tell them, for God's sake!'

She looked straight at him and mouthed, 'It's okay, I believe you,' before turning to remonstrate with the police officers. 'This is absurd! You've got this all wrong! Tim would never do this!'

But her protests were ignored, and her husband was led away.

TWENTY-FIVE

TIM

Now

Tim was woken on Monday by the sound of keys unlocking a barred metal door, and a tray containing a small baguette and plastic mug of black coffee being placed on the floor.

Being woken was perhaps not the right description of how his day started, since he had not actually slept. At night, the cells at the back of the police station were filled with strange banging and creaking noises, and the drunk inmate of one of the neighbouring cells shouted at regular intervals, even singing the 'Marseillaise' at one point.

Tim's expectation had been that he would be interviewed as soon as he arrived at the gendarmerie in Brignoles, and then released. But instead he was photographed, fingerprinted and swabbed for DNA, then locked in a nine feet square box with tiled walls and a small plastic-covered mattress on a concrete plinth. His own French was just about good enough for him to understand the custody officer when he explained that on a Sunday afternoon there were no lawyers available and he would have to wait until the following morning before he could speak to anyone. He had been offered food that evening but refused it, too shocked and miserable to contemplate eating. The thoughts crowding his brain were all of Louise. What the hell must she be going through right now? What was she thinking and feeling? He at least had an inkling of what was going on, but she would be completely in the dark.

By dawn, he was ravenous. He was tearing at the bread with his teeth and gulping down the coffee when Guillaume Hall appeared at the door to the cell, a look of sympathy on his face. Tim could barely remember being so relieved to see another human being. 'Thank God,' was all he could say.

'How are you doing?' There was genuine concern in Guillaume's voice.

'Oh, you know...' Tim managed a smile of his own. 'I'm not sure I'd recommend this place on Tripadvisor. I'm glad to see you though. Really glad.'

'I'm here in an official capacity. Under French law, you're entitled to an interpreter, and I've offered my services. You will be represented by a lawyer, obviously – that's also your right.' He was brisk, businesslike. 'They're just waiting on some new information, and then you'll be dealt with.'

He disappeared again and Tim was left waiting. His watch had been taken from him when he was processed – along with his phone and his passport – but there was a clock visible through the bars. An hour passed, then another, then a third. By now, he had been at the gendarmerie for around twenty hours. Wasn't there a limit on how long he could be held? And poor Louise must be frantic.

Eventually, he had to stop watching the hands of the clock as it was adding to his anxiety. At some point in the afternoon, he was led into a narrow, dusty interview room. It had windows set so high in the walls that it was not possible to see through them and a wall-mounted camera pointed towards his seat. He was introduced to his lawyer, Antoine Fabre, a pot-bellied man with grimy fingernails who smelled of Gitanes and whose shirt buttons strained across his abdomen.

After the tape was switched on and the time and names of those present stated, Capitaine Palomer started to speak. He paused periodically to let Guillaume translate.

'The results of the post-mortem show that the deceased died from being injected with a lethal dose of pentobarbital sodium. A vial of that drug was found in your possession, in the bag in your room. How do you explain that?'

'Quite easily,' Tim said. He managed to remain composed, even though his heart was hammering against his ribs. 'I'm a veterinary surgeon, and I use the drug to euthanise animals. I had some in my bag from a home visit I made a few weeks ago to put a dog to sleep, and I simply forgot to remove it before flying out to France. They're tiny amounts of fluid, so I guess the airport scanner didn't pick them up. But I didn't inject any into that woman. What reason would I possibly have to do that? I didn't even know her.'

Palomer snorted something in response, and Guillaume translated, without emotion. 'But you did know this woman. That is correct, isn't it?'

'No, I did not,' Tim protested. 'How can you even say that when nobody knows who she is?'

'We now have her identity confirmed. She is Hannah Messenger, a British national resident in London.'

As Tim stared back at the two men, Palomer now launched into a long volley of explanation, barely pausing for Guillaume to translate.

'Cotignac is a small place, and people talk, exchange information. As it happens, several police officers drink in Le Bar des Vignobles. Ms Messenger was working there as part of a six-month sabbatical travelling round Europe. In addition to a job in Cotignac, she had lodgings with Madame Garrigues, who owns one of the gift shops in the village. When she didn't turn up for her shift on Saturday night, and had not been back to her room, it caused some concern. Her landlady reported her missing. And then when an unidentified female of the same age was found deceased a few kilometres away, well... voila!'

Guillaume hardly needed to translate this last word, since Palomer had given it such a Gallic flourish.

Fabre, the lawyer, was making notes but otherwise contributing nothing to the proceedings.

Palomer continued, an expression of self-satisfaction on his face. *He's enjoying this,* Tim thought bitterly. *My life is on the bloody line, and he's just showing off, playing the big I am.*

'Of course, we still had to undergo the process of formal identification of the deceased. Ms Messenger's older sister flew to France this morning, and was taken to the mortuary at l'Hôpital Jean-Marcel here in Brignoles. She confirmed that the body was indeed that of her sister Hannah.'

He stared at Tim, waiting for his response.

Fabre leaned over and asked a question in French which Tim could not follow.

'Your legal representative has asked us to give some justification as to why we have stated that you know her.'

Palomer turned his laptop round towards Tim. On the screen, there was a grainy black and white image clearly taken from CCTV footage. 'For the tape, I am showing the suspect Exhibit 15/ACR... that is you, isn't it?'

Monsieur Fabre was shaking his head vigorously, indicating that Tim should not admit to this.

'I don't know. It's impossible to be sure.' This was true up to a point. The footage was of poor quality and you could only see the back of his head.

'But you admit that you were in Le Bar des Vignobles in Cotignac at around midday on Friday 28th July?'

Tim had watched enough TV crime drama to know that there was little point denying this. It would only make his actions seem more suspicious, if there was some third-party verification of him being there. 'Yes,' he answered pleasantly, trying to give the impression this was an unimportant piece of intelligence. 'I was doing some shopping in Cotignac and stopped to have a bite of lunch. I thought I'd go and check out the bar in case we ever came into the village in the evening. It had just opened up and I spoke to the barmaid, and since she was also English, she asked me where I was staying. We exchanged some small talk about the weather and how we were enjoying the area, and then I left.'

Fabre and Guillaume exchanged a glance.

'So, you told her you were staying at Le Mas des Flores?' The smug look had returned to Palomer's face. 'The same place where she died only twelve hours or so later.'

Don't get flustered, don't get flustered, said the voice in Tim's head.

'I may not have said the actual address. I can't honestly remember. I may have just referred to the direction of the villa, or the distance.'

Now he was overcomplicating things in his desperate attempt to obscure the true nature of his conversation with Hannah Messenger three days earlier.

'And you invited her to meet you there later? A rendezvous after dark?'

'I did not,' Tim said firmly. 'Look,' he leaned forward on the table, 'I'd just that afternoon signed a deal to go into business with one of the world's largest vet care providers. That puts my career at a peak. Things could not be better for me. So why on earth would I want to inject this poor girl with pentobarbital? And if for some bizarre reason I had done so, do you really think I'd just leave the rest of the drug there in my bag, ready to be found?' He appealed to Fabre, who had his arms crossed over his ample belly. 'Surely you can see how flimsy this theory is. Quite apart from the fact that I have an alibi: I was in bed with my wife all night. She can vouch for that.'

Palomer's response to Tim's calm rationality was to look annoyed. But he did switch off the recording device, and after a muttered conversation with Fabre, Guillaume told him that he was to be released on bail pending further enquiries.

'Does that mean I'm free to return to the UK?'

One of Palomer's superiors would have to make that decision, he was told, and it would depend on the progress of the investigation over the next few days. For now, he must forfeit his passport and remain at Le Mas des Flores.

What was Renée Weber thinking right now, Tim wondered as he was led out of the gendarmerie to a waiting police car. She had just gone into business with someone who, forty-eight hours later, was arrested on a potential murder charge. He could only hope that she still had trust in his innocence, but surely she could not be feeling full of confidence in him at this moment in time. He would absolutely have to play down his real involvement with Hannah Messenger, try to convince Renée that his arrest had been merely a formality due to his possession of a lethal drug, and that it was all satisfactorily explained away.

And then there was Louise. He had to somehow explain himself to his wife. Would she believe him?

TWENTY-SIX

TIM

Now

The tyres of the patrol car threw up clouds of dust as it made its way up the driveway of Le Mas des Flores.

As he climbed out of the back seat into the warm, scented air that Monday evening, Tim was reminded of arriving at the villa for the first time. That had been only twelve days ago, but it felt as though it had happened in another lifetime. This time, instead of being with him, his children were racing down the steps to greet him, flinging their arms around him.

Louise followed them outside but stood with her arms wrapped tightly around her body as he attempted to pull her into an embrace. He felt her flinch at his unshaven jaw grazing hers, aware he must smell awful.

'Am I glad to see you,' he murmured, smiling at her. 'How have things been here?'

'All right.' Her smile was tight.

'Let me go and grab a shower and shave and then we'll talk, okay?'

She nodded and once the children had been despatched to

the kitchen to eat their supper, followed her husband upstairs to their room.

'How have the kids been?' he asked once they were alone. The sallow shadows beneath her eyes told him that she had not slept any better than he had.

She shrugged. 'Harry's been a bit withdrawn, Elle more talkative, but tearful.'

'And everyone else?'

'Renée's been polite, but kept her distance... And who can blame her? It's horribly uncomfortable all round. The Staffords re-booked their flights and a car took them to Nice this afternoon. Until then they mostly stayed in their room. Keeping their distance. Again, who can blame them?'

Tim shook his head slowly. 'I'm sorry. Sorry we all had to go through this. It must have been awful for you, not knowing what the hell was going on.' He stripped off his grimy clothes and headed for the bathroom. 'Any wine in the fridge? I could kill for a drink.' He caught himself in this unfortunate turn of phrase and gave a hollow little laugh.

'So, is everything sorted out?' Louise asked him when he emerged wrapped in a towel a few minutes later. She handed him a cold glass of Sancerre, which he tipped back in one go. 'They haven't charged you with anything?'

He shook his head, pouring himself a second glass of wine.

'Then why did they need to keep you so long?'

'Just because there wasn't a lawyer available on Sunday night, that's all. They didn't speak to me at all until about three hours ago. And when they did, they just wanted me to explain on the record about the pentobarbital.'

'And that was all? They didn't want to talk to you about anything else?'

Tim shook his head.

'And they don't know who the dead woman is?'

He hesitated. 'They're still looking into all that.'

'So everything's okay now?'

He squeezed his wife's hand and leaned in to kiss her. 'Yes, sweetheart, I promise you: everything's okay.'

On Tuesday morning, Louise suggested that they should take the children out for the last day of the holiday.

'Not having the pool is hard for them when it's this hot.' The temperature gauge on the loggia was registering 34 degrees. 'And hanging around here after... what's happened... it isn't great for them. The atmosphere is pretty dark.'

Tim hesitated. He couldn't have agreed with his wife more, but there was the issue of him being bailed to Le Mas des Flores. He'd been told he had to 'remain' at the property. But surely that meant using it as his base, his *de facto* address in France? It didn't mean he was under house arrest, surely? No one had said that.

'I've just spoken to Renée and she completely understands,' Louise went on. 'She said we can have use of the BMW for the day.'

'All right, let's do it. Since the kids are desperate to swim and we're in the South of France, we should head to the beach, right?'

Tim spoke with levity, but his mind was still whirring. He was thinking of Hannah Messenger. Who had she spoken to before she died, and had she told them about him? If so, how on earth did that relate to her murder?

'You're quiet,' Louise observed, as they drove along the A8 to Fréjus Plage. The children, excited about their day release, were squabbling good-naturedly in the back seat.

'Sorry. I'm still tired. A sleepless night in a cell will take it out of you.'

He managed to collect himself sufficiently to give an impression of enjoyment at the palm-tree lined beach. The children dug in the sand and frolicked in the water like puppies let off the lead, and when they'd all had enough sun, they retreated to a beach restaurant. The four of them sat under a canvas awning enjoying salty fries with mayonnaise and a chilled carafe of the local rosé for the adults and for a while – just for a while – the trauma of the past two days was forgotten. It felt like a real holiday.

When they returned to Le Mas des Flores, Laurent had made a start on refilling the swimming pool. The children ran down to watch, but were disappointed to learn it would take at least another twenty-four hours.

'We'll be on our way back home by then,' Louise told them.

Except that I don't have my passport, Tim thought. He didn't want to air this concern out loud for fear of worrying Louise, following her upstairs to pack as though nothing was amiss.

To his relief, a police car arrived at the property just before they were about to eat their final dinner and a uniformed gendarme got out, accompanied by Guillaume Hall. They went into the dining room to talk, passing Renée in the hall-way. She forced a smile, but the expression in her eyes confirmed that she was having doubts about her latest investment.

Tim's passport was returned, and Guillaume took a few minutes to explain what would happen next. 'We have an inquisitorial system here, which means that in all but the most straightforward situations, the case is passed to an examining magistrate who acts as an official investigator. They can question witnesses, examine evidence and generally influence the course of proceedings, and in your case they will decide whether the public prosecutor should bring charges against you.'

'And how long is all that going to take?' Tim asked. He gripped the back of a dining chair to stop himself shaking. The possibility of being charged with murder was making him feel faint.

'It depends,' Guillaume said. 'It will be several weeks at least, but sometimes cases can be held up for months, or even years. I'm afraid that France doesn't have a great reputation when it comes to the speed of its justice system.'

Years? This could be hanging over me for years?

Guillaume saw the look of anguish on this face, and squeezed his shoulder briefly. 'Look, hopefully it won't come to that. And you're free to return to the UK, but I strongly advise you to retain legal counsel there as soon as you can. That's because the contents of your file can only be shared directly with a lawyer; you have no right to a copy of it yourself. So if you want to know what's going on, you'll need to be represented by someone with some experience of the French legal system.'

Tim balled his hands into fists and pressed them into his eye sockets, trying desperately to comprehend the magnitude of what was happening. If only they hadn't come to Provence, he thought. If only he hadn't been so keen to ingratiate himself with Renée Weber, and had simply told her that the Cutlers would be holidaying in Cornwall instead.

'The police will continue with other lines of enquiry in the meantime. Hopefully they'll find the person responsible and the investigation into you will be dropped,' Guillaume said.

Tim lifted his head and looked at him. 'And if they don't?'

'Then you'll be summoned to return to Brignoles to be formally charged. And probably remanded in custody in France awaiting trial. That can be for up to four years.'

'Four years! Jesus Christ,' Tim groaned. 'What a bloody mess.'

'Quite.'

Dinner that night was a subdued affair.

The Staffords were gone and Renée pleaded a tactical headache, so Pascale was only catering for the Cutlers and Jared. They ate their chicken escalopes and artichokes in near silence.

'I wonder if Jared and Shona are still in touch,' Louise said to Tim as they returned to their room to finish packing. 'Only, from what he was saying, he's perfectly happy to jet off to the States with Renée. Maybe she's asked him to marry her after all, and he's got his eyes on the financial prize.'

'Who knows?' said Tim, who privately didn't much care. His only concern was whether Renée was about to ditch the deal to purchase Fairlawn. The papers were signed and sealed, but did his indeterminate criminal status give her a get-out clause?

He got his answer the next morning when their luggage was being loaded into a taxi. Renée kissed them both formally and said coolly, 'It's so wonderful to get to know you both. Clearly with the recent... unfortunate events, we can't move things forward until I've had a chance to speak to VCM's legal department. I'm about to go on a business trip to New York, and I'm flying direct from there to Toronto, but I've scheduled a meeting with them as soon as we're back. On the 25th of August.'

That was a little over three weeks away. Tim had just twenty-three days to clear his name.

TWENTY-SEVEN

LOUISE

Now

The Cutlers' flight from Toulon was delayed for nearly three hours.

By the time they had retrieved their luggage, reclaimed their car and driven back to Winchester through heavy traffic, it was late afternoon. Louise loaded up the washing machine with a heap of dirty swimsuits, shorts and T-shirts and set about preparing a scratch supper of frozen burgers, oven chips and peas. The mood on the journey back was a stark contrast to their excitement at setting off for the South of France two weeks earlier. The children rallied once they were in contact with their friends again and social plans were being made, but Tim and Louise remained subdued, monosyllabic.

As they were loading the plates into the dishwasher and the children darted off to immerse themselves once more in the screen time they'd been missing, Tim announced that he was going into work.

'What, now?' Louise glanced at the clock on the kitchen wall. 'But it's seven forty-five.'

'I know that, darling,' he replied stiffly. 'But I'm the senior partner and I've been away from the practice for two whole weeks. I need to go and check what's been going on in my absence. I can deal with some paperwork and get a head start on tomorrow, since Amy tells me I've got a full list of consultations, followed by several operations.'

'All right,' Louise said quietly. She had her head bent over the open dishwasher and didn't look up at him. 'I suppose that makes sense.'

She watched a cookery show on the living room TV, and at nine thirty, once the children were in bed, decided to turn in herself. There was no message from Tim about his return and she decided against messaging him. Instead, she woke just before 1 a.m., to find him lying next to her in the bed. She knew intuitively that he wasn't asleep. So familiar was she with him after twenty years that she could tell just from the way his body was arranged.

'Tim,' she said flatly. 'Is everything okay?'

He leaned over and planted a kiss on the top of her head. 'Everything's fine,' he whispered. 'Go back to sleep.'

But she lay awake, because things did not feel fine. It felt as though there was something he wasn't telling her. And she needed to know what that was.

Louise eventually drifted off at around five, and when she woke, Tim had left for work.

She had the luxury of a slow start, at least until preparations for the new term started in another couple of weeks. Downstairs, she could hear the children arguing in the kitchen, and pulled on her dressing gown to go and referee. Her phone buzzed. 'Message from Shona Prentice', the notification said. The text itself was in all capitals.

WE NEED TO TALK!! X

This had to be about the terrible events at Le Mas des Flores, surely. While Louise didn't have any great desire to speak to Shona, she was experiencing an overwhelming urge to talk to someone about what had happened. To try to make sense of it. Once the children's petty argument had been settled and she had put some cinnamon rolls to heat in the oven, she replied to Shona.

Shall we meet for a coffee? Will have kids with me, so Abbey Gardens? 11.00? X

She named a small formal park in the city centre, that had a children's playground where Elodie and Violet would be happy enough on the swings. There was a restaurant in the converted mill that overlooked the park, which served coffees in the mornings and had outdoor seating.

Harry declared the playground 'babyish' and mulishly refused to go, and since he had just endured a fortnight in close daily contact with the two ten-year-old girls, Louise didn't really feel she could force him. After phoning round the school mums, she managed to secure an invitation for him to spend the day at his friend Noah's house, which was conveniently on the next street.

Once they were at the park and the girls had run shrieking to the play equipment, Shona and Louise bought iced coffees and settled on a bench within sight of their children. It was a lot cooler than France, but Shona was dressed in skimpy white shorts and an off-the-shoulder top that displayed the Provencal tan she had worked so hard for.

Her opening gambit was not what Louise had been expecting. Not at all.

'So, tell me everything!' she gushed. 'I want every scrap of info about Jared. D'you know where he is now? Are they together? Did he say anything to you about me?'

Louise shook her head. 'Not to me. He and Renée have flown back to Geneva, and then they were going straight on to the States. Well, Renée is. She did refer to when "we" were back, so I assume she meant Jared.' She tried to keep her tone neutral, but couldn't prevent a little frisson of schadenfreude.

Shona was staring at her stonily, as though Louise had somehow not done enough to prevent this development.

'Anyway,' Louise went on, taking a fortifying sip of her coffee. 'When I got your text, I assumed it was because Hampshire Police had been in touch with you about what happened. Did you and Kevin not know that a dead body was discovered by the pool, literally minutes after your taxi left?'

'Oh that,' Shona flapped her hand dismissively. 'Yes, the police came to our house on... when was it? Must have been Tuesday morning. Wanted to know if we'd seen or heard anything on the Friday night. Which we hadn't. We had a massive row after dinner when Kevin told me we were on the next flight home, but only once Jared and *her*...' she spat the word, '...were in bed, so I couldn't talk to him. We screamed all sorts at each other and Kevin ended up sleeping on the sofa in the salon. But there was nothing we could really tell them, since neither of us had ever even met the girl.'

Louise did a double take, confused. The Prentices had left before the body was discovered. 'Wait... how d'you know you didn't know her?'

'They mentioned her name. Hannah someone. What was her surname...? It's gone out of my head. But anyway, from what the police said, they knew who she was.' She shivered dramatically. 'I'm glad I wasn't there, to be honest. The whole thing creeps me out.'

The two girls ran over to get the packets of crisps and drink cartons that Louise had brought with her and rushed back to the swings with them, chattering happily.

'It's nice to see Violet so happy,' Shona said, with a trace of wistfulness. 'Kids pick up on stuff, don't they, and the last couple of weeks have been difficult for her, you know?'

'How are things with Kevin now?' Louise was genuinely curious.

'We're getting a divorce.'

'Oh God, I'm sorry, Shona!' She shook her head slowly. 'Is it really that final? Isn't there anything you can do to work things out?'

Shona shook her head and forced a smile. 'It's fine, honestly. It's not the end of the world: half the people in this country are divorced. Not that you and Tim will ever divorce, obviously. You two are rock solid.'

Back at home with Elodie, Louise set her bag on the kitchen table and rummaged through sundry tissues, receipts and biros until she found what she was looking for.

Guillaume J. Hall, Detective privé

She turned the card over and over in her fingers, then closed her fist around it and pressed it to her sternum as though it was some sort of magical talisman. Shona's relaying of events had made her uneasy. According to her, on Tuesday, the local police – at the request of the force in Provence – had named the dead woman. But Louise was sure that Tim had told her that on Monday they didn't know who she was. Or had he? She was now so confused that her head was pounding.

When Tim returned from work that evening, he uncorked a bottle of Italian wine and offered her a glass. She refused, since her headache was now starting to feel like the onset of another migraine. Instead, she placed Guillaume's business card on the table in front of him.

'I think we should ask Guillaume to help us.'

'Guillaume? Why?'

'Because he's a private investigator. He knows the system, and he also knows about the case against you.'

'But, sweetie, he's going to be very expensive.'

'We could find the money.'

Tim's expression shifted. His eyes were rimmed with red, and despite his tan, there were dark circles visible beneath them. He wasn't sleeping much; Louise was only too aware of that.

'Lou, I really don't think we should go down that route. I'm already going to have to pay a fortune to a lawyer who specialises in international law. I spoke to Peter Critchley – my contact at the practice's legal firm – but he only does commercial law, so he's helping me find someone at a specialist firm in London. We can't afford to pay Guillaume's retainer on top. We'd have to break into savings. Possibly even my pension account.'

He didn't look up, and there was no emotion in his voice as he spoke. Louise couldn't understand this flatness, this impassivity. He'd just been arrested, for God's sake. For murder. And yet he acted as though the whole business was just some bureaucratic inconvenience that had been added to his to-do list.

'I don't give a shit about the money!' Louise declared, with uncharacteristic anger. She rarely swore, and Tim now glanced up at her in surprise. 'If I understood Renée correctly, then you've got a couple more weeks to get the French police investigation into you closed, before VCM's legal team get cold feet and pull out of the purchase. That's not very long to come up with some information that will completely exonerate you.'

'Yes. I'm aware of that,' he said dully.

'So!' She slammed the table with the flat of her hand. 'Tim! Wake up! We've got to find a way out of this mess. And the way I see it, Guillaume's our only hope.'

TWENTY-EIGHT

TIM

Now

Fraser Armstrong was head of International and Cross-Border at Lovell Goddard. As of 7th August, he was also Tim's new lawyer.

Scottish born, he still had a faint Edinburgh accent, but was in every other respect an archetypal City lawyer, wearing pinstripes, silk socks and a cutaway collar. Despite being almost completely bald, he was a handsome man, with the physique of a rugby player.

Tim travelled up to London to see him at the large law practice in Gresham Street as soon as an appointment became available. He was led from the very glossy reception area which resembled the lobby of a five-star hotel to Armstrong's corner office with floor-to-ceiling windows. A cappuccino was brought to him by a smartly dressed PA, along with a plate of shortbread biscuits.

'They're Scottish,' Armstrong smiled. 'My dear mother sends them down from a little bakery in Morningside. I'm afraid I can't quite give them up.' Despite this admission, he refused the biscuits himself and got straight to the point, his style brisk and no-nonsense. 'You're aware of how the French judicial system works, I hope, Mr Cutler?'

'Tim, please.'

'Tim... as an individual, you are not entitled to a copy of any evidence or discovery paperwork, but I am. So you can view the material on your file through me, and me alone.'

Which will prove an expensive process, Tim thought gloomily, as he washed down the delicious buttery shortbread with his coffee.

'I've informed...' He put on metal-framed reading glasses and glanced at the papers in front of him, 'Capitaine Palomer that I am now representing you and we've just had the file sent through. There's not a lot you need concern yourself with, although I can see a recent development is that a search of the grounds of the property... Le Mas des Flores, it says here: is that right?'

Tim nodded.

'The search eventually produced a bag that had been thrown into a disused well, containing drug vials and a syringe along with clothing and shoes. Namely; a cotton dress, a pair of Havaianas flip-flops and some female underwear. Sure enough, subsequent trace DNA testing has proved that these were worn by the unfortunate Ms Messenger. Another thing that caught my attention is that the report states that the labels had been removed from the underwear and the dress.'

'Why would someone do that?'

'Good question.' Armstrong steepled his fingers. 'One assumption is that it's because our clothes tell a story about us. I've heard of similar cases where labelling is removed from clothing to obscure where it was purchased. Marks and Spencer knickers, for example, would strongly imply their owner was British.'

'Could that be why the body was found naked?'

Armstrong checked the file again. 'Certainly, there was no evidence of her being stripped for sexual gratification. She had not, according to the post-mortem findings, been sexually assaulted.' He paused and raised an eyebrow over the top of his glasses. 'Interestingly, the clothing was dry, indicating that when the victim went in the pool she would already have been naked. Naked and alive, since we know she didn't drown. So perhaps she removed her clothing voluntarily. It's not impossible that she was also the one who removed the labels, but I doubt it.'

Tim shook his head slowly and covered his face with his hands. Gathering himself, he said, 'I'm no criminologist, but doesn't this evidence also suggest that the perpetrator thought about this *a priori*? They planned it, in other words. It wasn't a heat-of-the-moment thing.'

'That would be my conclusion, yes. As far as I can see from the file, what they have against you is that you were responsible for the drug used to kill her being on the premises. Two empty vials of pentobarbital and a used syringe were also found in the well. Again, according to the PM findings, it was injected into her foot.'

Tim gave a groan of disbelief. 'Christ!' He looked up at the ceiling as he tried to compose himself. The thought of spending the next two decades in prison was unthinkable, but what if he couldn't prove his innocence?

'Now, the drug evidence is obviously not nothing, but nor is it enough. They're going to need more than that to convict you, or even to charge you. After all, any number of people could have taken the pentobarbital from your bag.'

'But no one knew it was there. That's what I can't get my head around.'

'No one? Not even your wife?'

'No!' Tim protested. 'Well, I suppose it's possible she could have seen it, but there's no way Louise could have anything to do with this. No way in hell.'

'Your faith in your spouse is touching,' Armstrong said drily. 'But trust me, in my experience, stranger things have happened.'

It was agreed that Tim would be kept advised of any relevant developments by email, but since no documents could be copied to him, he would have to go to the offices of Lovell Goddard LLP in person if he wanted to view anything.

On the train back to Winchester, he picked up a copy of the *Standard* that had been left on the seat and his heart sank.

British woman, 32, killed in France

The devastated family of Hannah Messenger, a London woman found dead in a luxury villa in the South of France on 29th July, have vowed to bring her killer to justice.

There was an aerial photo of Le Mas Des Flores, along with a headshot of Hannah herself.

Tim threw the paper back onto the seat, unable to read further. So it was out. It had only been a matter of time, but somehow he had not stopped to think about the implications of the story being in the press. How long until his name appeared in connection with the killing? And how would VCM view his suitability as a business partner then?

Tim spent a couple of hours at the surgery on his return from London, then went home to an empty house. This was such a rare occurrence in the Cutler household that he couldn't remember the last time it had happened. Louise was always there in the evening, supervising the children and preparing an evening meal. But today she had texted him to say one of the school mothers had invited her and the children on a trip to the cinema that afternoon, and they were going to go out for pizza afterwards.

He felt as though he was being punished for not seeing things from her point of view. Their relationship was more strained than it had ever been. As Tim poured himself a drink, he remembered something his mother had said on their wedding day (perhaps a little dig at the never less than perfect harmony of their union): 'Into every life a little rain must fall.' Was this their rain then? A light shower now, perhaps, but it could turn into a deluge if the truth came out.

As if the weather gods were reading his mind, a torrential summer downpour started. Tim looked out of the window at the cascade of water pouring off the patio sunshade and was reminded of that night in October 2010. The rainstorm that had led to this catastrophic sequence of events. The two girls at the party, one of whom he had had sex with and the other – her friend – who was now dead. And yet he had no idea why.

His thoughts were interrupted by the doorbell. He pulled the door open wide and there, under a huge black umbrella, was Guillaume Hall. The streaming umbrella and slick surface of his trench coat were illuminated from behind by the strange yellowish grey of the sky. This gave him an otherworldly appearance, like a male Mary Poppins.

After a few seconds of disorientation, Tim collected himself. 'Guillaume. Come in.'

'You weren't expecting me?'

'No,' Tim said heavily. 'No, I was not.'

He took Guillaume's soaking coat and umbrella from him and led him through into the kitchen.

'You have a lovely home.'

'Thank you,' Tim said stiffly. 'Can I get you something? Tea? Coffee? Or wine, perhaps?'

Guillaume accepted a cup of tea. 'My father was English,' he said, with his attractive eye-crinkling smile. 'I'm fully in on the tea thing.'

'So Louise asked you to come?' Tim said, as he boiled the kettle.

'Yes. She phoned me and engaged my services, and I agreed to fly over here to make some initial enquiries. I've just checked into the Premier Inn on the other side of the city.'

Which I am no doubt paying for, Tim thought with a trace of bitterness. But the money wasn't his primary concern. He knew it made him a hypocrite, but what disturbed him most about this situation was Louise taking matters into her own hands and going behind his back.

Would Guillaume be able to help make the case against him go away? Yes, probably. He seemed intelligent, insightful, experienced. But that was the problem. Because to achieve this he was going to have to dig into Tim's past.

And the things he uncovered might save him from prison, but they would destroy his marriage.

TWENTY-NINE

TIM

Now

'I'll need to start by talking to you both again,' Guillaume told Tim as he finished his cup of tea.

'Louise and the children are out, as you've probably gathered.'

'That's perfectly all right,' Guillaume said smoothly. 'In fact, it's probably better this way, since I'll want to talk to you each separately and in confidence.'

He turned his light eyes directly onto Tim's face, and Tim felt an uncomfortable sensation in the pit of his stomach. *He knows something. He knows there's more to what happened in Cotignac.*

'We can start now,' Tim said, with more sangfroid than he felt. 'Shall we go into the living room?'

'Whatever you'd prefer.'

They stayed in the kitchen, which felt less formal.

Guillaume held up his phone. 'All right if I record our conversation? It won't be passed on to anyone else. It's just for my convenience. I'll make written notes too, as backup.'

Tim nodded, and Guillaume set the phone between them on the kitchen island and set it to record.

'Can we please go back to your visit to Le Bar des Vignobles? And the conversation you had with Ms Messenger. You said it was just exchanging pleasantries about the weather, is that right?'

Tim paused for a long time. 'That wasn't really the whole truth,' he said eventually. 'I had met her before. Well, sort of. I can't say I knew her exactly, but...'

Guillaume didn't react, just waited.

'I came across her years ago, here in Hampshire. It was at a party... well, a work event. She and her friend were waitressing.' Tim had a sudden mental image of the two girls pointing at him and whispering behind their hands. 'I didn't speak to her – to Hannah – that night, but I noticed her because of the unusual colour of her hair. It was so pale, like silver. It stuck in my mind. And I caught sight of her in Cotignac, and immediately thought it must be the same girl.'

'And was it?'

'Yes,' Tim said heavily. 'I realised she must be working at that bar, so I went in to talk to her.'

Guillaume frowned. 'Let me get this clear... you went to speak to her in the bar because she was someone you had set eyes on once before, back here in Winchester?'

'Yes. Well, it was Basingstoke actually.'

'May I ask why?'

There was another long pause. 'Look, it's complicated.'

'These things often are.' Guillaume gave the merest hint of a smile. 'Especially when women are part of the narrative.'

'This goes no further, okay? You say nothing to Louise. That's incredibly important.'

As important as it felt to tell the truth to Guillaume now.

'Okay.'

Tim stood up and poured himself a glass of wine from the fridge. He held up the bottle to Guillaume, who shook his head.

Glancing at the recording, hesitantly, he went on. 'It was a long time ago. Many years ago. I had a... well, you couldn't even call it a one-night stand; it was barely that... with a friend of Hannah's. She was employed by the same catering company.'

'Do you remember the name of the company that employed them? I might need to speak to them.'

'Yes, Greenleaf Catering.'

Guillaume made a note.

'Louise has never found out about it, and the whole thing was over immediately. I mean, Christ, it was only about three minutes of my life. But when I saw Hannah... well, the coincidence alone was a shock. That she turned up in the same French village... it's bizarre. And it brought the whole thing back. So I wanted... I don't know, I wanted to find out if she knew anything about it.'

'I see. And did she know about it?'

'She did, yes, apparently. But she also told me she had lost touch with the girl in question a long time ago.'

'So that was it?'

'That was it. It was a pretty brief conversation, because there was really nothing else for us to talk about. We did talk about the weather and the villa, like I told the police. And then I left. The next time I saw her was when she was lying dead on the pool lounger. That's the truth, I swear it.'

'But when the body was discovered, you didn't say who she was. You let the police identify her instead.'

Tim gave a frustrated little exhalation. 'Because I didn't know her name at that point! I didn't ask it in the bar in Cotignac, and she didn't tell me.'

'But you knew where she worked, and that she was a British national. And that would have helped the police identify her,' Guillaume suggested reasonably.

Tim rubbed his hands through his hair. 'Of course, but I was scared that if I said I'd met her previously it would look really incriminating. But as it turned out she'd been killed with my drugs and I was arrested anyway.' He gave a shrug and gulped his wine. 'And here we are.'

'Indeed. So, just to be clear, you've never had sex with Hannah Messenger?'

'No!' Tim protested vigorously.

'But the other girl, the one you did have sex with; what was her name?'

'I don't see how that's relevant.'

'It probably isn't. But even so, for completeness, what was her name?'

Tim sucked in his breath. 'Tina,' he said eventually. 'Christina Locke.'

Guillaume wrote this down. 'And Louise knows nothing of you sleeping with Hannah's friend, this Tina?'

'Look, Guillaume...' He was rigid with frustration now. 'Sleeping with her is not what it was... she jumped me in my car, climbed on top of me. She seduced me. Like I said, Louise knows nothing. And whatever happens, you mustn't tell her.'

By the time Louise and the children returned from their evening of pizza and milkshakes at the local multiplex, Guillaume had left in a taxi for the Premier Inn.

Tim waited until Harry and Elodie were upstairs in their rooms before confronting his wife.

'Guillaume Hall came round. I take it you know about that?'

'Good,' was her defiant response as she helped herself to a glass of wine.

'I wasn't aware we'd agreed on hiring him. I've already got Fraser Armstrong on a hefty retainer, as of this morning.'

'We didn't agree,' said Louise calmly. 'But *I* decided I wanted his help with keeping *my* husband out of jail. I've sold some of the shares Granny left me to cover his bill.'

'Well, let's hope he can help, then.' Tim just about managed to keep his tone reasonable. He couldn't afford to antagonise Louise. Guillaume was going to be speaking to her in depth the next day, and Tim couldn't be one hundred per cent certain that he wouldn't betray his confidence on the subject of Tina. His wife was now picking up the private investigator's bill, after all: perhaps Guillaume would feel a greater sense of loyalty to her. He had also asked Tim's permission to view the file documents that would be lodged at Lovell Goddard with Fraser Armstrong. It seemed needlessly obstructive to refuse this, but for some reason Tim didn't feel completely comfortable with the idea. 'He told me he plans to start with doing some background checks on Hannah Messenger. Seems to think that will be helpful.'

Know your victim, was what Guillaume had actually said. *Your victim will lead you to their killer.*

THIRTY

LOUISE

Now

Two days later, Guillaume phoned Louise to discuss his preliminary findings.

'Of course, come over to the house,' she told him, then hesitated. It was a beautiful late summer day and both children were out with school friends. 'Or we could go out for coffee?' she suggested.

They met at Louise's favourite café at the foot of St Catherine's Hill. Built from timber, it looked and felt like being in a tree house. Louise chose one of the tables on the decked terrace, shaded by a canopy of branches, ordered a flat white and waited for Guillaume to appear.

'This place is very cute,' he said, giving her his familiar gap-toothed smile. He was wearing worn but expensive-looking jeans, leather loafers and a pale pink linen shirt. '*Très sympa*, as my mother would say.'

'Does she live in France?'

'Yes. In Paris. She's as Parisienne as they come, and my dad could not be more English. I guess that explains my ongoing identity crisis.'

Louise was curious to know if he had a wife or girlfriend, or even children, but felt suddenly inhibited. Apart from her colleagues at St Agnes, she never spent any time with single men. It felt strange. Guillaume, on the other hand, seemed completely at ease. He ordered black coffee and a croissant, then set a paper folder on the table between them.

'I'll go over what's in here briefly, but first, I should really re-interview you, like I did with Tim.'

'Oh.' Louise looked at him anxiously.

'Don't worry, it's not as intimidating as it sounds. Not like when I was working for the police in Brignoles. It's really just to make use of the time that's passed since we last saw one another. To see if you've had any further thoughts, or remembered anything that now seems significant.'

She sipped her coffee in silence for a few seconds. 'Not really, no,' she said eventually. 'Looking back, what stands out is how normal everything seemed. The day before, and the night that it happened, there was nothing that seemed different in any way. Apart from Tim going into Cotignac on his own. I suppose that was different.'

Guillaume narrowed his eyes slightly, but made no comment. 'Okay...' He pointed to the file. 'I've typed up some information about Hannah Messenger, which you can read later. And share with Tim, of course. Not that I found a lot. She seems to have led a pretty run-of-the-mill suburban life. Private school where she was an average student, stable home life in an upscale part of Basingstoke. Dad an engineer, mum a senior hospital administrator. No shortage of money. One sister, now married with kids. Hannah went to college and studied market-ing, moved to London and did a few jobs in that industry. After a recent break-up with a boyfriend, she chucked in her job and decided to take a belated gap year and do some travelling. And to pay her way she went back to working in hospitality.' He chewed on a piece of his croissant, before adding. 'Which, as Tim probably explained, is how he first came across her as a teenager. When she was waitressing.'

Louise felt a slap of shock, as though someone had just thrown cold water over her. 'I'm sorry...' she whispered. 'I don't think I follow. Tim *knew* this girl?'

Guillaume now looked mortified. 'Louise, *I'm* sorry. I just assumed Tim had already talked to you about this.'

She shook her head. 'When did he...? I don't understand.'

Guillaume put down his coffee and twisted slightly in his chair so that he was looking directly at her and their legs were almost touching. 'Please, don't worry, it's nothing sinister. Let me try to explain.'

His voice was gentle, reassuring, but Louise still stared at him with wild-eyed shock, her cheeks burning.

'After you and Tim discovered the body, he realised that he had in fact seen her before, serving him at a corporate veterinary event some years ago. He spoke to her at the Bar des Vignobles, in Cotignac after he recognised her from back in the UK.'

Louise was shaking her head. 'He actually *spoke* to her... when was that, the day she died? Then why on earth didn't he say anything?' Another thought dawned on her. 'Wait, do the police know this?'

No wonder they suspect him, she thought, appalled. *He was the only person at Le Mas des Flores who knew her.*

Guillaume hesitated for a long beat, and it was obvious to her that he was trying to craft his answer carefully. 'He didn't mention it to them to begin with, but they are now aware that he spoke to her in the bar, yes. That he knew her from the UK... I don't think so. I'll be liaising with the gendarmes working on the case shortly, and then I'll have a better idea of where they are with evidence gathering.'

'But why?' Louise wailed, so loudly that some of the other people on the terrace turned in her direction. 'Why start out telling a lie if you have done nothing illegal?'

'There are all sorts of reasons someone might lie, even if they're completely innocent,' Guillaume said reasonably. 'I see it all the time when I'm acting as a police interpreter. People get nervous, they feel out of their depth, they even worry that the truth might make them look guilty. My advice to you is not to get too hung up on a detail that will probably be unimportant.'

'He spoke to her hours before she was killed,' Louise had lowered her voice, but she was still angry and upset. 'How on earth can that be unimportant?'

'Because it's only a part of the picture,' Guillaume gave her that warm smile, as he picked up his coffee cup again. 'Think of it as just one piece in a jigsaw puzzle. When we know what and who make up the other pieces, this will fade into insignificance.'

'Do you promise?' She was aware she sounded plaintive, like a child.

'I promise.' He reached out and covered her fingers with his. It was the briefest touch, but she felt a shot of something – connection? comfort? – travel through her body. It felt like sinking into a hot bath.

'Now,' he said, taking out his notebook, 'I'm going to need the contact details for your friends the Prentices. I should go and speak to them while I'm here.'

'Sweetheart, I need to tell you something,' Tim said to her that evening.

It was a warm evening, and they had eaten supper outside on the patio. It had been a strained meal with Louise barely trusting herself to speak. Elodie was on the trampoline at the far end of the garden and Harry was kicking a ball about on the lawn in a half-hearted fashion.

'If you're going to tell me that you knew the dead woman was Hannah Messenger, then I already know,' she said flatly. 'Guillaume told me.'

Tim tipped his head back and swore.

'There's no use being annoyed with him, by the way. He only mentioned it in the context of me already knowing. He assumed we'd spoken about it.'

'And I was going to,' Tim said. He rubbed his hand over his dark stubble. 'I was. It was just a question of finding the right moment.'

'So you actually remembered a girl you saw once, serving at a function years and years ago?'

'Well yes. But only because her looks were so striking. You know, with that silver-blonde hair.'

'You found her striking?' Louise didn't know she could summon so much acid when it came to her husband. But this was uncharted territory.

'Only in the sense that she was unusual looking.'

'And are you sure there was no other reason you remembered her?'

'Jesus, Lou, of course not!'

She pulled him round to face her now. 'Tim, is there something you're not telling me? Because if there's more to this... this weird coincidence, then you'd better tell me now.'

'No, I swear it! You've got to believe me!'

She looked at him for what felt like minutes, examining his face. She could plainly see the anguish in his eyes, and yet for the first time in all the years she'd known him, she wasn't sure if she trusted him. It was profoundly disorientating. Who had they become?

She stood up abruptly. 'I'm going to sleep in the spare room tonight. I'll go and make up the bed.'

'But, darling, we never sleep apart from one another. When we got married, we agreed we'd never be one of those couples that do that.'

'We also agreed we'd never lie,' she said sadly, turning and walking into the house.

THIRTY-ONE

TIM

Now

Tim woke at 2 a.m. and swung an arm across to the other side of the bed.

It was empty, the patch of sheet on his right cool to the touch. So Louise hadn't relented and come back to their bed. He lay on his back for a while, feeling wretched with guilt. Out in the garden, a fox screeched and there was a clatter as a dustbin lid was dislodged. Then silence descended again.

Groping for the switch on his bedside light, Tim pulled himself up into a sitting position. He sat on the edge of the bed for a while, hunched and miserable, then left the bedroom and headed along the landing towards the guest bedroom. He went to open the door and then stopped, his hand hovering over the door handle. What was he going to do, wake Louise and order her back to the marital bed? Break down in tears and beg her? No, he should leave her to sleep. Instead, he tiptoed down to the kitchen and put the kettle on.

What he must do, he decided as he made tea, was come

clean. About everything. About Tina Locke, about the black-mail, about the true nature of his conversation with Hannah Messenger. Only once everything was out in the open could they set about restoring trust. It would be impossibly hard, but it was the only way of moving forward.

And yet the next morning, despite having rehearsed the conversation over and over in his head, he found he was unable to go ahead with his confession. It was Louise who stopped him in his tracks.

She started by apologising for abandoning him and taking refuge in the spare room.

'It was a cowardly thing to do,' she said flatly. She looked as though she had slept as badly as he had. 'We're better than that. I went over and over it in my head last night, and I've made a decision. For everyone's sake – especially the kids'– we're not going to talk about the Hannah business anymore. I have no choice but to trust what you say, and so for now we'll carry on as normal and let Guillaume do what he needs to do. Other than that; I don't want to know.'

Tim inhaled a long breath. 'If you're sure that's what you want.'

She nodded curtly. He tried pressing his hand in the small of her back as she walked past him to put bread in the toaster, and while she didn't pull away, she stiffened at his touch. 'The truth will come out.' Her tone was brisk as she flicked the switch on the coffee machine. 'It always does.'

Tim could only nod helplessly, his own plan to drag the truth into the light of day abandoned.

Things were quiet at Fairlawn Veterinary Clinic, with a lot of their clients still away on their summer holidays.

As he caught up with his paperwork, Tim wondered whether he should make contact with Renée Weber. Quite what he could say he wasn't sure, but he was feeling an unfamiliar sense of paranoia. In the end, he decided to err on the side of caution and wait until her meeting with VCM's lawyers was a little more imminent. Even so, he felt restless, unable to settle to anything other than the most straightforward task. He certainly couldn't bring himself to look at the practice accounts.

It was a distraction, if not exactly a welcome one, when Guillaume Hall phoned him that afternoon.

'Can we talk? I have some important developments I need to discuss with you. And with Louise, of course. I've spoken to her, and she suggested I come to the house this evening. Is that okay with you?'

Normally his wife would have messaged him about this already, but Louise had said nothing about the arrangement. She hadn't been in touch with him all day. And now, it seemed, she was doing so via a third party.

'Sure,' he said, with a cheerfulness that he didn't feel. 'If that's okay with Lou, then it's okay with me. We're not busy today, so I should be back from work around six. Perhaps we can have a quick chat before we need to feed the kids.'

'I'll see you around six.'

Tim arrived home at ten past six to find Guillaume had already arrived. He was sitting in the garden with Louise, drinking a beer and looking entirely comfortable in her company. As she did in his, Tim noted as he watched them for a few seconds through the kitchen window before heading out to join them. She was wearing a smart white linen dress with a pleated skirt that she usually only chose for formal occasions, her wavy brown hair was tamed with a sparkly clip and she was wearing cherry red lipstick. To his eyes she was beautiful, perfect. And yet he'd never felt so distanced from her.

'Ah Tim, good evening,' Guillaume said with his easy charm. 'Lovely to see you.'

Tim merely nodded, before sitting down at the patio table.

Louise got up and fetched him a beer, placing it in front of him wordlessly.

'As I was just telling Louise, there have been a couple of developments I want to discuss with you both,' Guillaume said.

He was wearing a plain white T-shirt under a leather biker jacket, and the combination made him look young and stylish. Tim found himself wondering with a flash of envy how old he actually was.

'I'll put this all in my written report, as always, but this is the gist of what I've uncovered, and I think you'll find it interesting.' Guillaume swigged his beer from the bottle. 'I spoke to your friend Kevin Prentice this morning, and he told me something he'd remembered. The night of Friday 28th July was the Prentices' last night at the villa, as you know. Kevin argued with his wife, which led to him leaving their room and going downstairs to sleep on the sofa in the main salon. He told me he'd woken and gone into the kitchen to fetch some water at around 1 a.m. There were no blinds or curtains drawn on the French windows in the salon, and when he came back into the room, he recalls seeing a very bright light, like a security light being tripped on. He went and looked out of the window, and says he was sure the light was coming from the direction of the Staffords' room, which was a distance away from the main house. He watched through the window for a few seconds until the light eventually switched off, then went back to sleep on the sofa. He admits he'd had a bit to drink, and by the next morning had forgotten all about it.'

Guillaume leaned back in his chair and waited for a reaction.

'Is that really significant?' Tim asked. 'Surely if it was a security light it could have been tripped by anything: a fox, a deer, a boar even. There was plenty of wildlife around the grounds.'

'Agreed. But he also says he thought he heard splashing in the pool. Which puts a different complexion on things, given we know that Hannah Messenger had been in the pool at some point.'

Louise was looking at her husband expectantly, as though he should somehow be able to explain this new information.

'Ah,' said Tim. His mind was racing. 'But it all seems fairly... circumstantial, I suppose is the word.'

Guillaume nodded. 'Or possibly it represents another piece of our metaphorical jigsaw puzzle. On that note, I also tracked down his friends, the Farrows, but from Thursday to Saturday of that week, they were at Euro Disney with their children, having driven up there from the Cotignac area. They even sent me a time-stamped photo of the whole family on the Thunder Mountain rollercoaster.'

'So that rules out their involvement,' Louise said.

'It does. After I'd spoken to Kevin, I took the train up to London and went to the offices of Lovell Goddard to review your file. And there was a new piece of footage from the security camera at the Bar des Vignobles.' He set his laptop on the table and opened it, pulling up a slightly blurry black and white image. 'Now, as you know, your lawyer can hold copies of any evidence that the French police have unearthed, but you can't. And, officially, I can't take a copy away either. But I did manage to take a screenshot with my phone, which I've uploaded here so you can see it slightly better.'

Both Louise and Tim leaned forward to examine the image. It showed Hannah Messenger behind the bar, dressed in white shirt and black trousers, her pale hair tied up in a ponytail. Facing her across the bar, and seemingly in conversation with her, was a woman with a luxuriant mane of hair, wearing a crochet dress.

'That's Merry Stafford,' said Tim and Louise in unison.

THIRTY-TWO

LOUISE

Now

'Do you know when that was taken?' Louise asked, after a few seconds of stunned silence. She looked very pale.

Guillaume nodded. 'Yes, the footage was date-stamped. It was Wednesday 26th July at 1.34 p.m.'

'Wow.' Tim exhaled, shaking his head.

Louise looked at the image again, thinking to herself that Guillaume's jigsaw theory was exactly right. Here was another piece that could shift the completed image.

He closed his laptop. 'Clearly this could be quite innocent. Maybe Hannah was just admiring her dress, and they got into a conversation about where she'd bought it. Or perhaps Merry had lost her sunglasses or a credit card and was asking if anything had been handed in. There are countless scenarios whereby a tourist might speak to someone serving behind a bar. But if—'

'If you add in what Kevin said he saw and heard that night,' Tim interrupted, 'Which suggested there was more than one person out there by the pool...then it could be more significant. '

'Exactly.' Guillaume put his laptop in his bag and stood up to go. 'Right: I'll leave you guys to get on with your evening now that you're up to speed. Obviously, I'm now actively sourcing intelligence on the Staffords. Also, with your consent, this might be the moment for me to head back to Cotignac and make some further enquiries. Talk to people who could have seen or heard something.'

'Of course,' Tim said, also getting to his feet. 'I agree that seems like the next logical step.'

Louise, still seated, suddenly spoke. 'I think I should come with you,' she said firmly. 'To Provence.'

Guillaume did a slight double take. 'Well, yes, of course, if you can spare the time. In fact, it might even prove useful. There are some situations in which people are more comfortable opening up to a woman than a man.'

She nodded. 'In that case book me on the same flight, and send me the details.'

'Are you really just going to hop back on a plane to the South of France?' Tim asked incredulously, once Guillaume had left.

They had come back into the kitchen and Louise was dicing up tomatoes to put in a salad.

'Why not?' There was an unfamiliar chill in her voice. 'I don't have to go back to work for another two weeks.'

'But what about the kids?'

'You'll have to look after them for once.' She chopped angrily, smacking the knife blade onto the board. 'It's the weekend anyway, and I'm only going to be gone a couple of days or so. Harry can hang out with his friends, and if you need to pop into work, Elodie can go with you. You know she loves seeing the animals. Or you could ask Shona Prentice to have her.'

Tim closed his eyes briefly. 'All right,' he said eventually. 'It doesn't look like I have a choice.'

'We're doing this for you,' Louise hissed, throwing the sliced tomatoes into a bowl and starting on a cucumber. 'Don't let's forget that.'

Flights from Gatwick to Toulon were all full for the next few days, but Guillaume managed to secure two seats on Saturday's pricier British Airways scheduled service to Nice.

They didn't speak much on the journey. Guillaume busied himself with paperwork while Louise sat rigid with misery the entire way. She wanted to do this, but at the same time hated the fact that she was having to do this. Her speech to Tim about letting go of what had happened and moving on had made her a hypocrite. Because she had not let go and she felt incapable of moving on. The simple fact was that she neither believed nor trusted her husband. And when she said she was making this journey for Tim's benefit, she herself had been lying. She was doing it to find evidence against him.

She had been over and over it in her mind, but the shocking fact was that she no longer completely trusted her husband. No one was more dismayed about it than she was, but there was a glaring crack in the perfect façade of their marriage. And the problem with façades was that they were not what they seemed. Things could be hidden behind them.

They took a hire car from Nice to Brignoles, where they were booked into a hotel that was part of a budget chain. It was a low-rise, featureless modern building with equally featureless rooms, but it was at least spotlessly clean and had a swimming pool. After they had been given their key cards, they agreed to drop their bags and meet downstairs in the restaurant. Louise showered and changed into denim shorts, a T-shirt and trainers, opting for practicality rather than glamour.

Guillaume was waiting for her when she got down to the restaurant. In reality, it was more of a cafeteria; its Formica tables and plastic chairs reminding Louise of the dining room at St Agnes. He had a detailed map of the local area spread out in front of him, and was poring over it.

'We can get a coffee here, I think.' He nodded in the direction of a machine stationed next to the buffet-style serving area. 'Shouldn't think it's up to much, frankly.' Louise was bestowed with one of his warm, gap-toothed smiles, and she felt herself relax a little.

'No thanks, I'm fine.'

'Good,' said Guillaume briskly. He folded up the map and strode off in the direction of the car park, with Louise trotting at his heels.

'Where are we going?' she asked, as he unlocked their hire car.

'Le Mas des Flores.'

'Won't there be people staying there?' The idea of walking into the place with a new group of VCM's guests in situ – lounging on the pool terrace and dining on the loggia – made her feel anxious.

'Probably,' said Guillaume, sounding unconcerned. 'Don't worry, I'll explain when we get there.' He flicked on the radio and for the twenty-kilometre drive the car was filled with French pop music that all sounded like Eurovision entries to Louise's ears.

When they reached the narrow country road to Le Mas des Flores, Guillaume drove a hundred yards or so past the entrance to the property and pulled into a lay-by opposite its perimeter fence. He switched off the radio, and took out the map he had been examining.

'This is the IGN map of the area – the *Institut Geographique National*. It's the French equivalent of our

Ordnance Survey maps, and it's extremely detailed. Much more so than an online map.'

He wrestled with the folds in the paper and pointed out something to Louise, although to her it just looked like a tangle of fine lines and gradients.

'See here,' he tapped the map. 'That's the boundary of Les Mas des Flores' land. And here, dissecting it at an angle...' he pointed to a different patch of land, 'is a track that leads to the vineyards. I suspect it would once have been for the grape pickers to come and go without disturbing the people at the main house. And it looks from this as though...' He squinted at the map again, '...there's a gate allowing access to the track from the road, which should be just about...' He looked out of the window of the car and pointed. '...There. D'you see?'

Sure enough, set into the wall and partly overgrown with creepers was a latched timber gate.

Louise nodded.

'Now, we know that when the police first arrived at the house on that Saturday morning two weeks ago, one of the first things they did was to check the CCTV from the main gate. But it showed nothing. Or rather, no one. They know that Hannah Messenger came from Cotignac by scooter, because it was found in a ditch on this stretch of road a couple of days after her body was identified. She had to have got onto the property somehow that night, and if not through the front entrance, then I reckon it had to have been this way. Come on.'

He opened the driver's door and got out of the car and, with Louise following him, crossed the road to the gate. The latch was stiff, but it was not locked. Guillaume pushed it open and stepped onto the track that led up a slight slope. Ahead of them and to the right was the stand of oaks that shaded one side of the pool terrace. And a little further along and to the left was the outbuilding that housed the fourth guest suite.

'That's where the Staffords' room was,' Louise said, her voice barely above a whisper.

Guillaume pulled out his phone and started taking pictures when a burst of laughter erupted from the other side of the hedge, followed by a loud splash as someone dived into the swimming pool. 'Come on, we'd better go.' He gestured back in the direction of the gate. 'We're trespassing, and we don't want to complicate things with the local cops.'

Once they were back on the road, Guillaume strode off past their parked car and back in the direction of Cotignac, his head swivelling as he took in his surroundings.

Louise followed him, having to break into a trot to keep up. 'What are we looking for?'

'Cameras.'

Louise glanced around her. There was nothing but tilled lavender fields edged with rows of Italian cypress and punctuated by the occasional honey-coloured farm building. Eventually, they reached a stone barn at the edge of the road and Guillaume pointed.

'Look. Up there,' he said triumphantly.

Sure enough, there was a security camera fixed to the side of the building and trained in their direction.

'I expect the farmer's put it there to discourage would-be thieves. He's probably got some expensive machinery in his barn, and if it's anything like the UK, that stuff regularly gets stolen.'

They had now turned up the farm track and were heading towards the farmhouse, Louise still working hard to keep pace with Guillaume's purposeful stride.

'A tractor costs as much as a luxury car, so I guess it's not surprising.'

The farmer, a Monsieur Guerin, intercepted them in the yard and interrogated Guillaume at length before reluctantly allowing them into the farm office. He was a wiry, weather-beaten man with the complexion of a walnut and callouses on his hands accumulated during what must have been decades of outdoor work.

Louise's French was just about good enough to follow snatches of the conversation, which seemed to be about thieving bastards taking the mechanical harvester used to pick his wine crop. Eventually, he agreed to search for footage of the early hours of 29th July, on the type of computer terminal Louise hadn't seen in years. He clicked on a file on a list and there it was, the images surprisingly clear.

'*Il y avait une pleine lune*,' Monsieur Guerin offered by way of explanation.

And, sure enough, Hannah Messenger's Vespa appeared on the road at 12.08 a.m. Streaming out from under her helmet, her hair was turned pearlescent in the moonlight. Goose pimples broke out on Louise's arms as she watched the girl and her scooter vanish from view. She herself had been lying asleep in bed merely metres away at the time this was recorded.

And Hannah Messenger had been going to her death.

THIRTY-THREE

LOUISE

Now

Guillaume knocked on the door of Louise's room at six o'clock.

She'd spent the afternoon lying by the hotel pool while Guillaume went to speak to the gendarmes in Brignoles. The loungers were the most basic white plastic kind, and she found herself thinking back to the ones at the Le Mas des Flores, made from slatted teak with padded cushions. And then, inevitably, she could see Hannah Messenger's body all over again, water from her drenched hair leaching onto the linen cover of the cushion. The thought made her shiver, despite the heat.

As usual, she had positioned herself in the shade and made sure her face was obscured by her hat. Smoothing sunscreen onto her skin and settling down to read a novel, she'd told herself that she did not feel guilty. There was no reason to, after all. The children were fine. Harry had gone to a waterpark with Noah's family and Elodie was having a wonderful time helping nurses Claire and Magda care for the cats and dogs who were in-patients at the surgery, while Tim caught up on paperwork.

As for Tim himself; well, he would just have to manage without her.

He had sent her a full update about the children's activities and asked her to do the same, but she'd replied simply 'Tell you later'. Although she was notionally in France to try to help her husband, she was relieved to be away from him, away from the festering anger and resentment towards him.

She climbed off the narrow double bed with its vinyl-covered headboard and answered the door. Guillaume was there looking scrubbed and shaved and smelling of a dry, spicy aftershave. 'Fancy a drink?' he asked her.

'Downstairs?'

'No, over in Cotignac. I was thinking we could call in at Le Bar des Vignobles, kill two birds with one stone, as it were.'

Louise was rapidly getting used to being in Guillaume's company, but going out for a drink with him felt different some-how. She hesitated for a few seconds. 'Sure,' she said eventually. 'Give me ten minutes and I'll meet you downstairs.'

She changed into the one dress she had with her; lilac gingham with a full skirt, and switched her trainers for strappy sandals. Who was this woman reflected in the bathroom mirror, she wondered, as she applied mascara, blusher and lipstick. This woman making herself pretty for another man. It wasn't just that she no longer knew her husband anymore; she barely knew herself either. She paused with the bottle of Coco Made-moiselle in her hand. The scent that Tim had bought for her last Christmas, the scent he claimed to love smelling on her. Then she sprayed it: once, twice – onto her wrist and her neck – picked up her bag and headed downstairs.

The bar in Cotignac was full, despite it being early, and it became apparent that they were hosting an event. A poster outside announced that it was 'La Nuit de Ceroc', and there would be live music as well as dancing.

'Have you ever done ceroc?' Guillaume asked, as he opened the door for her and ushered her in. He was, as ever, quite unphased by this turn of events. 'It's kind of a blend of swing and ballroom.'

'Never.'

'You should give it a try. It's a lot of fun.'

The bar was panelled with dark wood and had a dozen or so classic bistro tables covered with red checked cloths. They had been pushed to the edges of the room to clear space for a makeshift dance floor.

Once Guillaume and Louise had managed to secure one of the few remaining free tables, he went to the bar, returning with a carafe of the local rosé and two glasses.

'So dancing isn't Tim's thing?' he asked once the wine was poured.

'I wouldn't say that,' Louise said carefully. 'Of the two of us, I'd say he's actually the more confident.'

Guillaume raised an eyebrow.

'We might seem like two peas in a pod, but in some ways we're very different. The way we grew up for example.'

'Go on.'

'Tim has the archetypal nuclear family – mum and dad and the two boys: all very stable.' She thought back to how alluring this had seemed to her as a young, rootless student. A cosy world of pet dogs, tennis lessons and skiing holidays. 'But my dad left when I was three, and my mum... well, she was troubled. Had problems. She died when I was thirteen.'

'I'm sorry.'

Louise shrugged. 'There was no one else to take care of me, so I spent several years in foster care. That's why the thought of losing Tim makes me so... desperate.'

Guillaume nodded slowly, patting her hand, before leaving her to her thoughts for a few minutes. She watched the band set up, while he went to speak to the manager about Hannah Messenger.

'How did it go?' she asked when he returned fifteen minutes later.

Guillaume turned down the corners of his mouth and gave a Gallic shrug. 'I asked him what he could remember about the day that Merry Stafford came into the bar. He wasn't all that keen to help, but let's say a fifty-euro tip helped refresh his memory.' He picked up the wine that Louise had poured for him and knocked it back in one gulp.

'So?...'

'He checked back through the old staff rosters, which confirmed that in addition to Hannah, there was a woman called Celine on shift that day. Another fifty euros scored me her address and phone number.'

'You'd better add that to your list of expenses,' Louise said drily, earning herself another of his grins.

Their carafe of wine was finished now and the band had started playing, fast rockabilly-style music, and a handful of couples had started to dance. To Louise's untrained eye, the steps looked like a hybrid of jive and tango, with a lot of twirling and some close, sultry holding.

'So you say you've never done this before?' Guillaume asked.

She shook her head.

'It is a peculiarly French obsession. Come on.' He held out a hand.

'I can't. I'll look a complete idiot.'

'Nonsense,' Guillaume insisted, pulling her to her feet. 'The idea is just to let go and have fun.'

Let go and have fun. How long had it been since Louise had been able to do that? Probably only no more than a couple of months, but it felt so much longer since she'd been able to relax and laugh. As if it was a different lifetime.

And here she was, now dancing with someone other than Tim for the first time in two decades. Guillaume moved easily, with perfect rhythm.

'You've done this before,' she said accusingly.

'Of course,' he said smoothly. 'My friends and I used to go to ceroc clubs in Paris all the time.'

He spun her away from him and then pulled her close, just as the music slowed. She was pressed against his chest, his arms on her back, and it felt... good. Confusingly good. Her tipsiness from the wine was part of it, for sure. Seeing him through rosé-coloured glasses. She looked up at him and he held her gaze just a fraction too long for it to feel entirely platonic. Her heart sped up and her cheeks burned hot and pink as though she had caught the sun on her face.

Why was she feeling like this? Like she wanted him to kiss her. Was it just because she was angry with Tim; some kind of perverse rebound?

Guillaume dipped his head and she sensed that he was, indeed, about to kiss her.

She swallowed hard, and broke from his embrace. 'Can we go back to the hotel?' she mumbled. 'It's been a really long day, and to be honest I'm pretty tired.'

Yes, their flight had left Heathrow very early that morning, but at that moment there was so much adrenaline coursing through her blood, there was no way she would be able to sleep.

'Sure,' said Guillaume smoothly, adding ambiguously. 'It's probably a good idea to turn in.'

Celine Besson lived on the fourth floor of a narrow terracotta building with shutters painted in a faded blue.

When she and Guillaume arrived there the next morning,

Louise had been expecting someone in their twenties, but Celine was somewhere in early middle age, with badly dyed red hair and the skin of someone with a lifelong Gitanes habit.

She held a lit one between two fingers as she led them into a bare, sparsely furnished apartment, and coughed fulsomely as she gestured for Louise and Guillaume to sit down at a small round table. She served them black coffee and continued to both smoke and cough as Guillaume spoke to her. Her English was non-existent, so Louise's contribution was minimal, adding to the discomfort she already felt after her close encounter with Guillaume on the dance floor. Now that she was completely sober, she could see that it had been a bad idea, for so many reasons. They were here to find answers, and for that they both needed completely clear heads.

Celine spoke fast, guttural French with a strong Provencal accent, but Louise managed to pick out the odd word: '*En colère*' and '*en désaccord*'. Once they had forced down their strong, bitter coffee and thanked Celine (which involved another fifty-euro note, Louise observed), they emerged onto the main square in Cotignac.

'I think I got the gist of that,' Louise said, as they went to a café to order croissants and more coffee, this time with milk. 'There was some sort of an argument?'

'Yes.' Guillaume did not shy away from eye contact, seemingly quite happy to overlook what had happened the night before. 'She said from the way Merry approached Hannah at the bar, it was clear that the two women knew one another. Celine said not only that, but she got the sense that they had seen each other recently, rather than just then bumping into one another after many years.'

'Interesting.' The waiter brought their coffee and pastries, and Louise thanked him.

'Obviously the issue we have is that Celine doesn't speak any English, so unfortunately she has no idea what was being discussed.' Guillaume tore into his croissant with his usual gusto. 'But she did say that when Merry left, Hannah abandoned the bar and followed her outside. Celine could see them through the window in what appeared to be an intense discussion, if not an actual row. Merry held out her phone at one point, as though telling the other woman she'd call her, then Hannah came back into the bar. She seemed a little quiet, but otherwise carried on as though nothing was wrong.'

Louise took a mouthful of her coffee. Her third of the day now, and she needed it. 'So what are you thinking now?'

'Well, one of the jigsaw pieces we already have is that Hannah ended up at Le Mas des Flores two days later. The place where Merry Stafford was staying. That simply can't be a coincidence, can it?'

'So Merry asked her to come? If so, why so late at night?'

'Or Hannah showed up anyway, uninvited?' Guillaume mused. 'Either is possible. But what we do know is that there seems to have been some issue between them that needed to be resolved.'

Louise set down her cup and stared at him. Her heart was pounding so hard she could barely catch her breath.

'Are you all right?' Guillaume asked her, reaching out a hand. 'You've gone very pale.'

She nodded. 'Do you mean... Are you saying it was a big enough issue for Merry to want Hannah dead?'

'I don't know. But that's what we need to find out.'

THIRTY-FOUR

LOUISE

Now

They returned to the hotel and Guillaume left Louise sitting by the pool while he went to try to arrange flights back to the UK.

'I've managed to book us on the early flight from Nice tomorrow,' he told her when he came down to join her for a swim an hour later. 'I think we've done all we can here for now. At least until after I've spoken to the Staffords.'

He stripped off his T-shirt, revealing a surprisingly muscular torso and dived into the pool, swimming a few lengths with a powerful crawl. As Louise watched him, she remembered Merry Stafford carving her way through the pool at Le Mas des Flores. Remembered her surprising strength.

'I've got some more phone calls to make. Shall we convene in the restaurant for some dinner later?' Guillaume asked as he heaved himself out of the pool. Rivulets of water streamed down his chest and dripped onto her from the hem of his shorts. Louise shifted away fractionally on her plastic lounger.

She shook her head. 'I've got a bit of a headache coming on,' she lied. 'And I need to catch up with what the kids are up to. I'll probably just have something in my room.'

Back in her room, she showered and lay down on the bed to FaceTime the children, but exhaustion caught up with her and she fell asleep for a couple of hours. When she woke up, there was a missed call from Tim. She pressed 'Call back'.

When he answered, he was in the kitchen cooking something in a pan on the stove. Elodie was perched on a stool next to him, stirring the contents with a wooden spoon. The wholesomeness of the scene made her stomach lurch and she felt sick.

'Hi, darling.' He smiled warmly, but looked tired.

'We're making pasta sauce,' Elodie interjected. 'I put the herbs in.'

'Well done,' said Louise, trying to inject some brightness into her voice. 'I bet you're being a great help. Is your brother there?'

'Nah, he's playing football.'

'Why don't you go and set the table outside, sweetie? That would be really helpful.' Tim took over the stirring and Elodie scampered off. 'How's it going?' he asked once he was alone. 'What have you two managed to achieve?'

'We went back to the bar to find out more from the other employees.'

'Really?' Louise instantly picked up the shift in Tim's body language. His jaw tightened. 'And what did that lead to?'

To me slow dancing with another man. To me feeling like I wanted him to kiss me.

Louise's gaze shifted to the side, so she was not quite meeting her husband's eye. 'We found out some things that could well be relevant, but Guillaume will go over it all with you tomorrow. We're flying back first thing.'

'You'd better get an early night then.'

'Yes,' Louise agreed. 'I will.'

. . .

And yet ten hours later, at just after midnight, Louise found herself standing in the corridor outside Guillaume's room.

A curious guest glanced at her as they used the key card to unlock the door of their own room. Her body language must have seemed highly unusual. Rather than the seductive air of someone seeking a late-night tryst, she was wired, manic even, her arms held rigidly at her sides. There was a burning sensation in her throat and her mouth was dry.

Swallowing hard, she knocked at Guillaume's door.

Seconds later, it was wrenched wide open and Guillaume stood there in only his boxer shorts, his hair tousled. 'Louise! Are you all right? You look like you've seen a ghost!'

'Can I come in for a second? There's something I need to tell you.'

'Sure.'

He stepped aside. The blinds were down and the bed rumpled, indicating he had already been in it.

'I've woken you up, I'm sorry.'

'No problem. I'm good at coming round quickly, and I never have problems falling asleep again.' He grinned, switching on the light over the narrow shelf that doubled as desk and dressing table. 'Put it down to my special forces training.' There were twin beds in the room, and he indicated the one he hadn't just slept in. 'Sit down.'

'There's something I need to tell you. I just can't sleep unless I get it off my chest.'

He sat down next to her and turned to face her. From his expression, she could tell that he was expecting a confession of a personal nature. That she fancied him, or even wanted to have an affair with him.

'It's not about you and I,' she said hurriedly. 'It's about the case.'

His mouth twitched slightly. Was that disappointment? 'Go on.'

Louise took in a long breath. 'You know that the pentobarbital was found in our room at Le Mas des Flores? In Tim's bag.'

He nodded.

'Well, Merry had lent me some medication when I had a migraine and she asked for it back. And on that last Friday afternoon, I told her she could go up to the room and fetch it. She was in our room alone. So she could have taken the pentobarbital. She had the opportunity.'

Guillaume looked at her sceptically. 'And you've only just remembered this?' There was an edge of sharpness in his tone.

She shook her head slowly, closing her eyes as she did so to try to quell the tears she could feel coming. 'No. I realised a while ago. I've... I've started to realise a lot of things lately,' she added cryptically.

'But you didn't say anything? Even though it was such a vital piece of evidence. You didn't tell the police? Or Tim's new lawyer?'

Louise shook her head again and tears escaped onto her cheeks. 'I was angry with Tim.' The words came out as a strange gasp. 'I felt so let down by him that I wanted to punish him. To make him suffer by remaining under suspicion. So I kept what I knew to myself. I know that sounds harsh, but, like I said, I've been learning that there's a lot about my marriage I never knew. About my husband... But then, after what we discovered this morning about Merry knowing Hannah... I knew I had to say something.'

There it was. She was left feeling grubby and pitiful by what she'd done, but Tim had been her best friend and he'd betrayed her.

Guillaume laid his hand over hers and squeezed her fingers. 'You've been put in a very difficult position by all this, I understand that. But it's really vital that you tell me everything you know. *Anything.*'

He stood up and fetched a tissue, handing it to Louise before sitting down again.

'Can you remember what the drugs were that Merry Stafford lent you?'

She thought for a minute. 'They were... diphenny something.'

'Diphenhydramine?'

'Yes, that's it. Why, is that relevant?'

'It could be. I phoned Richard Stafford's London office this morning, and they said he was travelling, but I managed to get a mobile number for him. I spoke to him briefly, just as he was boarding a flight, and asked him about that night of the 28th of July. And guess what he said.'

'What?'

'That he hadn't heard anything, because he was out cold. In fact, he slept so soundly, in his words, it was "as if I'd been drugged".'

Louise stared at him, her mouth slightly open.

'And diphenhydramine is a very powerful antihistamine that's commonly used as a sedative.'

'Oh my God... the stuff knocked me out when I took it for my migraine... so you think, Merry could have given it to him? Was she with Richard when you spoke to him?'

'No, I'm pretty sure he was alone. And don't worry, I don't think he suspects anything at this point.'

Louise was very still, the implications of this conversation only just sinking in. 'Oh my God,' she repeated.

'Our next move's pretty obvious,' Guillaume said grimly. 'As soon as we get back, we need to locate his wife. And find out what part she's played in this.'

THIRTY-FIVE

TIM

Now

Tim was at the surgery on Monday morning when Louise texted him to say that her plane had landed at Heathrow and she would be home in a couple of hours. It was, like all her recent communications, practical and devoid of affection. She used to end every message with three kisses. Now there were none.

I'll see you when I get back from work, he replied. *Elle playing with Violet P, Harry at soccer camp at sports centre xx*

See you later, was all he got in response.

It was strange, he reflected, that when he returned to the house that evening and found Guillaume already there, he was relieved. Things had become so strained between himself and Louise that it now felt as though they needed a third wheel, a mediator.

'Hi,' he said as he walked into the kitchen and tossed his messenger bag onto a chair. He pulled Louise into an awkward one-armed hug and shook Guillaume's hand.

Both children were hovering within earshot, on the hunt for

snacks, so after pouring beers for each of the adults, Louise suggested they go out into the garden. Tim listened as Guillaume summarised their findings: that having seen CCTV of Hannah Messenger heading to Le Mas des Flores in the early hours of 29th July, they discovered her likely access point to the property. And that they spoke to one of her fellow bartenders, who claimed that she and Merry Stafford appeared to have a prior relationship. That Louise had not been necessary to any of these enquiries seemed obvious. And yet they were now acting as though they were the couple and he the third party, completing one another's sentences and glancing at each other frequently for affirmation of what they were saying. He felt excluded, isolated.

'My urgent priority is now to speak to Merry Stafford,' Guillaume finished.

Talk about stating the bleeding obvious, Tim thought bitterly. Out loud he said, 'Have you any idea where she is currently?'

Guillaume shook his head as he lifted his beer glass to his lips.

'Where do they even live, anyway?' Louise asked. 'I don't think they ever said. Richard talked about them having met in Switzerland, but they clearly travel a lot.'

'It looks like they have several homes,' Guillaume said. 'One in Basel, one in Florida, one in London. So she could be anywhere. But I'll be on to that straightaway, and I'll speak to Fraser Armstrong first thing tomorrow, fill him in on everything.' He stood up. 'And now I'll leave you two in peace.'

'So what do you make of the confrontation between Merry and Hannah Messenger?' Tim asked as they got themselves ready for bed. 'Strange, huh?'

'I don't really want to talk about it,' Louise said quietly. She was sitting on the edge of the bed tugging off her shirt, and her back was to him. 'Let's just see what Guillaume can come up with.'

'So you have faith in him to get to the bottom of it?' Tim addressed his wife's naked back.

'Yes.'

She did not head to the spare room once she was in her pyjamas, and Tim was grateful for this, at least. But they did not touch once they were in bed. Louise always used to roll over towards Tim and wrap her legs around his, resting her head on his chest. Now she lay facing away from him, giving the impression that she was asleep. But he knew she wasn't. He could always tell. She was not acting out of spite, because Louise was never spiteful, but her disappointment and confusion were palpable. They were usually so in synch that he was feeling exactly what she was feeling. But now he could not bridge the gulf between them because it had been created by his own dishonesty. The only way of closing the gap was by coming clean.

After his consultations the following morning, Tim told Amy he had a doctor's appointment and left the surgery. With the VCM deal still uncertain and Fairlawn's profit margins vanishing, the last thing he could afford to do was take time away from work. And yet his ability to concentrate was so compromised he was like a zombie anyway. He was no more use to his patients than he was to his wife.

He turned his car onto the M3 and drove north, taking the exit for Kempshott. He didn't really know why he was going there or what he hoped to find, but some sixth sense propelled him in that direction. Perhaps it was because the murdered woman had come from the area. He had some sense that returning to the place would give him answers.

Without really knowing why, he pulled over on Harebell Close in the exact spot where he had parked on that fateful night. Even as he did so, he was telling himself it was pointless. Tina Locke's family had moved away over a decade ago, and Hannah Messenger had left the area for London. He let out a groan and sank forward, resting his head on the steering wheel as he realised what he was doing. He was trying to revisit the past, as if that would somehow allow him to make a different decision. To create a sliding doors moment.

His mobile rang and he fumbled to answer it.

'Tim?' It was Guillaume. 'Are you at work?'

He let a silence play out before he said finally. 'No, I'm not, as it happens.'

'Can we meet up to talk? Just the two of us.'

'Sure.' Tim straightened up and checked his watch. 'Meet me at the Cathedral Café in half an hour.'

Guillaume was already at the café when Tim arrived, sitting at one of the tables in the pretty walled garden that faced the cathedral itself.

'Does Louise know we're here?' he asked without preamble, as soon as the server had taken their order.

Guillaume shook his head. 'No. I wanted to talk to you alone this time.' His eyes were obscured by aviator shades, but there was a calmness, a steadiness in his manner, which was a stark contrast with Tim's uneasiness.

'Go on.'

Guillaume waited until their coffees had been brought to the table before continuing. 'When you spoke to Hannah Messenger in the Bar des Vignobles, what did you really talk about?'

Tim set down his coffee cup abruptly, making it clatter on

the saucer. 'What do you mean? I told you, I wanted to know if she was aware I'd had sex with her friend, Tina.'

'Is that all?'

'Of course.'

'Listen, Tim,' Guillaume leaned back in his chair and inspected his fingernails. 'I've been an investigator for a while, and I can tell when someone is holding back on me. There's something else, isn't there?'

Tim hesitated a few seconds.

'Yes. Yes, there is.' He sighed, twisting uncomfortably in his chair. 'But I need you to understand, I wasn't trying to deceive you in any way, I just didn't think it was relevant.'

'What was?'

'I... She was blackmailing me, back in 2010. Tina Locke.'

'I see.' Guillaume chewed his lip. 'Was this to prevent her telling Louise that you'd slept with her.'

'Yes, partly.'

'What do you mean by partly?'

Tim breathed out hard. 'Louise had just had a miscarriage and was in a very fragile state. If it weren't for that I would probably have bitten the bullet and told her what happened. Begged for her forgiveness. And I thought hard about doing it, but then we found out she was expecting Harry and I just couldn't risk it. And then Harry had some health issues, so I was afraid to rock the boat.' He shook his head and added bitterly. 'Like all blackmail victims, I took the line of least resistance and paid up.'

'You said partly. So what was the other part?'

Tim looked around at the tourists and holidaymakers on the nearby tables and lowered his voice. 'I found out that she – Tina Locke – was only fifteen. I'd had no idea of course,' he said hurriedly. 'She looked older. She was the one who seduced me, that's the awful fucking irony.'

Guillaume let out a low whistle.

'So even if Louise had been able to forgive me for a five-minute episode of infidelity, there was the small matter of criminal charges and a life on the sex offenders register. Losing my job. So while it wasn't exactly easy to scrape together the fifteen hundred quid a month she was demanding, it was the less grim option.'

'I see. So it was a case of Hobson's choice.'

'Just a bit,' said Tim wretchedly.

'How long did this go on for?'

'Years. I tried to end it once, but she made more threats. And then suddenly a few years ago, it stopped. The payments were returned and the account was closed. Never heard another thing about it.'

'And you mentioned the blackmail to Hannah Messenger?'

'Yes, I did as it happens.' Tim's tone had become defensive. 'I asked if she'd known that Tina was extorting money from me and she said she had no idea. She seemed glad I'd told her though. Interested in what I had to say.'

'And you believed her? That she hadn't known previously?'

Tim frowned. 'I had no reason not to. And, like I said, I didn't mention it to you because it didn't seem relevant.'

'Not relevant? Seriously?... And you still haven't told your wife the whole truth.' There was more than a hint of disapproval in Guillaume's tone.

'No, I haven't.' Tim pressed his hand to his forehead. 'Look, I was about to when she gave me this whole speech about leaving things alone and focusing on the investigation. She pretty much told me not to talk about it.'

Guillaume took a mouthful of coffee but said nothing.

'Have you had any joy finding where Merry Stafford is currently?' Tim was now eager to change the subject.

'Up to a point. I phoned the Stafford residence in Basel and the housekeeper told me that Mrs Stafford is in Italy. But exactly where in Italy she couldn't say.'

'So that's what you're working on?'

'It's one thing, yes.'

'If it was even Merry that was responsible for Hannah's death. I'm still trying to work out why on earth Merry of all people would want to harm her. It makes no sense.'

'That,' Guillaume tossed his napkin down on the table and stood up to leave, 'is the million-dollar question.'

THIRTY-SIX

LOUISE

Now

For the past few years, Tim and Louise had spent every fourth week of August with Tim's brother Phil and his wife Serena. They were based in Oxted most of the year, but once Phil's haulage company had started doing well, he and Serena had bought a holiday home on the Studland peninsula in Dorset, and it was there that the Cutlers usually had a relaxing week in the house overlooking the bay, with the children romping happily in the sloping garden or playing beach cricket on Knoll Sands.

'D'you think we should go this year?' Tim asked Louise on the Friday before they were due to set off.

'Why not?' She raised an eyebrow.

'Renée's meeting with her lawyers next week and things are going to be pretty tense. Do we really want to bring the mood down with our troubles?'

'I think that's exactly why we should go,' Louise said firmly. 'It'll help take our minds off things. Anyway, the kids will be devastated if we don't go. You know how they love Dorset.'

And so on Monday 21st August they crammed Tim's Land Rover with wetsuits and bodyboards and ball games of various descriptions and set off to Studland. If the atmosphere between the adult Cutlers was a little strained, it was barely noticeable amid the high-spirited chatter coming from their children.

'Dad, can I go to the surf school and learn on a proper board this time?' Harry wanted to know.

'We can look into it, certainly.'

'Excellent!' Harry pumped his fist.

'Can I?' Elodie clamoured. 'Please, Dad, can I?'

'You're too young,' Harry scoffed.

'Let's wait till we get there and see what ages they take,' Louise said soothingly. 'But if you're too young, Elle, I'm sure there are other things you can do. Maybe we could go to that place just outside Swanage that does pony riding.'

'That would be awesome!' Elodie wriggled with pleasure.

'Pony riding!' Harry snorted. 'That's for losers.'

'Harry!' Tim admonished.

The conversation continued in this vein for the whole journey. The bickering was largely of the good-natured variety, and provided a smokescreen for the Cutlers' marital fragility.

And by lunchtime they had arrived at the house, with Harry and Elodie barrelling down the path to be hugged by their uncle, aunt and cousins. Phil Cutler was a heavier, slightly balder version of Tim, naturally louder and brasher than his brother. Louise had always thought Serena was a very fitting name for his wife. She was a willowy, languid blonde who presided over their brood of tow-haired children, now aged three, five and eight.

As soon as they had eaten lunch, a beach visit was planned for all five children. The older ones were bodyboarding and the younger making sandcastles, but all ended up equally tired by the time the sun started to set. The entire party trudged back to the house with sunburnt shoulders, salt-crusted skin and the special glow that comes from spending several hours in the fresh air. The younger children were put straight to bed and Harry and Elodie retired to the games room, leaving the adults sitting on the terrace drinking gin and tonics.

'Is Tim okay?' Phil asked Louise, while his brother was inside refereeing a dispute between his children.

'Yes, he's fine,' Louise said, rather more briskly than was necessary. 'Why do you ask?'

'He just seems a bit quiet, that's all. A bit subdued.'

'He's still in the thick of the practice sale,' Louise said with what she hoped was a reassuring smile.

'Ah yes, the good old corporate sell-out.' Phil narrowed his eyes thoughtfully as he helped himself to crisps. 'I expect that'll be it then. How's it going?'

'Should all be settled soon,' said Louise vaguely. Tim had not spoken to his parents or his brother about his arrest, insisting it would distress them unnecessarily. She waved a hand in the direction of the spectacular sunset: a sky burnished with apricot, rose and violet. 'And in the meantime, what better place to help him relax?'

And little by little, they did manage to relax.

Being in the company of others – which Tim had initially been worried about – proved beneficial. Serena and Phil were generous hosts, and in addition to endless outdoor activities, there was an abundance of good food and alcoholic drinks. The children all got along well despite the age gap, and to their delight both Harry and Elodie were able to attend the local surf school. Evenings were filled with laughter, as Phil and Tim reminisced about their childhood.

'This is how it's supposed to be,' Tim said to Louise as they climbed into bed on the third night in Dorset, after a particularly delicious dinner of freshly caught fish.

How we used to be, Louise was thinking, but she did concede to let him wrap his arms around her for the first time since France.

The next morning, there was more encouragement in the form of an email from Guillaume. Louise read it out to Tim as they sat in bed drinking tea.

Hi Louise,

I wanted to send you a quick update as things are now moving swiftly in the Messenger murder case.

I have spoken to Capitaine Palomer on the phone and sent him a formal summary of my findings for his own paperwork. I included the developments that we uncovered while we were in Cotignac together…

Louise paused for a few seconds. She was grateful that Guillaume didn't reveal that these 'developments' included her own prior knowledge that Merry Stafford had been in the Cutlers' room. How crass he must have thought her, withholding such a critical piece of information out of a petty need to punish her husband. But then again, he had never been married himself, and therefore would never have experienced the depth of betrayal that had gripped her.

…and I'm pleased to report that they are now focusing on Merry Stafford as their primary suspect.

They wouldn't yet confirm that the investigation into Tim has been formally dropped, but I'm pretty confident he'll hear something to that effect any day now. They will also want a revised statement from you, Louise.

From what I understand, Merry has been staying at a

resort in Sicily but has now flown back to the Staffords'
home in Palm Beach, Florida. Obviously as soon as there are
any more developments, I will update you, but for now I am
pausing my active enquiries on your behalf and have
attached my final invoice.

My very best wishes to you both, G.

'Wow.' Tim leaned back on his pillows and tipped his head
back. 'What a bloody relief. But Merry Stafford...' He pressed
his eyes shut with his fingers and shook his head.

'I know,' Louise said, staring at her phone screen as though
it would give them some sort of answer. 'Why? That's all I can
think. Why would Merry do something like that? It makes no
sense.'

'Except that there was clearly some pre-existing link
between her and Hannah Messenger.'

'Yes, but what could that possibly be? Perhaps we'll never
find out.'

Louise climbed out of bed and sat down at the dressing
table, teasing a hairbrush through her hair. The salt and sea
breeze had left it matted in stiff dreadlocks. Although she had
her back to him, she could see Tim reflected in the mirror. He
suddenly gave a violent shudder, and his throat convulsed.

'Are you okay?' she asked sharply.

'Fine, sweetie.' He smiled, collecting himself. 'Someone just
walked over my grave, that's all.'

THIRTY-SEVEN

TIM

Now

After the email from Guillaume arrived, Tim decided that updating Renée Weber about the status quo was a priority. He phoned her office in Geneva and arranged a video call for that afternoon at a time when the others would be at the beach.

'Good afternoon, Tim,' Renée said briskly as she appeared on the screen. She was wearing designer athleisure wear and her usually rigidly sprayed hair was damp and slightly tousled. It made her look younger. 'It's good to see you. How are you? You'll have to excuse me looking dishevelled, but I have cut short a session with my trainer to take your call.'

Pleasantries exchanged, Renée was keen to get to the point.

'Tell me everything that's been happening, but speak slowly please, so that Elisa here can make a note.' She indicated a smiling young PA with a shorthand pad, just visible in the corner of the screen,

Tim outlined the substance of Guillaume's investigation, concluding with Merry Stafford's new status as suspect.

'Frankly, I am shocked by this,' Renée's voice quivered

slightly, confirming that the shock was genuine. 'I have known Richard for years and Merry since they married, and I have never seen any hint of such a thing. She has always been devoted to Richard and to me has never been anything other than polite and well... rather inoffensive.' Emphasis was placed on this last word. 'Certainly there was never any suggestion of anything criminal, her background seemed quite unremarkable.'

'Quite,' Tim said noncommittally.

'Anyway, enough of that; the police will deal with it. This is excellent news for you, Tim, and we must concentrate on that. Not that I ever thought you capable of murder, but you understand that for the lawyers there are certain boxes to check.'

'Of course.'

'I'm meeting with them tomorrow, as you know, and they will need to confirm everything with the gendarmes leading the case, but as far as I am concerned, the purchase of Fairlawn can go ahead as planned.' She beamed at Tim. 'I am so relieved.'

'Not half as relieved as I am,' he said, with genuine feeling.

After supper that evening, Tim and Louise left Phil to supervise Harry and Elodie and went for a walk on their own, inhaling night air filled with that special seaside smell of salt and ozone. As they strolled the mile-long path that took them down to the beach, Tim reached tentatively for Louise's hand, and she let him take it. It felt good. It felt normal. It felt as though they could move forward after all.

'I'm so pleased that VCM are going to go ahead,' she said as though reading his thoughts. Perhaps she was: she always used to do so.

'I don't think I've ever felt relief like it,' Tim agreed. 'Unless perhaps it was when you read out Guillaume's email this morning.'

'Thank God he came through for us.'

'Hiring him was a great judgement call.' Tim squeezed her hand. 'What would I do without you?'

'You'll never have to find out.' Louise then added soberly: 'But I never want to go through anything like this again. Like the past four weeks.'

'Agreed.'

It was almost dark when they reached the sand, the sky streaked with a band of gunmetal grey that threatened rain. The holidaymakers had long since left for their hotels and caravans, and there was no sound, apart from the sighing of the waves as the tide came in. They took off their shoes and carried them, the damp sand oozing between their toes.

Tim had a sudden flash of memory, and once more Louise read his thoughts. 'Are you thinking what I'm thinking of?' she asked, leaning in so that her head was on his shoulder. 'It reminds me of when we were at uni and we used to go down to White Sands beach after dark and have beach barbecues. And everyone used to go skinny-dipping.'

'Those were happy times.' Tim's tone was wistful.

'We can have happy times again though.' Louise turned to face him and her eyes shone in the half-light. 'Can't we?'

'Of course we can.' He attempted a laugh. 'If we can get through me being arrested for murder, we can get through anything. As long as we still have each other.' There was a question in his voice.

'Of course we do,' Louise insisted. 'That will never change. Come on!'

She let go of his hand abruptly and raced towards the water's edge, arms outstretched like a child. Stripping off her sweatshirt and shorts, she ran into the sea in her bra and knickers, splashing through the shallow waves until the water was up to her waist.

Tim hung back for a few seconds, then pulled off his own shirt and shorts and followed his wife into the water.

'We should really be taking off our underwear too,' Louise said. 'To recapture the original experience.'

'I wanted to take my boxers off, but I thought we might get arrested.'

'And for you that would be twice in one summer,' Louise laughed.

Tim joined in, and as he did so he experienced a sense of release, as though a bad spell had been broken.

It was raining now, sheets of steady drizzle dripping on their faces and soaking their hair. He took Louise by the hand and led her back through the shallows to the water's edge, falling to his knees and tugging her down with him until they were both sprawled on the sand. He rolled onto his back and pulled her wet body on top of his, and they were kissing like teenagers, or like the undergraduates they had been when they first met. Louise squirmed on his crotch and he could tell she was thinking of having sex with him right there on the beach, just as he was. His hands explored her body in a way they hadn't for weeks and it felt natural. It felt right.

'Later,' he murmured in her ear after a couple of minutes. 'Remember the not getting arrested thing.'

'So I'm on a promise?' she said playfully, rolling off him and standing up.

'Definitely.'

They pulled their damp clothes on and walked back up the beach with their shoes in their hands.

'You know what I'm thinking now?' Louise asked.

'How quickly can we get Harry and Elle to go to bed?'

'Exactly!' she said happily, and linked her arm through his.

The following afternoon, Renée emailed confirmation that, following consultation with the French police, VCM's lawyers had indeed rubber-stamped the acquisition of Fairlawn Veterinary Centre.

That initial message was duly followed by a flurry of further emails with contract paperwork attached and requests for information from the Fairlawn end. While Louise took Harry and Elodie to surf school and Phil and Serena went on a supermarket run, Tim sat down at the dining table with his laptop and made a start on his new to-do list. He needed to go over the heads of terms for the sale agreement, provide copies of the current staff's contracts, plus an inventory of drug stock and equipment. But the first thing he did was to send an email to Fraser Armstrong and thank him for his services, requesting a final account. He copied the email to practice lawyer Peter Critchley, and also emailed Glen Beane to request a meeting. Fairlawn's accounting would be handled by VCM's team in the future, but Tim felt he owed Glen a face-to-face talk first.

He would not show him the 'real' accounts from the past – the ones that showed money going out to Tina Locke's account – but he would go over them in detail himself and use the generous signing bonus he was about to receive to make up any outstanding amount left after he'd factored in the earnings from his on-call moonlighting. As he typed away on the keyboard, he felt the muscles in his shoulders loosen as though a weight was being lifted from them. It was going to be all right. He and Louise were going to be all right.

His phone buzzed with a text. It was from Guillaume Hall.

Can you find a moment to call me when you're on your own.

There was a plummeting sensation in Tim's stomach. He pressed the call icon.

'I'm actually on my own now,' he said when Guillaume answered. 'Catching up on some admin while the others are out.'

There was a brief, loaded silence.

'Tim, have you told Louise about your one-night stand yet?'

'No. I haven't,' Tim said heavily. 'I admitted to her that I knew who Hannah Messenger was and how I'd met her, but now that everything's sorted out, I decided it was unnecessary to upset her by going over all that.'

Another silence. 'Here's the thing, Tim.' Guillaume inhaled sharply. 'There has been a further development. When we got back from the trip to France, I ordered a copy of the Staffords' marriage certificate.'

'Were they not married?'

'Yes, they were. They married in 2020. But, as you know, a marriage certificate gives the full names of both parties, as recorded on their birth certificates. And what it revealed...'

Even before Guillaume had completed his sentence, Tim knew what he was going to say. He felt a falling sensation, a crashing as though his whole life was crumbling into pieces. Because there could be no hiding it now: the whole sordid truth would be exposed. He had probably known it subconsciously all along, but the truth had only penetrated his conscious mind yesterday when Louise had questioned the possible connection between Hannah Messenger and Merry Stafford.

Even so, it was still a shock to hear Guillaume speak the words out loud.

'...is that Merry Stafford was born Christina Meriel Locke.'

PART THREE

THIRTY-EIGHT

MERRY

Four weeks earlier

As a rich and childless couple, summer for the Staffords meant drifting from one luxury Mediterranean resort to another. Merry – as Richard called her – was reluctant to go and join Renée Weber's party in Provence. There would be families there, Richard told her, probably with young children. Merry did not like children. Too much of her life had been taken up with looking after her younger siblings and step-siblings, and she had no desire to be around anyone else's. But Renée was an important business contact of Richard's and, as ever, she wanted him to be happy.

When they arrived at Le Mas des Flores on 18th July, only Renée and her boyfriend were in residence, and the four adults had champagne on the roof terrace and a civilised dinner on the loggia. It was all very pleasant. But the next morning a family called the Prentices arrived with their young daughter. Kevin Prentice was a crass, gormless sort of man and his wife Shona reminded Merry uncomfortably of her own mother. Once she and Richard were alone after lunch, she observed that the Prentices did not seem at all the sort of people Renée would have as friends.

'Oh, they're not,' Richard said airily. 'They were invited by some other guests. A guy from Hampshire whose veterinary practice Renée is about to take over.'

Merry felt her heartbeat skip slightly.

'Do you know what his name is?'

'Ummm...' Richard met so many people through his business empire that he struggled to retain names. 'Tom something, I think. Or was it Tim?'

It must be a coincidence, she told herself, her mind lurching towards blind panic. It couldn't be the same man, could it?

She had her answer soon enough. As she was lying on a lounger next to Richard, he appeared on the pool terrace with his children, to be introduced to the other guests.

Tim Cutler.

Thank God it was bright enough for her to keep her sunglasses on, even though she was partially shaded by an umbrella. She favoured the oversized, visor shades that were in fashion that summer and had pairs by Gucci, Dior and Dolce & Gabbana. They obscured most of her upper face, and her nose, teeth and lower face looked quite different, thanks to the handiwork of Mr Christakos. She had a lot more hair now too, her own gold and amber highlights bulked out with real hair extensions that she'd had expertly fitted at a salon in Knightsbridge. There was no way he would recognise her, surely?

'Everybody, this is Tim Cutler, and Harry and Eloise,' Renée said.

'Elodie,' said the little girl.

'This is my partner, Jared Frayn. And these are my friends Richard and Merry Stafford.'

Merry let Richard stand up and shake hands, and as soon as the children had colonised the pool, she used them as an excuse to retreat to their room. Thank God they weren't in the main house, and she could stay out of sight most of the time. She knew she would have to remove her sunglasses at dinner because by the time they ate it would be growing dark. The eyes and the voice were the things people recognised, she knew that. As long as she didn't speak much, she would probably be all right, and when she changed, she attempted to disguise her eyes by applying dark, smoky eyeshadow and false eyelashes. Apparently it worked. Even though he'd once had sex with her in his car, and sat across from her in a coffee shop, Tim Cutler was completely blind to her true identity.

His wife was due to arrive three days later, and Merry convinced herself that this was a good thing. They'd probably do things as a couple or a family and stay out of her way. But no sooner had Louise Cutler arrived on Saturday evening, than there was a knock at the door of their room.

Merry, who was on her way to shower for dinner, let Richard answer it.

'Hi, Tim, come in.'

She darted into the bathroom and pushed the door to.

'Sorry to disturb, but poor Louise has come down with a horrible migraine and doesn't have her medication with her. Do either of you have anything she could use?'

'Merry!' Richard called. 'Did you hear that? Have you got anything suitable?'

Merry pulled a cosmetic bag out of the drawer and found a blister pack of tablets. They were sleeping pills, but she was anxious to get rid of Tim. 'In here,' she called, hoping her voice was sufficiently muffled. Richard stuck his head through the bathroom door and she gave them to him. 'These work for me.'

The tablets were handed over and Tim disappeared again. At breakfast the next morning, Louise appeared, and was at pains to thank Merry for her help. She seemed lovely, Merry thought, prettier in person than in the online photo she'd seen all those years ago. And Tim, over forty now, was still a very attractive man. She felt the traces of the desire he had stirred in her all those years ago, but this only strengthened her resolve to stay out of his way. The life she had now was better than anything she could have dreamed of back in Kempshott. Nothing was going to threaten that, not even the presence of Tim Cutler.

On Sunday, the housekeeper had the day off, and the guests had to cater for themselves. Merry did not volunteer to help, leaving that to Louise and the irritating Shona Prentice. She stayed away from the communal meals as much as possible without raising suspicion. Sports had always been her thing and she loved to swim, but now avoided using the pool unless the other guests weren't there.

'Fancy coming into Cotignac with me, sweetheart?' Richard asked the next morning as he dressed for breakfast. 'I'm going to go and order some wine. Plenty of wonderful producers round here.'

'Yes please.' Anything to get out of the villa and away from the Cutlers.

'Shall we ask the others if they want to come too?'

'No,' said Merry quickly. 'It'll take them forever to get organised. Let's just order a taxi and get going now, before it gets too hot.'

Choosing wine was a process that Richard took very seriously and that didn't interest Merry in the slightest. Knowing that she would just be standing there while her husband earnestly discussed terroir and barrel-fermenting, she opted to wait for him outside, finding a seat in the dappled shade under one of the huge plane trees that lined the central square and removing her sunglasses to rearrange her ponytail. She was just congratulating herself on how well the holiday at Le Mas des Flores was going in the face of potential disaster when she heard a familiar voice.

'Hello, Tina.'

THIRTY-NINE

CHRISTINA

Then

The payments from Tim Cutler continued, for the rest of 2012, and into 2013. In the spring one of the surgeons who had led the aesthetic medicine training course, a Mr Georgios Christakos, offered her a job in his Harley Street clinic.

He offered cosmetic surgery to rich women who were a step up the socioeconomic ladder from the bored housewives of Purley. These women expected more minor tweaks to be available in the same opulent consulting rooms and this would be Tina's job: injecting well-preserved faces with botulinum toxin and hyaluronic acid, zapping them with lasers and peeling them with acid.

Mr Christakos – who had taken a shine to Tina – gave her a generous discount on the treatments the clinic offered, and soon her skin was as smooth and tanned and glowing as that of their clients. She saved up enough for a dental colleague of Christakos' to fit her teeth with veneers, turning them into an immaculate white row. Christakos himself reshaped her chin and – after she had slept with him, of course – performed rhinoplasty on her to make her nose smaller and neater.

In 2016, she was headhunted to perform a similar role in the clinic of a luxury spa on the outskirts of Zurich. Tina had not really travelled much, apart from a couple of drunken girls' trips to the Costa del Sol, and she hesitated over accepting the job offer. What swung it was the very generous salary and the comfortable accommodation provided on site. She very quickly came to be glad she'd accepted. If she hadn't, she would not have met Richard Stafford.

At the start of her third year working at the spa, he arrived there as a guest. Tina was booked to give him a manicure in his suite. She was already aware that the President's Suite cost thousands of euros per night, and there were numerous other clues to Richard Stafford's wealth. The exquisite diamond cuff-links and Breitling watch that he removed before he dipped his fingers in the bowl of warm, scented water for a start. Then there was the monogrammed Louis Vuitton luggage stacked neatly in the dressing area. Having been surrounded by five-star luxury for two years, she could spot the signs easily. But there was nothing brash or showy about Richard. He was well-spoken and confident, but his manner was self-deprecating, even humble. As she worked on his cuticles – he had nice hands: she'd always noticed men's hands – they fell easily into chatting about her life as an expat, her struggle with learning Swiss German, the things that made her homesick for the UK.

'Your name's Christina, is that right?' he asked her. The concierge always gave guests the name of their therapist in advance.

Something in her made her hesitate at this most basic of questions. She found herself telling him something she hadn't until now voiced out loud. He had a manner that made you want to confide.

'I've been thinking about using my middle name instead.'

'And what's that?'

'Meriel. It was the name of one of my mum's favourite aunts.'

'Meriel...' He turned the syllables around in his mouth. 'That's pretty. A pretty name for an extremely pretty girl.'

She lifted her face and their eyes met. And that was it: the moment on which her life pivoted. Her Cinderella moment.

'You should do it,' Richard said, as she looked away again, colour flooding into her cheeks. 'Start using your middle name. It's much more distinctive than Christina.'

Fifteen minutes later, as she was packing away her kit, he asked if she would be allowed to join him for dinner in his suite. Although it was strictly against the rules, she lied and said she would. What else was she going to do? In a world of male trophies, this was the biggest of big game.

Tina spent the night with him, and, sure enough, she lost her job. But it didn't matter, because she'd won Richard. He asked her to come back to Basel, where he had an apartment overlooking the Rhine: one of several homes. Away from the suited corporate world, he turned out to be more of a cowboy boots and faded jeans sort of man, who had a surprising love of stockcar racing and house music. He was generous and easygoing and not in the least stuffy, and she was surprised to find that she wanted to please him. To take care of him, even. She had never been happier than playing at house in his immaculate apartment, feeling that finally there was a place where she belonged. After being at the beck and call of rich women and their whims for so many years, this was a place where *she* had status.

That Richard was nearly twenty years her senior and twice divorced did not concern her at all. Whatever happened, he would look after her. Yes, she was fully aware that she had abandonment issues in general and daddy issues specifically. But for this very reason, in her mind, they were a match.

After only a few months of living together, it became clear that he was about to propose to her. Only then, in a panic, did she close down the account into which Tim had been making his payments. She had allowed them to continue long after she needed his fifteen hundred pounds a month, perhaps out of some twisted need to maintain the link with him. But now, as she became Mrs Meriel Stafford, she told herself that she could afford to forget all about her extortion of money from Tim Cutler. She was never going to see him again.

Until, in July 2023, she did.

FORTY

MERRY

Three weeks earlier

There was no mistaking who it was.

It might have been drawn back in a ponytail and mostly hidden by a baseball cap, but the hair was exactly the same, that amazing silver blonde that she had envied so much when they were young. Hannah Messenger. Of all the people to see here in Cotignac. Merry could hardly believe it.

'It *is* you, isn't it, Tina?' She sounded doubtful now. 'I wasn't sure at first, but then when you took off your shades... Only you look really different.'

What could she say? She couldn't exactly deny that she was Tina Locke. Her voice would give her away, and that would just make her seem extremely dodgy. The last thing she could afford now was to start acting suspiciously.

'Hannah! Hi,' she said, forcing her mouth into a smile. 'Yes, I've had some tweaks along the way. Perks of the job.'

She took in the other woman's appearance now. In contrast to her own Miu Miu dress and Aquazzura sandals, Hannah was wearing denim cut-offs and a tie-dye vest. She was deeply tanned, which made her hair colour even more startling.

'Yes, I heard you were working in the beauty field.' Hannah's eyes were now darting over her face, no doubt trying to work out exactly what she had changed. 'And you're married too.' She pointed to the five-carat cushion cut diamond engagement ring and the platinum wedding band on Merry's left hand.

'Yes. Are you?'

'No.' Hannah shook her head. 'I came close, but then we broke up. And I decided to do some travelling for a while, hence me being here. I'm working at that bar.' She pointed to a striped awning in the corner of the square. 'Using our old catering experience.'

'Ah, nice.'

'And you're here on holiday, I take it?'

'Yes.' Merry stood up. She had to end this conversation and get away. She did not want to start swapping reminiscences with Hannah Messenger about their juvenile pastiche of the Forty Elephants gang. 'If you'll excuse me, I need to—'

'Darling!'

Oh Christ. Too late. Richard had come out of the wine merchants and was striding towards them.

'Hi,' he said to Hannah, extending a hand. 'I'm Richard, Merry's husband.'

'Merry?' Hannah was predictably confused.

'I use my middle name now.'

'Oh yes!' Hannah broke into a smile. 'Meriel. I was always jealous of you having such an exotic name when my middle name is just boring old Anne.'

'You're a friend of Merry's?'

'Yes. Very old friend. Hannah Messenger.' She extended her hand.

'What a fantastic coincidence!' Richard could not have

been more pleased, making Merry's heart sink like a stone. 'You must come up to the house. We're staying a few kilometres up the road. Le Mas des Flores, it's called.'

Merry shot her husband a look, but he was oblivious.

'How about dinner tomorrow?' he was saying. 'Our hostess is going to be away on business, but I'm sure she won't mind. There are other guests staying at the house too, but they're all perfectly nice.'

'That would have been lovely, but I'm working a late shift tomorrow.'

'Wednesday then. Sweetheart, give Hannah your mobile number and you can send her the details of where we are.'

Merry hesitated as she took the proffered phone. She could put in a fake number, but Richard had already told Hannah the name of the property. Hannah could show up unannounced, which would be worse.

Having sent a text to herself so that she had Hannah's number too, she looked pleadingly at her husband.

'Can we get going? I'm getting a splitting head.'

Her head was fine, but she wanted to get away from Hannah Messenger as fast as possible, before there could be any more reminiscing about their former life in Hampshire. Above all, she needed time to think.

Having stewed over the problem for nearly forty-eight hours, on Wednesday Merry invented a shopping trip and arranged for Laurent to drive her into Cotignac.

She browsed the shops for an hour or so while waiting for Le Bar des Vignobles to open, but was too distracted to actually buy anything. When she eventually walked into the bar, there was an older woman with red hair cleaning tables but no sign of Hannah. She felt a stab of panic. Yes, she had Hannah's number now but leaving this to a message felt far too risky. She needed to look her former friend in the eye, to know she was getting through to her.

The woman did not speak English, but at the mention of Hannah's name, she tapped her watch and held up all of her fingers, which Merry interpreted as meaning Hannah would be there in ten minutes. She ordered a glass of blanc de blancs and sat down to wait.

Sure enough, exactly eight minutes later, Hannah appeared with her pale hair tied up and wearing a white shirt and black trousers, just as they had in their waitressing days. Having picked up a cloth and started polishing glasses, her face lit up with a smile when she spotted Merry.

'Hi!' She put the glass down and approached the table. 'I was just about to text you about tonight. About what time to come, and directions to the house.'

Merry chewed her lip. 'Dinner's off, I'm afraid.'

Hannah's face fell.

'Look, I'm sorry, but there's a bit of a situation at the house. One of the guests has started a fling with our host's boyfriend. It's all a bit awkward. A bit tense, you know. Maybe we could meet up for a drink here in Cotignac before I leave. Just the two of us.'

'I suppose so.' Hannah didn't try to hide her disappointment.

'Great. Well, maybe see you soon.'

Merry set down her glass abruptly, spilling some of the fizzy liquid onto the table. The older woman, muttering under her breath about having to do it twice, darted forward to wipe the table again.

As Merry walked outside there were footsteps behind her, and her heart sank.

'Tina, wait.'

Gritting her teeth at the use of her old name, Merry spun

round and faced Hannah. In her wedge heels, the two of them were the same height.

'Have I done something wrong? Or offended you in some way? Only if I have I'm sorry.'

Merry shook her head. 'No, nothing like that.'

'But you don't want me at your holiday place. You extend an invitation, and then retract it.' Hannah's tone was bullish.

'I didn't invite you, my husband did,' Merry pointed out coldly.

'Look, if you're worried about me bringing up the old Forty Elephants stuff in front of your friends, don't worry. I won't say anything about all that. We were young and stupid; no big deal.'

'It's not that. It's really not.'

Except that it was. It was exactly that. And the fact that, having failed to recognise that she was Tina Locke, Tim Cutler might still recognise Hannah.

She pulled out her phone. 'As I said, things are fraught at Le Mas des Flores at the moment. It's a timing thing. But I've got your number.' She waggled her mobile as if to demonstrate this. 'I'll text a time to meet up here. And if not, Richard and I have a place in London, so maybe we can meet up there.'

Hannah shrugged. It was clear she did not believe this any more than Merry did, but was forced to outwardly accept her narrative. 'Sure,' she said eventually. 'If that's what works for you.'

And having given Merry a long, cool look, she turned on her heel and walked back into the bar.

FORTY-ONE

MERRY

Three weeks earlier

Merry's relief at blocking Hannah's visit was short-lived.

On Friday, just as she was starting to relax in the certainty that Tim Cutler had no idea who she was, she received a text.

I know you said not to come but I think we really need to talk

Just one sentence. One sentence from Hannah.

'Everything okay?' Richard asked, glancing in her direction. He had just come out of the shower and was surveying the row of colourful designer shirts on the wardrobe rail, trying to decide which one to wear that evening.

'Fine.' She forced a smile. 'I just need a bit of fresh air, I think.'

Merry slipped out of their suite, closing the sliding door behind her. Outside, the air was anything but fresh; close and humid and saturated with the sickly scent of jasmine and bougainvillea. They had a private terrace with its own seating area, and she sank down onto one of the patio chairs, still staring at her phone screen. She badly wanted a cigarette. Richard disliked smoking so she'd given up three years ago, but now found herself wondering if she still had any, an odd one left at the bottom of one of her bags perhaps.

Sucking in her breath, she typed back. *I explained that it's not a great time*

Hannah must have been on her own phone because her reply was instantaneous. *Tina, this is important. Something major has happened. I'll come to the house*

Merry's heart started thumping in her chest, and she felt queasy. Something major? What on earth did that mean? From the tone of the message, it clearly wasn't anything good.

Don't come here. I can meet you in town, she typed hastily.

Hannah's reply was swift. *No I'll come to you. Give me a time we can talk alone.*

She clearly was not going to be deterred, and if Merry did not take control of the situation by naming a time, she might just show up anyway. Possibly during dinner when Tim was there.

It will have to be after 11.30 when the others are in their rooms. Make it midnight to be sure.

Merry hesitated, her mind racing ahead. If Hannah came through the main gate and up the drive it would be picked up on the security camera and her arrival would alert Laurent. She couldn't have that. She sent a second message.

Don't come in the front entrance, use the side gate further along the lane, on the right when you're heading towards L'Eveque. The path brings you out by the pool. I'll meet you there.

It would be fine as long as Richard was asleep, she told herself. Then Hannah would be able to say what she needed to say without them being overheard, and she could leave again via the gate with no one being any the wiser. But to guarantee that Richard wouldn't wake up and come looking for her, he would need to have taken a sleeping pill. And Louise Cutler still had Merry's.

She stuck her head round the door and told Richard she was going to fetch more ice cubes. As she passed the swimming pool, she saw Elodie and Violet hanging around at the water's edge.

'Are you girls all right?' she called.

'We're just waiting for my mum,' Elodie said. 'We're not allowed to swim without an adult present.'

They looked at Merry hopefully, as if she might be prepared to play lifeguard, but she ignored them and continued into the main house to look for Louise. Sure enough, she and that idiot Shona Prentice were in the kitchen, talking in raised voices. Merry could guess what they were talking about. She'd seen Shona pawing at Jared Frayn with her own eyes. Now it occurred to her that the Shona/Jared circus could potentially prove a useful smokescreen. At the very least it would be a reason for her to have a conversation with Louise, who she had largely ignored thus far.

She intercepted Louise as she was following Shona out of the kitchen, looking distinctly rattled. Merry waited until the ridiculous Prentice woman was out of earshot and placed a hand on her arm.

'Look, tell me if I'm speaking out of turn, but I wanted to say something about your friend. About Shona...'

Louise turned to look at her, surprised.

'...A couple of days ago I went back to the pool to fetch my sunglasses case, and I saw her and Jared on one of the loungers. You know, in a clinch.'

'Yes. I'm aware of the situation.'

'Poor you. This must be terribly difficult for you. Awkward, I mean. You're kind of stuck in the middle, aren't you?'

'I am rather.' Louise, who had initially stiffened under the pressure of Merry's arm, now smiled at her. This signalled her opportunity.

'Actually, Louise, I'm glad I found you. I was going to ask if I could have my tablets back. I've got a headache coming on.'

'Yes, sure. I'll just pop up and get them.'

'No need. You've only just come downstairs, and I know the girls are waiting for you. Just tell me where they are, and I'll go and fetch them.'

'Sure. Our room's the one at the far end when you turn left. I think they're on the bathroom vanity unit, to the right of the sink. Excuse the mess.'

Merry left her in the hall and went up the main staircase to the Cutlers' suite. Of course it wasn't messy. Why would it be, when Pascale and her team serviced all the rooms every morning. She found the diphenhydramine pills where Louise told her they would be and slipped them into one of the pockets of her dress. Richard was in the habit of having a cognac or a whisky just before bed, and it would be easy enough to slip the contents of a couple of capsules into his drink. Yes, he would sleep more heavily than usual, but he'd be none the worse for wear in the morning.

As she was leaving the room, she saw a leather bag, too large and masculine to be Louise's. She experienced a sudden, vivid flashback to being in Tim Cutler's car and asking him about his medical kit on the back seat. And him telling her he always carried drugs. Unable to resist, she opened the flap of the bag and looked inside. The first thing she found was his passport. His date of birth put him at forty-two, but the photograph must have been an old one. He looked innocent, boyish. There was a travel agent's paper wallet stuffed with euros, a pen, a phone charger, some AirPods, a packet of chewing gum. And then, at the very bottom, her fingers hit something hard and cold. She reached down and pulled out a plastic Ziploc bag containing three small glass vials and a pack of syringes. There was a red lethal drug warning label on the vials. *Euthasol (Pentobarbital sodium) 5 ml.*

She hadn't intended to go looking for them when she headed up the stairs. Her plan had been simply to retrieve her own sleeping tablets. But now here they were, in her hand. And something deep in her subconscious was telling her she needed to keep them.

They were simply an insurance policy, she told herself as she slipped the vials and needles into her other dress pocket and let herself out of the Cutlers' room. The whole point of insurance was that you didn't intend to use it.

But it was there. Just in case.

FORTY-TWO

MERRY

Three weeks earlier

Before Merry could even think about her meeting with Hannah, there was a celebration to get through, of Renée's company buying out Tim's veterinary practice. She would have much preferred to avoid it, but the naturally sociable Richard was looking forward to it, and not attending would have drawn more attention to her. So she dressed in her favourite Tom Ford satin slip dress and went up to the rooftop terrace to drink Dom Perignon and listen to Renée deliver a very predictable speech about the joys of going into business with Tim Cutler.

Tim himself was not behaving any differently towards Merry. So whatever Hannah needed to talk about, it couldn't be anything to do with Tim, surely? Why would it? There was the special dinner to endure afterwards, featuring lobster and Shona Prentice drinking enough champagne to float a small boat. She had been blocked from sitting anywhere near Jared and sat next to Richard instead, shooting filthy looks at Renée. Merry was fearful that a row might break out that would mean everyone going to bed later than usual, but soon after eleven, the party dispersed and everyone headed back to their own quarters.

'Shall I pour you a brandy?' Merry asked Richard once they were alone.

'I wasn't going to have one, sweetie, but if you'll join me...?'

Merry did not much like brandy, however expensive, but she smiled brightly and said, 'Sure. You go and sit on the terrace and I'll bring them out.'

Once alone, she poured two glasses of cognac and darted to her bag, taking out two of the sleeping pills. After emptying the powder directly from the gelatine capsules into one of the glasses, she lifted the amber liquid to her nose and sniffed it. It didn't smell of anything except alcoholic spirit.

'I'm done in, darling,' Richard said with a yawn, once he'd drained his glass. Merry took only a few tiny sips from her own. The last thing she wanted was a fuzzy head. 'Must be all the sun. Coming to bed?'

'I'm just going to have a quick shower, then I'll join you.' She smiled sweetly at her husband. 'Unzip me, will you?'

Once she was out of the shower, Richard was asleep and snoring heavily. She checked her phone: 11.43. She didn't have long. Dressing in a swimsuit, gym shorts and a T-shirt, she picked up the cotton tote bag where the vials and syringes were hidden under a towel, slipped her feet into her beach slides and headed to the swimming pool to wait for Hannah.

She sat under a sky the colour of a bruise, the silence broken only by the rhythmic thrumming of cicada wings.

Ten minutes or so passed, and for that short period, Merry felt strangely at peace. Their ten days at Le Mas des Flores – a holiday she had neither wanted or needed – had been filled by noise and commotion. Yelling children, quarrelling spouses, endless communal meals. Now, in this moment, it was just her.

Rousing herself from her moment of reflection, she pulled the two vials of pentobarbital from the bag and drew them up into a syringe. Her work as an aesthetician administering Botox and filler had made her confident with injections, and she completed the process efficiently. Making sure the syringe was sealed with a silicone cap, she looked around for somewhere to put it.

Just in case, she repeated in her head. *It will be there just in case.*

She settled on the space underneath the feet of one of the long low planters of geraniums that flanked the shallow end of the pool. The floodlights were on, and the violet glow of the water beckoned her. Walking slowly down the steps, she turned and leaned backwards, letting the water envelop her before starting to swim in a steady backstroke.

Another sound joined the whining of cicadas, the faint buzz of a single cylinder engine. Two minutes later, Hannah appeared on the poolside decking. Her hair was loose now and she was carrying a motorcycle helmet.

She stood watching Merry complete her length and haul herself out of the pool.

'You always did like swimming, I remember,' she observed.

'Still do.' Merry reached for a towel and wrapped it round her torso. She pointed to the crash helmet. 'Is that how you got here?'

'Yes, I've rented a scooter, just for while I'm here. So I can explore the area.'

Merry sat down on one of the loungers and indicated that Hannah should do the same. 'So how long do you plan to stay in Cotignac?'

Hannah shrugged. Her hair was turned almost white in the moonlight. 'Till the end of the summer season probably. Then I was thinking I might go back to Australia.'

'Oh yes,' Merry nodded slowly. 'I remember now. You went there with Levi.'

Hannah laughed. 'God, Levi. That's a name I haven't heard in a while.'

Merry did not join in with the laughter. 'So what's this about, Hannah? What's so important that you have to talk to me right away?'

There was a strained silence for a few seconds. Hannah was no longer smiling either.

'You remember when we did the Forty Elephants thing? Screwing money out of all those unsuspecting men?'

'Of course.' Merry kept her tone neutral, unbothered, even though her heart was racing.

'We agreed to split all the money down the middle. Fifty-fifty, remember?'

'And we did.'

Hannah laughed again, only this time it was hollow, bitter.

'Except for the small matter of around one hundred and sixty-five thousand pounds paid to you by that guy from the vets' conference. Tim Cutler.'

For a few seconds, there was silence, apart from the incessant cicada chorus.

'How long have you known?'

'I found out this morning!' Hannah spat. 'This morning when he came into the bar and said he wanted to talk to me. I didn't know him from Adam, but he remembered me, apparently, from when we waitressed at that event.' She corrected herself. 'Actually, I did vaguely remember him once he'd reminded me of the occasion. I remember us noticing him and saying he was better looking than most of the middle-aged losers there. But what I did *not* know was that you'd slept with him and then extorted thousands and thousands of pounds from him. Over nearly ten years, he told me.'

'Does he know?' Merry interrupted urgently. There seemed little point denying it had happened: Tim had clearly been completely credible. 'Does he know who I am?'

'Oh yes, that was the absolute icing on the cake!' That bitter laugh again. 'Not only does he tell me what you got up to back then, but he tells me where he's staying and I realise it's the exact same holiday villa you're also staying in.'

'Does he know?' Merry demanded again.

'No, he doesn't,' Hannah said. 'At least, not yet.'

'And he didn't refer to me by my name when he told you what I'd done? Because I made sure never to tell him what it was.'

Hannah frowned. 'No. He just said, "your friend from the catering company".'

'And you didn't tell him what I was called? Because we said no names back then, remember?'

'No, I didn't, I promise.'

Merry exhaled hard. 'Look, Hannah, if you're pissed off about the money, then that's fair enough. But it's easily remedied. Give me your bank details and I'll make a transfer of half of what he paid me. How about a round hundred thousand; surely that's more than enough.'

Hannah was staring at her, shaking her head. 'How long have you been rich, *Tina*?' She placed heavy emphasis on the name. 'It can't be all that long, but you're already doing that thing where you think you can fix any problem just by throwing money at it. This isn't about the money. Although if you're going to pay money back, then it should be to him, not me.'

'What is it about then?' The cool night air was settling on Merry's wet skin and she started to shiver. This was turning out to be more difficult than she had anticipated. Why was Hannah pushing back like this? 'Think what you could do with that much money,' she insisted.

Hannah shook her head firmly. 'That money's tainted: I'd never touch it. You know as well as I do that the only reason Tim Cutler paid it to you was because you told him you were fifteen years old. Fifteen!'

Merry pulled the towel more tightly around herself. 'So?'

'So? You and I both know that in October 2010, you had just turned nineteen. You left school in July 2010.'

The silence stretched for what felt like minutes.

'All that time, the poor man thought he could be prosecuted for underage sex and it was a pack of lies.' Hannah glanced around her and lowered the volume on her angry hiss. 'You were an adult.'

'So what do you want me to do?' Merry pulled off the towel and walked down the steps of the pool and back into the heated water. 'Sorry, I'm going back in; I'm getting cold.'

'You've got to tell him! Ideally pay his money back too, but at the very least tell him what you've done.'

If she was forced to confess to Tim, there was a very good chance that she would be prosecuted. And even if she wasn't, Richard would find out. He would leave her, just as her father had done. Her safe, comfortable, happy life would be over. Just like that, it would be gone.

Merry looked back at Hannah calmly, and it was in that moment that her mind was made up. A strange, burning sensation overtook her, as though battery acid was circulating in her veins in place of blood.

'I'm going to give you twenty-four hours,' Hannah was saying. 'And if you haven't told him by then, I will.'

'All right.' Merry slowly swirled her arms through the water, making shadows in the beam of the pool lights. 'I'll tell him. You can check with him. In twenty-four hours.' She bent her knees and let the water stream over her shoulders. 'Since you've come all this way, you may as well have a swim.' She beckoned. 'Come on in.'

Hannah hesitated. 'I'm serious about this, Tina. After what you've put him through, that poor man deserves to know the truth.'

'Of course,' Merry replied calmly, swooshing the water to and fro with her palms. 'What choice do I have?'

FORTY-THREE

MERRY

Three weeks earlier

'The pool does look lovely,' Hannah said wistfully, looking at the sparkling, rippled surface. She reached out her foot and let her toes trail in the water.

'Come in,' Merry repeated.

'I suppose this is pretty normal for you,' she added as Merry flipped onto her back and floated, chin tilted up towards the starlit sky. 'I expect you've got your own pool now.'

'We do,' Merry replied dreamily. 'At our house in Florida.' Her mood was calm now, almost trance-like. Straightening up again, she said, 'If you want to borrow a swimsuit, there are a few spares in the pool house there.' She pointed. 'I expect there'll be something that will fit.'

'No need.' With one smooth movement, Hannah tugged her dress over her head, tugged off her knickers and plunged naked into the water. 'God, that feels amazing!' she spluttered as she surfaced. 'I love skinny-dipping. We used to do it all the time in Sydney.'

Merry held a finger to her lips, reminding Hannah not to

raise her voice, then trod water, watching the other woman. She still felt calm, the acid in her veins now displaced with something colder and more brutal.

Hannah dipped her head and started to swim a length underwater, her hair a streak of silver as it flashed past the spotlights. And it was then, while she was submerged, that Merry acted. She waded to the shallow end and reached under the planter for the syringe, wedging it between the two foam pads in the bra part of her swimming costume. Hannah broke the surface of the water and waded abruptly to the edge of the pool, as though suddenly coming to her senses and realising why she had come to Le Mas des Flores.

'I'd better get going,' she said over her shoulder, and proceeded to haul herself up so that she was balanced on the edge of the pool, the light gleaming on her naked buttocks. She flipped her body weight so that she was seated with her feet dangling in the water.

'Oh don't go.' Merry swam closer so that she was less than a metre from Hannah's feet. She grabbed Hannah's ankle in what she hoped seemed a playful gesture.

'I really have to. But don't forget: I'll be in touch tomorrow. After you've spoken to Tim Cutler.'

She made to pull herself free, but Merry was still holding on firmly to her left ankle. Her heartbeat had sped up now, and she was breathing heavily – panting almost – as she expertly inserted the needle between Hannah's big toe and second toe. She had spent months of her life using a needle like a magic wand to plump and smooth, so this was easy work for her, the contents of the syringe emptying in less than three seconds.

She found herself speaking out loud as she did so, giving voice to the single thought in her head. 'No, Hannah. You're not going to do this to me. It's not going to end like that.'

She had had to take a gamble on the dosage but pentobarbital, she knew, would act quickly. Sure enough, the grappling of the fingers on Merry's right wrist stopped almost instantaneously. There was a long gasping sound, and the whole of Hannah's body twitched and shook as she started to have a seizure.

Merry closed her eyes and put her fingers in her ears.

Let it be enough, she thought. *Let it be enough.*

Eventually, she sensed the stopping of Hannah's heart in the ensuing silence. She opened her eyes. Hannah was lying on her back, her legs still in the water, her own eyes also open. Merry was frozen to the spot. She wanted to get out of the pool but she couldn't get her legs to work. Finally, the fear of discovery became too strong, and she managed to wade back to the shallow end. There were things she needed to do. Tracks that must be covered.

Firstly, she used two fingers to gently close Hannah's eyes. She wanted to dress her again, but tugging the sundress over the wet, heavy limbs was simply too difficult. Also, the rational part of her brain reminded her, without clothing she would take longer to identify. She considered tipping the body over the edge of the pool and into the water, so that it would look like a drowning, but this did not feel right. Hannah would float, bloated and inert as a blow-up doll, and this struck Merry as too macabre. Supposing one of the children discovered her like that?

The ideal solution would be to hide the body and let people assume Hannah had left for Australia earlier than planned, but it was simply not going to be possible, not with limited time and one pair of hands. As it was, it took all her strength to half drag, half lift the heavy limbs onto one of the loungers and arrange them as though she was sleeping, covering her lower torso with a towel. She looked beautiful, Merry thought, even though her hair was so sodden it was now dark ash blonde.

They hadn't had anything to drink, so there were no cups or bottles to deal with. Merry found a pair of scissors behind the drawer in the pool house and cut out the labels from Hannah's dress and knickers, pocketing them before bundling the clothes into the tote bag with her flip-flops, the empty vials and syringe. There was an old disused stone well at the top of the track near the boundary of the vineyard and she hurried up there now and dropped the bag inside it. It was only as she was returning down the track that she remembered the crash helmet, which Hannah had left under the lounger she had been sitting on. And there was the scooter too, somewhere in the vicinity. Christ, she'd almost forgotten about that.

Shaking with adrenaline, she headed along the track in the other direction and towards the gate in the perimeter wall. The rubber sliders were not ideal for moving in a hurry, and she cursed herself for not wearing trainers. Parked a few feet from the gate was a Vespa, that was probably bright red but looked brownish in the moonlight. She had no idea how to ride the thing, and was worried about the noise that starting the motor might make. Kicking up the stand, she managed to wheel it a few hundred yards to a place where the ditch conveniently widened where it ran in parallel to a lavender field. Pulling off her T-shirt, Merry used it to wipe the handles, helmet and keys and then rolled the Vespa into the ditch. She scoured the edge of the verge for branches and tossed a few on top of the scooter. It was barely concealed at all, but she didn't dare linger on the road any longer, in case someone drove past her and wondered at the sight of a woman in swimsuit and shorts with soaking wet hair at whatever time this was. One a.m.? Two?

Reaching their own suite again, it was as though she'd had an out-of-body experience. She collapsed against the wall and slid down it, her legs unable to hold her up any longer and shaking so hard that her teeth chattered. With the wave of adrenaline draining from her body, she was barely able to move, but somehow she pulled herself through the sliding doors, which she'd left slightly ajar. Still shaking violently, she stood and listened. No sound, apart from the rumbling sound of Richard's snores, and a glance through the bedroom door confirmed that he hadn't moved. She tiptoed on bare feet to the wardrobe in the dressing area and pulled out one of her Louis Vuitton cases. Once she had stripped naked, she thrust the damp shorts, T-shirt and swimsuit inside it and pulled on clean pyjamas. The wet clothes would join all the other laundry from her holiday, probably to be sorted and washed by the house-keeper in whatever home they returned to.

If only that could be tomorrow, she thought, as she slipped under the sheet next to her husband. She curled against his back, warming her cold body on his, comforting herself with his solid, reassuring presence. This was what Hannah had been asking her to lose, and she had not been able to risk it. She wondered briefly if she could tell Richard she wanted to leave Le Mas des Flores earlier than planned, but that would clearly be a wrong move. *Don't draw attention.*

It was only then, as she lay awake watching the curtains moving in the breeze, that Merry realised the glaring flaw in what she had just done. She had removed and hidden all the items that might identify Hannah so that no one would know who the dead woman was.

But there was one other person here who knew her. Tim Cutler.

FORTY-FOUR

TIM

Now

'But why?'

That was the only thought that Tim could vocalise. He leaned back in his chair, head tipped back with his phone still to his ear, eyes closed. 'If it really was Merry Stafford, why would she do something so terrible. And to a friend?'

'Fear of discovery,' Guillaume said baldly. 'The four most common motives for murder: love, money, revenge, silence. This falls under silence. As Meriel Stafford, she had an awful lot to lose. That's quite some lifestyle that Richard Stafford's providing. We know that she and Hannah spoke before she came to Le Mas des Flores that night, so my guess is she told Merry – Tina, let's call her – that you'd spoken to her about the blackmail. And Tina decided she had to silence her. Of course, that's just supposition at this point, and would need to be proved in a court of law. But it's where the evidence is strongly pointing. Louise told me that Tina went to your room to fetch some pills that afternoon. So she had access to the bag with the pentobarbital in it. And we know she had experience with injections from her former line of employment.'

'It was me that told Hannah about what she'd done all those years ago.' Tim's voice came out as a croak. 'This is my fault.'

'It's not your fault,' Guillaume said firmly. 'You were as much a victim of Tina Locke as Hannah was. Let's not forget the tens of thousands you gave her.'

When Tim tried to protest, Guillaume cut across him. 'Listen, Tim, there's something else you need to know. I also ordered a copy of Tina's birth certificate.' He paused. 'She was born on 27th September 1991.'

It took Tim a few seconds to make the calculation, but Guillaume was ahead of him.

'When you met her in October of 2010, she wasn't fifteen like she told you. She blackmailed you for having sex with a minor when all along she was nineteen years old.'

Tim's mouth felt dry, and his pulse pounded. He pictured the school blazer, the pleated skirt. 'She was wearing school uniform,' was all he could say, his voice barely above a whisper.

'She may have been, but she'd left school the previous July.'

'Jesus Christ!' Tim groaned.

'The positive here is that you did not commit a criminal offence, and you won't wind up on the sex offenders register. But, Tim, I think you know what I'm going to say next...'

'I need to tell Louise.'

'You do. All of it, including the one-night stand. Because when this investigation becomes public, you'll be firmly at the centre of the narrative and what happened between you and Tina Locke back in 2010 is highly likely to come out. You need to be the one who breaks it to Louise, if you have any respect for her at all.'

'Bloody hell, of course I do!' Tim shouted. Outside, he could hear the car draw up and the sound of voices raised in happy chatter, including Louise's. 'But this is going to destroy her.'

Guillaume adopted a gentler tone. 'Look, you two are a strong couple, as strong as any I know. She'll be angry and upset, but she'll forgive you.'

Let's hope you're right, Tim thought grimly.

The Cutlers had three more days left in Dorset, and Tim decided he could not embark on his confession while they were still there. There was a beach picnic and a barbecue planned as well as a trip to a waterpark that all four children were excited about. Disclosing his sordid secret to Louise would not only ruin their own holiday, but the atmosphere that would ensue would make things miserable for Phil and Serena too. And after hosting them generously for a week, his brother and sister-in-law did not deserve that.

But as soon as they got back to Winchester, Tim resolved, he would arrange for the children to be out of the house, and then he would sit down with Louise. He'd lay out the facts for her in as straightforward and unemotional way as he could, and assure her he would do anything to get their marriage back on track. What happened after that was up to her.

'That was such a great week,' she said happily, as they were driving back up the A31. 'In fact, I don't think we've ever had a better one in Studland. The weather was perfect, wasn't it?'

'It was.' Tim kept his eyes on the road, his arms rigid, jaw clenched.

'And you've got an exciting time coming up at Fairlawn once we get back, haven't you?' she went on. 'I expect you'll be able to make plans for improving the practice now you've got the Mondiale money coming in. Will you hire more people?'

'Maybe.'

'And when will you be paid the signing bonus? Only I was thinking that we could build one of those garden offices out at the back. There are loads of companies that do them now, properly insulated, with heating and power.'

'Why do we need a garden office?' Tim asked, careful to avoid meeting his wife's eye. 'You have your own office at school and I have a desk at the surgery, plus we've already got a study in the house.'

'I know, but it's nice to be able to separate home and work, isn't it? Or when the children get older and they need a quiet space for revising or whatever. Some of them are gorgeous; really stylish.'

She was so enthusiastic that Tim felt even more wretched.

'That would be sooo cool,' Harry piped up from the back seat. 'I could set up my gaming in there.'

'Hold on, hold on, let's just wait until the money's in our bank account first.'

'At least it looks like we won't need extra money for legal fees anymore,' Louise added.

Her hopeful smile stabbed at Tim's heart. 'Like I said, let's just wait and see, shall we?'

The following Monday he returned to work at Fairlawn and Louise went back to St Agnes to start preparations for the upcoming September term. Life fell back into its normal rhythm and for a few days Tim allowed himself to cling to this brief slice of normality. Was he putting off the dreaded task of telling his wife the truth? Of course he was. But it still hung over him with the crushing inevitability of a death row inmate's date with the electric chair. He repeated Guillaume Hall's words to himself like a mantra. *She'll forgive you.*

He considered booking dinner for the two of them at one of their favourite restaurants and telling her there. But on reflection this would be cowardly and not really fair to Louise. Yes, they would be on neutral ground, but she would be trapped there under the watchful eyes of the other diners, unable to raise her voice or even to leave the room without running out onto the street. No, he would have to do it at home. It was only right.

On Saturday, with Harry away for a week at a residential football camp and Elodie on a sleepover with her friend Samira, he could put off the inevitable no longer.

'We could go out,' Louise suggested. 'I'm dying to try that new Mexican place on Chesil Street.'

'No, let's stay in,' Tim said, forcing his face into a cheerful expression. 'We can open one of the bottles of plonk we brought back from Cotignac. And maybe look at some brochures for garden offices,' he added as an extra inducement, hating himself for the manipulation as the words left his mouth.

'Okay great.' Louise leaned in and kissed him on the lips. 'I'll make that pork and mustard dish you love. And, actually, I've got a surprise for you. I can give it to you then.'

As if he needed to feel any worse.

FORTY-FIVE

MERRY

Three weeks earlier

For a fleeting few minutes after she woke on Saturday, Merry managed to convince herself that last night had been a dream; a murky fever dream. Hannah Messenger was surely still alive, cleaning tables in the bar in Cotignac, or having coffee with friends in the square. Merry could walk down to the pool area now and there would be no dead body there. It didn't happen.

Richard was stirring beside her. His face was creased and puffy, his focus uncertain.

'Christ, I slept like the dead last night.'

She flinched at his choice of words.

'I was completely zonked. That brandy you poured me must have been a treble, darling.'

Merry nodded, but she was on high alert, listening. The bedside clock said 9.06. And now there it was: the faint sound of voices outside, then feet running, and raised voices. So it wasn't a dream. Someone had found... her. There was no going back and undoing what she had done, however much she might want to.

'What the hell's going on out there?' Richard asked, getting up off the bed and tugging on his bathrobe. 'I'm going to go and take a look.'

He disappeared, giving Merry the opportunity to gather herself. She sat in front of the mirror for a minute or two, then set about restyling her hair extensions, which were bedraggled from their immersion in the pool. Last night had been an aberration. She had been in... what was the expression? A fugue state. For that couple of hours, she had gone back to being the Tina Locke with a massive chip on her shoulder. The Tina Locke who felt inadequate with her cheap blonde highlights and her small, overcrowded home. The Tina Locke who compared herself unfavourably with the classier, more confident Hannah Messenger.

But as far as the rest of the world knew, she was just Mrs Meriel Stafford. Tim Cutler might have recognised Hannah from the bar, but if Hannah had been telling the truth about not using her name, he would have no reason to connect the girl who had seduced him with the Merry who was a guest at Le Mas des Flores, just as long as she kept her nerve. No reason at all.

Once her hair was styled and she had applied some make-up, she threw a silk kimono over her pyjamas and walked slowly towards the pool terrace. If she was the only one who stayed away from the crime scene, it would look odd.

The first thing she saw as she approached was that someone had draped a towel over the body, obscuring the face. She still shivered violently as she positioned herself next to her husband's side. Had Richard seen her before the towel was placed there? Because it occurred to her now that he had met Hannah when they had gone to buy the wine. She had been wearing a hat and sunglasses so it seemed unlikely he would make the connection. As for the dinner invitation; Merry had simply told him her friend had made other plans and he accepted it without further question.

There would be questions now, though, inevitably. Richard told her the police had already been called, along with Renée's lawyer.

'I mean, she didn't drown, did she?' Jared was saying. He had an arm around Renée, whose face looked drawn. 'Otherwise how the hell did she get out of the pool and onto the lounger?'

'Someone dragged her out and put her there?' This was Richard's contribution.

'Exactly. Foul play.'

Louise Cutler was shaking her head. 'That makes no sense. There's only us here, and none of us could have done this. Someone else must have been here too.'

Merry seized this opportunity to redirect the conversation. 'Where are the Prentices?'

'They were picked up in a cab about an hour ago. At least I think they were,' Tim said. To Merry's relief, he hadn't looked in her direction once. If he had recognised the body as that of Hannah Messenger, there was nothing in his behaviour to give this away.

And then, before the speculation could escalate, the police arrived. Four armed gendarmes came down the path to the pool terrace and took control of the scene, ordering the guests to stay in the house. They watched through the windows of the salon as first a van containing dog handlers drew up, and then a team of forensic specialists in white suits. The sniffer dogs started combing the grounds. Would they find the clothes in the well? Merry wondered, her heart in her throat. Surely their sense of smell wasn't that good? And if her scent was detected in the pool area, well, she'd been using the pool for nearly two weeks, along with the other guests. What would that tell them? They'd find the Vespa before very long, but for now the focus was firmly on the house and grounds.

Renée disappeared for a few minutes and came back with an update. The swimming pool would need to be drained, apparently, and already there were officers checking CCTV from the front gate. Thank God she had had the foresight to direct Hannah to use the side gate where there was no camera surveillance.

They were all forced to wait there in one room, like the players in a reality television challenge. One by one, they were all summoned into the dining room to be questioned by two of the investigating officers. Merry was polite but detached, and the whole process was remarkably straightforward. Did she recognise the deceased? No, because the body had been covered by the time she reached the pool. Had she left her room during the night, or heard anything unusual? No, she and her husband had retired at 11.30 p.m. and stayed in bed until 9 a.m.

'I'm very sorry,' she had said with a regretful smile. 'But there's really nothing else I can tell you.'

And then came a development that she had never once anticipated.

Tim Cutler was arrested for the murder and taken away for questioning.

'I can't believe that of him, can you?' Richard asked her when they heard the news on Sunday. 'I mean, why would he kill that woman? Nobody even knows who she is. It makes no sense.'

Merry agreed that it did not.

'And he seems such a lovely chap. And she's delightful too: Louise. They're both lovely. The perfect family.'

And his arrest gives me the perfect alibi.

. . .

'I'm thinking we should try to leave early,' Richard said, when they returned to their room after breakfast.

Merry had never been so relieved to hear her husband's words. She was desperate to leave that wretched place, but she could not appear to be desperate. She merely nodded.

'The pool area's out of bounds after all,' he went on. 'I'm sure no one's in the mood to play tennis, nor do I particularly want to mooch around in Cotignac. I think we've exhausted its charms.'

'Agreed.' Merry wound her arms round his waist and rested her head on his shoulder. He kissed the top of her head in a paternal gesture.

'I'll get on to Hermann now and see what he can do.' Hermann was Richard's executive assistant, based in Basel. 'If necessary, I suppose we could charter private.'

In the end, they secured the last two first-class seats on a flight from Nice to Zurich, and Hermann arranged for cars both to take them to Nice and pick them up at the other end. With Tim still detained in Brignoles, Merry's escape couldn't have worked better. There would be no need for further eye contact or awkward silences as Merry struggled not to give herself away. She kept up her outward show of calm, but was inwardly vibrating with nerves until their luggage was loaded into the car and the others came to wave them off.

The sight of Louise's quietly stoic face made Merry's insides twist.

'I hope you understand,' she told her, 'But it seemed for the best to cut our trip short.'

Louise nodded and forced a smile.

'God, I really hope Tim will be all right,' Richard said as their car slid down the driveway, tyres rumbling over the gravel and Renée, Jared and Louise waving in the rear-view mirror. 'Poor bastard. But surely they can't really pin this on him, the

idea of him murdering anyone, let alone a complete stranger, is
preposterous.'

'Agreed,' said Merry.

But she was hoping fervently that the French police
persisted in pursing Tim Cutler. Because as long as they were
focused on him, they would not be looking in her direction. She
would be safe.

FORTY-SIX

TIM

Now

'Why don't you have a bath?' Louise asked at 6 p.m.

Tim pulled a face. 'Baths are really more your thing, darling. I'll have a shower.'

'No, treat yourself to a bath for once,' Louise said firmly. She gave him one of her twinkliest smiles, her dimples showing, and his insides ached from what he was about to do to her. 'Take as long as you like.'

As he was tipping one of Louise's bubble bath bottles into the water, his phone pinged with an email. It was from Fraser Armstrong who had – Tim noted – attached an invoice for his fee.

Sorry to disturb you at the weekend, but I thought you ought to know as soon as possible that I've received a communication from the investigating officer in Brignoles formally revoking your status as a suspect in the Messenger case. They also sent a copy of the forensic examination of the clothing and vials found, which found fingerprints and trace

DNA, neither of which was a match with yours. As I understand it, the investigation has now been handed on to Inter-
pol's National Central Bureau in Paris, which suggests that
the focus has moved outside of French jurisdiction. I'm sure
you will be very happy to hear this news and I wish you and
your family all the very best.

Yes, he was relieved, Tim thought bitterly as he switched off
the taps. But happy? Happy he was not. He still had to tell his
wife the truth.

Thirty minutes later, he emerged from the bath he hadn't
really wanted and felt obliged to put on a clean shirt. Dressing
up for the executioner, he thought grimly. When he headed
down the stairs and walked into the kitchen, his heart sank like
a stone. Louise had changed into one of her favourite dresses,
white cotton dotted with small blue hearts, and had applied
some lipstick. The table was set with fresh flowers, there were
lit candles on every surface and some vaguely Brazilian-
sounding lounge music was coming from the Bluetooth
speaker.

'Wow,' was all he could say, failing to inject the requisite
tone of delight. 'You shouldn't have gone to so much trouble.'

You really shouldn't, given what I'm just about to do.

'I thought we could treat it as an early anniversary celebration,' she said, pouring him champagne. Champagne: of course
there was champagne too. 'I know it's still a couple of weeks
away, but there is method in my madness. I thought I'd give you
your anniversary present now.'

She handed him a folded computer printout, her face alight
with happiness. As Tim read it, his self-disgust was complete.
Flights to Venice and a reservation at the Gritti Palace, for the
end of October.

'I wanted to give you plenty of notice given how busy
work's going to be. And it had to be half-term week, I'm afraid,

because of work, but Phil and Serena have already agreed to have the kids.'

'That's... amazing,' he said weakly. 'You're amazing.'

Maybe they could still go. Maybe given another couple of months Louise would have been able to get her head around what had happened.

She was busying herself with the food, heaping green vegetables onto the plates, ladling out mashed potato. Tim, unable to bear the wretched guilt a second longer, gently put his hand on her wrist and forced her to set down the serving spoon.

'I'm almost finished serving up.'

'Stop.' Her expression as she turned to look at him was one of horror, and he realised that he had tears in his eyes. 'Lou, there's something I need to talk to you about. It can't wait.'

He led her to the table and they both sat down.

'What is it, Tim? You're scaring me.'

'I...' He didn't even know how to begin explaining. *Start at the beginning.* 'I... had sex with someone,' he blurted. This was not how he had intended to tell her. Not at all.

She paled slightly, but kept her gaze steady. 'Who? Who was it?' she said eventually, her voice thick and faltering.

'Merry Stafford.'

Her hand flew to her sternum, and she pressed it there hard as though she feared she was about to have a coronary. 'You mean, when we were on holiday?'

'No!' He shook his head violently. 'Not then. It was only once, and it was a long time ago. She wasn't Meriel Stafford then, she went by her first name of Christina. Tina. Her surname was Locke.'

And he told her then, about the night of the Curadex party and how he had stopped to give Tina Locke a lift because of the storm. As he did so, he experienced a rush of sensory memory and he was suddenly back in the car with her. The smell of wet clothing mingling with cigarette smoke and sweet vanilla perfume. The taste of cherry lip gloss. The strange sensation of the gem glued to her incisor as it scraped his tongue. The rain battering the car roof like gunfire.

'Did you kiss her?' was the first thing she wanted to know.

'No. I, well... She kissed me.'

'Why didn't you try to stop her?' Louise demanded angrily. 'Why? I don't understand.'

'I tried, but it all happened so fast, I couldn't react. I just froze.'

'Well, obviously not all of you froze,' Louise snorted. 'I presume you managed to get it up.'

He dropped his head into his hands.

'So this was thirteen years ago, and you're just telling me now? Presumably because the same woman is probably going to be arrested for murder?'

'Yes...' Tim shook his head desperately. 'Well, no. That's not all there is to it. She... After I had sex with Tina, she black-mailed me. She told me she was fifteen.'

Louise groaned, and stood up from the table, started pacing the room.

'She wasn't fifteen, she was nineteen, but I didn't know that.'

He told her the details of Tina Locke's scheme, and how it had all come to the surface again when he spotted Hannah Messenger in Cotignac and had sought her out to talk to her.

Louise tipped back a glass of champagne and an unfamiliar look came over her face. It was as if his wife had receded and someone else had appeared in her place. 'You gave her all that money,' she said coldly. 'Enough money to put both our children through university. And yet you never thought to mention it to me. It was *our* money.'

'I was afraid, Lou.' He tried to make eye contact, but she had averted her face. 'When it happened, it was just after the miscarriage, and you weren't in a good place. And then you got pregnant again and I was so afraid of what the shock would do to you.'

'Oh, so it's my fault, is it?' She poured more champagne, gulped it back.

'Of course not. And I took on extra locum work to cover the payments.'

'What a hero,' she sneered. 'For ten years, Tim. *Ten. Years.*'

'I suppose I just got used to it. I'd set up the payments from the practice account and they went out month after month, and I suppose after a while I stopped noticing it. Just like any regular payment.' As he spoke, he realised how craven this sounded.

'Oh, so to you it was just like paying the electricity bill, or the council tax. Hush money to the little tramp you'd shagged by mistake.'

He ground his fingertips into his temples. 'Louise, sweetheart... I don't know what else I can say to make you see how sorry I am.'

'And did you know?' Louise took a swig of champagne from the neck of the bottle, tipsy and belligerent now. 'When we got to the villa, did you know that Merry Stafford was the girl you'd fucked?'

'No!' Tim insisted. 'She's clearly had a ton of plastic surgery because she looks completely different. Her hair's different, her teeth... everything. And she and I barely exchanged two words.'

'Yeah, and now we know why,' Louise snorted. 'I'm sure she didn't want your affair being public knowledge any more than you did.'

'It wasn't a bloody affair!'

Louise slammed the bottle down on the countertop and rounded on him. 'Tim, you haven't even mentioned the worst thing about this whole squalid episode.'

'What do you mean?'

'That by confiding in Hannah Messenger you effectively

signed her death warrant. Merry has to have killed her to shut her up. It's *you* who's responsible for her death!'

Tim slumped forward at the table, unable to respond. There was no point in arguing with Louise. In a way, she was right.

'And do you know what the second worst thing is about this?' Louise's eyes were wide and manic, her expression one he had never seen before.

He did not respond.

'I'll tell you, shall I?' she spat. 'You were supposed to be different. Different from the rest. But you're just the same as every other bloody man.'

Tim shook his head sadly. Again, there seemed little point arguing. 'So what do we do now?' he asked. 'How do we get past this?'

'We don't.' Her composure had returned, but her voice was devoid of emotion. 'I'm leaving you.'

FORTY-SEVEN

MERRY

Two weeks earlier

'We've got Sicily coming up, darling, don't forget.'

Merry stared at the empty cases she had just unpacked in the Basel apartment, making sure to bundle the swimsuit, shirt and shorts she had worn on Friday night into the washing machine herself, along with some of her underwear and Richard's T-shirts and boxers. It was churning away in the tub now, washing away any trace of suspicion.

They invariably spent around a week at the San Domenico Palace in Taormina in the spring or summer, and while Merry felt that, on balance, switching locations was probably a good idea, the reality proved different. Whole sections of time were lost in those first two days, as if she wasn't really there. She admired the spectacular views of the Ionian Sea from their balcony, wandered the building's pristine white marble colonnades and ordered poolside drinks along with all the other wealthy guests, but her mind remained in Le Mas des Flores. She replayed the events of that night over and over in her mind, as if she was watching a film and rewinding the tape would change the outcome. As if it would make Hannah alive again, and not lying in a coffin in some funeral home somewhere.

But if she was still alive, then Tim would now know the truth of what she had done. She would be facing a criminal prosecution herself, and given the length of time her blackmail had played out, she would be looking at a substantial prison sentence. There was no way she could pay off Tim Cutler. He wasn't the type to be bought off, unless perhaps it was for a huge sum, one that she couldn't raise without Richard noticing. And if he found out, Richard would definitely divorce her. He'd divorced two other women for less. He was wealthy and agreeable company, someone else would snap him up. Objectively, yes, the sentence for murder was stiffer even than for blackmail. But by never telling Tim Cutler her name when she blackmailed him, she had made sure she was bulletproof. When the police dug around for a connection to Hannah Messenger, Tim would never make the link. That girl he had sex with was long gone. There was no reason for Merry Stafford née Locke to want Hannah Messenger dead: none at all.

Yet still, at night, when she closed her eyes, all she could see was Hannah's dead face. When she eventually fell asleep, it was all she dreamed about. What if she had not stumbled on Tim's cache of pentobarbital? she asked herself during her waking hours. Would she have tried to talk Hannah around? Or would she have resorted to a less clean and clinical solution. A blow on the head with a heavy object, perhaps. Since she couldn't imagine herself doing something so crude and messy, she could only blame the availability of the lethal drug. It was really Tim Cutler's fault, she convinced herself after two days stuck in the same exhausting mental feedback loop. Even if no one else would ever see it that way.

And then on the third day, as they were eating a room service breakfast on the balcony and Merry was scrolling news headlines on her phone, she saw it.

Family of murdered Hannah speak out

As a man arrested for the murder of British citizen Hannah Messenger is released without charge, her family say they are cooperating with the authorities as they start to investigate other lines of enquiry.

Hannah, 32, was found dead at a luxury villa in the South of France on 29th July, but for now the circumstances surrounding her killing remain a mystery. 'The police are now turning their attention to the UK, and finding new witnesses who can help build a picture of my sister's life,' said Olivia Haynes, 34. 'Obviously we will do all we can to help them bring the killer to justice.'

Bile rose in Merry's throat, and she took a quick gulp of her orange juice.

Richard threw her a glance. 'Are you okay, darling?'

'I feel a little bit off,' Merry said, pressing a pristine white linen napkin to her forehead. 'I think there might have been a dodgy clam in that seafood pasta we had last night.'

'Why don't you go and lie down for a bit? Spend the morning in bed,' Richard said, with an indulgent smile. 'I'll get the staff to bring up something that will settle your stomach. Or I can ask them to call the doctor.'

'No, it's all right.' Merry pushed her plate away and stood up. 'Actually, I was thinking I'd like to head out to Palm Beach for a bit. We had almost two whole weeks in Provence and now it's more of the same: olive oil, local wine, lounging by the pool, siestas... To be honest, I'm a bit over the whole summer in the Med thing.'

She was aware as she spoke how spoilt and entitled she sounded, but she felt a desperate need to get away. Even further away. Their Palm Beach house was in a gated compound, and felt safe, impenetrable.

Richard frowned. 'Okay, I get that Sicily feels a little samey after the South of France, but Florida in August is not ideal. You know you hate the humidity. Why not spend some time in the UK?'

'No!' Merry protested, then moderated her strident tone. 'I'll stay in the air conditioning in the day and swim at night. It'll be fine.'

I can hide away from the world, was what she really meant.

'Okay, if you're sure, sweetheart.' He kissed her forehead. 'As it happens, that suits me quite well, because I've got some business in Frankfurt I really need to take care of.'

So that evening Merry flew from Naples to Miami, leaving Richard to travel to Germany the following morning. When she landed at Miami International and switched on her phone, her heart sank when she saw three missed calls from her stepsister Jodie. The two of them had irregular and largely superficial contact – wishing one another happy birthday and Christmas – so three calls must mean something was wrong. Having found Merry's phone switched off, Jodie had eventually resorted to sending a text.

Merry shoved her phone back into her pocket, her heart hammering against the wall of her chest. Only when she was in the back of the car being driven up the coastal I-95 to Palm Beach did she take it out and re-read it.

Hey, something weird ...you know my friend Amber does work on and off for Greenleaf, well she said a detective had been to the office asking questions about Hannah M. Apparently they wanted to know about her connection with you from back when you two both worked there. Like I said, bit weird, but maybe they're speaking to anyone who knew her. Just thought you'd want to know xx

Although she managed to remain still and composed behind

her Gucci shades, every muscle in Merry's body twitched and flickered. She started counting inside her head to avoid alarming the driver by crying out. She was surprised that the authorities would go to speak to employees of Greenleaf Catering given that had been more than a decade ago, even though the company had long been a mainstay of casual work for teenagers in Kempshott. Jodie herself had done some waitressing stints for them, as had several of her acquaintances. Had someone tipped them off about this pre-existing link between herself and Hannah Messenger? If so, was that Tim Cutler, or someone else?

As Jodie had suggested, perhaps police were aiming to speak to anyone and everyone who had known Hannah Messenger. But 'they wanted to know about her connection with you' was more alarming. They wouldn't seek out someone who had worked with Hannah for a mere nine months thirteen years ago unless there were some ongoing connection with the circumstances of her death. They must somehow know that Hannah's presence at Le Mas des Flores was linked to Tina Locke, an ordinary working-class girl from Kempshott. Who was now Richard Stafford's wife .

Had she really been so arrogant to think that a desperate Tim would not work out the connection for himself? Only now, with a horrendous sinking feeling did it become obvious. That if she could work out who he was back in 2010, then he could have somehow discovered the name she withheld from him. The name she withheld from him. Her bank account only had her initials but that would have been more than enough if he'd wanted to work it out.

The car turned onto the causeway that led out to the island and slid past the rows of endless royal palms and the large coral-roofed mansions, eventually turning into the gated development where the Staffords owned a house. She would have plenty of time to think now, Merry reflected bitterly. She was not sure how long she had, but eventually the parallel strands of her long-standing extortion, her real name and Tim's recent meeting with Hannah would all converge. When they did, she could only pray they failed to find the hard evidence that would make a charge stick. That was her only chance.

Her phone rang in her hand. Richard.

'Hi, darling, just checking you arrived safely. How was the flight?'

'Fine. We're just pulling up at the house now.'

The driver got out and opened the front door and she walked up the steps and onto the white marbled portico.

'Sonny and Nicole are around, if you're in need of company. And Brad and Kathleen, I think.'

He named neighbours on the estate that they sometimes socialised with.

'Sure,' said Merry, though she had no intention of doing so.

She waited until the driver had deposited her luggage in the cool, lofty atrium, the ceiling fan swirling lazily overhead, and returned to the car. Then she locked the front door behind him. She would stay here in her luxurious fortress, until such time as they came for her.

Because come for her they would.

FORTY-EIGHT

LOUISE

Now

Louise forced herself into practical mode, as abruptly as though she had flicked a switch. Tipping the rest of the champagne down the sink and scraping the half-served plates into the bin, she walked straight out of the kitchen and up the stairs.

Tim, who had been sitting at the table in stunned silence, followed her to the foot of the stairs. 'Lou, what are you doing?' he called.

The quiver in his voice infuriated her. 'What does it look like?' she snarled.

She fetched a small suitcase from the top of the spare-room wardrobe, flung it onto the bed she had shared with her husband for as long as she could remember, and started putting essentials into it: her bathrobe and washbag. She was methodical: folding a change of underwear and T-shirt neatly, rolling jeans. Being orderly soothed her, allowed her some semblance of control over the forest fire of rage in her brain.

'Please don't tell me you're moving out.' Tim had appeared in the doorway.

'No,' she said coolly. 'You are. But just for tonight, I need to be somewhere else. I'm going to go to Yasmin's.'

'You can't drive. You've drunk half a bottle.'

'I know that.' She slammed her make-up bag and hairbrush onto the folded clothes. 'I'll get an Uber.' The case was zipped shut and dragged off the bed. 'Elle's being dropped off tomorrow morning around 11, so I'll aim to be back here by then. I won't say anything to the children yet, but obviously we can't keep it from them for long. They're going to notice pretty quickly that you're living somewhere else.'

Tim flapped his arms against his sides. 'Darling, please. Can't we at least talk about this?'

'You talked, I listened. And this is what's happening.'

She opened the ride share app on her phone and tapped in her request, then wheeled the case to the top of the stairs. Her phone bleeped.

Without even turning back to look at her husband, she said calmly, 'My car will be here in two minutes. I'll wait outside.'

She was grateful, at least, that Tim took her seriously. When she returned the following morning, he had already left, having first stripped the sheets off the marital bed and loaded them into the washing machine. An inspection of the wardrobe revealed that some of his clothes had gone, and his toothbrush and shaving kit were no longer in their en suite. Now that her champagne-fuelled anger had dissipated, she simply felt a deep, deep sadness.

She attempted to keep busy with work and grocery shopping and entertaining Elodie, but it was as if she was in the middle of a prolonged bad dream. At the end of the afternoon, she received a simple message from Tim saying that he would be staying at a bed and breakfast in town for a few nights, and then from the end of the week he had arranged to rent a furnished studio flat a short walk away from Fairlawn. He didn't give the address, and she didn't ask for it. She replied saying that they would need to make some arrangement for access to the children and got a one-word response: 'Yes.'

And that was it. Her marriage was over.

Over the following few weeks, she and Tim worked out an efficient, if bleak, arrangement that would allow him to spend time with Harry and Elodie. He would see them after school every Wednesday and every other weekend. Since there was no way for him to accommodate them in his depressing studio flat, his contact weekends would be spent at the marital home while Louise absented herself at her parents' house, or with friends.

It was a relief once the September term had started and the children had school to distract them from the bewildering state of affairs between their parents. Parents who had always been overtly affectionate and never argued and yet suddenly couldn't live with one another any longer. Louise tried to explain that she and Tim had had a difference of opinion over something that had happened in the past, but even to her ears the justification seemed weak and flawed.

Back in the company of their schoolfriends, the children gradually adapted to the unwelcome new status quo. Louise herself was grateful for the sanctuary of her job and working hours that meant she was rarely at the school gates to collect her children. She did not want to be the object of pitying looks and whispered gossip, although she had no doubt there was plenty of that doing the rounds. And once it reached the ears of Mandy Fielding, there might as well have been an article in the *Hampshire Chronicle*.

'Did you hear the Cutlers have split up?' people would be saying. 'Of all people!' Or 'If it can happen to them, then there but for the grace of God.' She could hear it all, even if she wasn't there.

She also had no doubt that one of the chief disseminators of the news would be Shona Prentice. Tim would have updated Kevin during their squash games, and although he and Shona were still separated, they were still in contact because of Violet. The news would have been passed on.

Sure enough, a couple of weeks after the start of the September term, Louise got a text from Shona.

Hi! Now we're both single ladies, why don't we go out for a girls' night out on the town? Let me know when works for you xx

As she read it, Louise gave an involuntary shudder. The idea of drinking in a badly lit bar with a leopard-print-clad Shona Prentice as she scouted for younger men filled her with horror.

Not sure I'm up to a girls night just yet, but how about we meet for coffee? X

It was a compromise she was prepared to live with. She could just about manage a brief daytime meeting if it gave her the opportunity to squash the idea that the two of them were now Winchester's answer to Thelma and Louise. Shona and Louise.

In the end, she and Shona met at a coffee shop in town one Saturday morning when Tim had the children.

As soon as she saw Shona, she could tell from her body language that she had news to impart. She had that bristling, self-important air that people had when they're in possession of important information.

After she had kissed Louise, she thrust her phone screen in her face. It was opened on the BBC News site. 'Have you seen this?' she crowed.

BREAKING: British woman arrested for killing of Hannah Messenger

Christina Stafford (32), formerly Christina Locke, has been arrested at the home in Palm Beach that she shares with her businessman husband, Richard Stafford (54). Detectives from Scotland Yard flew back to London with Mrs Stafford in their custody, and she appeared in Westminster Magistrates' Court, where she pleaded not guilty to the charge of murder. Hannah Messenger, also 32, was found dead on 29th July at a luxury property in the South of France where the Staffords were holiday guests.

'Can you believe it?' Shona crowed, as she tugged off her purple faux-fur jacket and waved a waitress over. 'Merry Stafford! I never would have guessed it. I mean, she was a bit of a stuck-up cow. But murder!'

'It is unbelievable,' Louise agreed. She was not going to tell Shona that she had known for several weeks that Merry Stafford was the primary suspect. And certainly not that her husband had once had sex with her.

'And to think they started out by arresting poor Tim!' Shona spooned sugar into her cappuccino and stirred with gusto. 'It's outrageous. Still, at least it looks like she'll get what she deserves. That's the main thing, right?'

Louise nodded, but didn't even try to raise a smile. Yes, justice would be done, and that was a good thing. But, in the process, her marriage had been destroyed. The marriage that turned out not to be so perfect after all.

FORTY-NINE

LOUISE

Now

'Nobody is really who you think they are.'

That was something Louise's mother had told her not long before her death. She may have been a profoundly damaged woman, but she had been right, Louise reflected, as she read a news update on her phone that Merry had changed her plea to guilty and been sentenced to twenty-four years.

Nobody staying at Le Mas des Fleurs had really been what they seemed. She included herself in this statement, because she, too, was guilty of harbouring a secret.

Once the children were in bed, she took a deep breath, picked up her phone and sent Tim a message.

Can you come over please? There's something I need to say.

Her phone bleeped with a text, but it wasn't a reply from Tim. It was from Guillaume Hall.

I'm in the area, and I'd really appreciate the chance to talk x

. . .

When she answered the door thirty minutes later, it was Tim who stood on the doorstep. She saw with a pang how thin he looked and – underneath his dark stubble – how pale. That had been her own reflection in the mirror for the past few months: a thin, anxious facsimile of her former self. Still, his eyes lit up when he saw her.

He followed her into the kitchen. 'Are the kids asleep?'

She nodded.

'So what's this about?'

Louise took a very deep breath. 'I don't know where we go from here, Tim. I don't know if we can salvage our marriage. But I do know that I need to be honest with you.'

He sat down at the breakfast bar. 'I'm listening.'

She gripped the edge of the countertop to quell the shaking. 'I know,' she said eventually. 'I've known for a while. About you and Tina Locke.'

He stared at her, his face growing paler still. 'I don't understand. How could you have done?'

'It was about a year ago. Your mum phoned and we were chatting about the cost of possibly extending the house and she mentioned a bequest from your great-uncle when he died. She had no idea you hadn't told me about the thirty thousand pounds; why would she? So...' She took a gulp of wine. 'That was the start of it.'

Tim looked down at his hands.

'I should have said something about it to you, I know I should.' She pressed her lips together, with a slight shake of her head. 'Instead, I brooded about it for a few weeks, then went through the desk drawer until I found a load of bank statements from about a decade ago. Fifteen hundred pounds a month, payable to a C.M. Locke.'

Tim flung his head back. 'Lou... Jesus! Why didn't you say anything at that point?'

'I don't know. I was scared, I suppose. Scared of breaking up the family. We'd been through so much to have our perfect family, and we were all so happy. The children were thriving... how could I spoil all that? It occurred to me that you'd been blackmailed. But for doing what? I turned it over and over in my head for months. And then we end up in the South of France with you being arrested for murder. And I'm left thinking that I don't know who I'm married to.'

'Nor do I,' Tim said quietly. He raised his chin and looked straight at her. 'I never would have believed you capable of keeping something like that to yourself. Not my Lou.'

Louise shrugged. 'I'm not that Lou any longer. And you're not the same Tim any more. That person's gone.'

As she looked at her husband, another thing that her mother had said to her suddenly came back to her. *In life, you get what you deserve.* Was this what she deserved, then? To struggle on as a single parent? Yes, Tim had fallen short of the image she had of him, but did that have to mean their marriage was doomed? Or would festering resentment mean that it was better to find something new, to start again?

'The problem is, I wanted to believe our marriage was perfect,' she told him.

'Perfection is overrated,' Tim said with a sad smile.

Car tyres crunched on the driveway outside and a car door slammed. Louise walked from the kitchen to the family room and glanced out of the window. Guillaume was walking purposefully towards the front door. She was frozen for a few seconds; torn between two worlds. Between the shock of the new, the comfort of the old.

It was time to decide.

EPILOGUE

January 2024

Renée Weber read the online news headline and smiled to herself with satisfaction. There would be plenty to entertain the clickbait consumers and social media sleuths, she thought. The case had all the components of the perfect story: wealthy people, a glamorous location, and both a victim and a killer who were young and good-looking. And now would be the perfect time to contact poor Richard. To offer a shoulder to cry on.

What were the chances, people would speculate, that these two former friends who had not met for years would end up in the same small Provencal village at the same time? But Renée knew that it was no coincidence, that it had all been a set-up. Because she had been the one to do it.

It had started when Richard Stafford separated from his second wife. This, Renée was convinced, was their moment. They had had a brief but intense fling when they were in their twenties, brought to a halt by the company promoting her to their Dusseldorf office. She was fiercely ambitious and nothing would have persuaded her not to go, but it brought to a screeching halt the star-crossed lover narrative she was spinning in her head. He would wait for her, she reasoned. Or come and join her. But instead he met a Slovenian girl called Monika and married her. She had only just heard about them splitting up when he announced his second marriage, to Camille.

That marriage also proved short-lived, and Renée reached out to Richard. They had a single drunken night of passion in Zurich, but then... silence. A few months later, Renée heard through her contacts that Richard had moved in with a much younger woman, a British girl this time, called Meriel Locke. Sure enough, a year or so later, his third marriage was announced. Fury and frustration overwhelmed Renée. This had been *their* time, finally. Hers and Richard's. All right, so she was now seeing Jared, but he was just a plaything, a distraction. This time, she resolved, she would not be passive. She would take matters into her own hands. The girl was a masseuse, for God's sake. There must be something in her past that would make Richard think twice. She just needed to find it.

As the CEO of a huge international company, she had limitless resources at her disposal; teams of people working under her. Legal staff and professional researchers on tap. Renée had no need to get her own hands dirty, but the work was done nonetheless, discreetly and expensively. She found out all there was to know about the former Tina Locke from Hampshire, England. All the way back to her teenage years. And that included the name of one of her former friends. Hannah Messenger.

It was convenient that Hannah was at a crossroads in her life, at a loose end. It didn't take much – an airfare and a generous amount of spending money, to persuade her to take a detour on her travels and come to Cotignac. Renée's minions even found her the job at Bar des Vignobles, and a place to stay.

Hannah was to 'bump into' her former friend by chance, to arrange to spend time with her, ask her questions, and feed anything she found directly to a specially dedicated, untraceable phone. And, sure enough, on Friday 28th July, Hannah had messaged her.

I've found out something extremely interesting about T. Think you'll find it useful!

Only Renée never received confirmation of her suspicions about this intelligence, because, hours later, Hannah was lying dead next to the pool at the house where both Renée and Merry Stafford were staying. Renée knew she had to stay tight-lipped and give nothing away. Tell no one she knew who Hannah Messenger was. She had never met the girl in person, so had plausible deniability.

And there'd been another unexpected stroke of luck. The expensive dark web hackers she had bankrolled as part of her research had managed to get into Tina Locke's former bank accounts. There had been regular payments for years from one Tim Cutler. A married man who, by a stroke of luck, happened to be a vet.

Yes, VCM was in the process of buying up independent veterinary businesses anyway, but this small struggling clinic in Winchester wouldn't really have been of interest to the acquisitions team unless Renée herself had insisted. By taking over the negotiations in person, she created the opportunity to get both Tina Locke and Tim Cutler under the same roof at her company's villa. If the subsequent turn of events had put Tim Cutler in a jail cell... well, that had been unpleasant for him, but the benefits that came with the sale of his practice surely more than made up for it.

That Merry herself would eventually be charged with the murder was a gift from the gods. Yes, Hannah Messenger was dead as an indirect result of Renée's intervention and that was unfortunate. Extremely unfortunate. But Merry could not have been removed from the picture in a more decisive fashion had Renée planned it that way, leaving Richard finally on his own after all these years.

With the satisfied smile still playing on her lips, Renée picked up her phone and dialled Richard Stafford's number.

A LETTER FROM ALISON

Thank you so much for choosing to read *Just The Nicest Family*. If you enjoyed it and want to keep up to date with all my latest releases, just sign up at the following link. Your email address will never be shared and you can unsubscribe at any time.

www.bookouture.com/alison-james

Family summer holidays are special, bonding times. They're also flashpoints of stress that can put the happiest of couples under pressure, and it was this idea that I wanted to explore *in Just The Nicest Family*. Throw in heat, alcohol and competition with other holiday guests, and even a seemingly perfect marriage might start to fall apart...

I really hope you enjoyed reading this novel, and if you did I would be so grateful if you could write a review. I'd love to hear what you think, and it makes such a difference helping new readers to discover one of my books for the first time.

I love hearing from my readers – you can get in touch on my Facebook page, Twitter or Goodreads.

Thanks,

Alison James

KEEP IN TOUCH WITH ALISON

goodreads.com/author/show/17361567.Alison_James

[facebook] facebook.com/Alison-James-books
[X] x.com/AlisonJbooks
[tiktok] tiktok.com/@allyjay855

PUBLISHING TEAM

Turning a manuscript into a book requires the efforts of many people. The publishing team at Bookouture would like to acknowledge everyone who contributed to this publication.

Audio
Alba Proko
Melissa Tran
Sinead O'Connor

Commercial
Lauren Morrissette
Hannah Richmond
Imogen Allport

Cover design
The Brewster Project

Data and analysis
Mark Alder
Mohamed Bussuri

Editorial
Natasha Harding
Lizzie Brien

Copyeditor
Jade Craddock

Proofreader
John Romans

Marketing
Alex Crow
Melanie Price
Occy Carr
Cíara Rosney
Martyna Młynarska

Operations and distribution
Marina Valles
Stephanie Straub

Production
Hannah Snetsinger
Mandy Kullar
Jen Shannon
Ria Clare

Publicity
Kim Nash
Noelle Holten
Jess Readett
Sarah Hardy

Rights and contracts
Peta Nightingale
Richard King
Saidah Graham